Jo

Monsters Unleashed
Book 1

City of Flames

This is a work of fiction. Any similarity between
people, events, or otherwise is purely coincidental.

ISBN: 9781719542487
CreateSpace Independent Publishing Platform
Copyright © 2021 Jocelin Deneweth

As cliché as it is, this is for my parents. They have always supported me in whatever dream I had, especially this one.

I also want to dedicate this to Mrs. Nelson. She was the first one to read my story and one who inspired me to become a teacher.

So, Mrs. Nelson, thank you.

City of Flames

Monsters Unleashed: City of Flames

Ryder Skye

Mind Reader/Bender
Hater of Liars
Lover of freedom

1

Hidden memories and those who seek them out

Help *me…*
Save me…
Kill me…kill everyone…
Die, you darkling scum…

The agonized voices echo through the dark walls every time I brush against them, something that is impossible to avoid considering how small the space is. They make it impossible to sleep, haltering any attempts with their tragic stories and forcing me into the pacing mess I am. Hence why I keep brushing up against the walls. Standing still, though I'd be away from them, seems somehow worse.

No one else can hear them, leaving me to my own personal hell. Most days I can ignore them. I've spent my entire life learning how to muffle my abilities but today…

Today has my mind all sorts of messed up.

I should probably be grateful for the distraction. It's either the voices or…facing the painful memories that stem from…well, past mistakes.

No, I stop myself, but it is too late. *His* face flashes before my eyes, reminding me of what I lost. This day…this *pain* always comes today. The same day it happened three years ago, tormenting me over and over again as soon as the anniversary comes along.

My heart jumps into my throat and tears well up in my eyes as I push his image, these thoughts, out of my head. I plop down on my cot, it's barely better than the cement floor below, as tears threaten to fall down my face.

I should be over this. It happened three years ago. The mere thought of him shouldn't be enough to warrant such a reaction.

"Grow up," I mutter to myself, repeating the words often used on me by my so-called superiors. Swallowing the lump back down, I glare at the walls and wonder as I always did when days like these interrupted my sense of calm.

Is it worth it to give into temptation to stop these horrid feelings from wrecking me? Their tragedies have to be better than mine, or at least easier to deal with. I lift my hand toward the wall, ready to welcome the voices and their stories when a knock sounds from my door.

Yay, a better and far safer distraction.

The door slides open without my consent, something that always leaves me feeling uneasy. However, when a short, dark skinned shifter steps in, a sense of calm rushes over me. Rodriguez, the officer assigned to my hall, is the only decent lightling I have ever met. He looks almost...proud of himself.

Yes, he's a lightling and I am a darkling. An odd combination of friends but it kind of works.

A large smile decorates his face as he holds out a small box and steps closer to me without a word. My first instinct is to refuse and if it was anyone else, I would have. However, I know him well enough that, despite our people's hatred for one another, he would never willingly hurt an innocent soul.

"I know you don't like today for reasons you won't disclose," he says as I take the box from him, "but it's your birthday. What kind of friend would I be if I didn't get you something?"

"I didn't know you were allowed to celebrate our birthdays. Anything from the outside is considered a potential threat," I mutter as I pull at the bright red ribbon.

"There's nothing saying we can't," he grins, looking expectantly at the box, "and I already approved it with the higher ups."

With a sigh, I slowly toss the lid onto the cot. Inside is a cupcake with a single candle it. I take it out, Rodriguez already armed with lighter. I watch as he lights it, the fire dancing to life with little sparks from the infused magic.

"I know it isn't much," he shrugs, "but, happy birthday."

"You didn't have to do this," I say as I blow out the candle. He laughs as the fire goes out only to jump back to life. I roll my eyes as I blow it again and again until it finally dies.

"Wait," he says, "you aren't allergic to anything, right? I totally forgot to ask."

"We'll see," I shrug as I pull the small wrapper on the bottom away, "but, thank you. It's been a while since I got a birthday gift."

"Don't worry about it," he shrugs as he takes a step backward to the open door. As he moves, I take a bite out of the small cake. I groan with pleasure and he lets out a chuckle, "my wife is a master baker and takes every opportunity she can to make something yummy. My shift is starting soon so I better head out. I'll see you later."

Just as he makes it to the doorway, two sour-faced officers stomp in. He stumbles as one of them runs into him, the other just sending him a pointed look before he turns toward me.

"There's a new assignment," the other agent, his nametag read Jones, says, "be ready and downstairs in fifteen."

"Understood," I nod as they immediately spin on their heels and leave in response. Of course, I see the nasty looks they shoot at Rodriguez, but he doesn't seem too bothered.

"Is that really all the information they give you?" He asks.

"Usually," I shrug as I carefully place my cupcake on the small dresser top before stepping over toward the small closet. I change into a pair of jeans and a white shirt before turning to face curious look.

"That sucks, man."

"Not really," I tell him as I slide on my boots. My coat sits draped over the end of the frame and I yank it up over my shoulders before stuffing the rest of his gift into my mouth. He laughs at my stuffed face before giving me a wave and leaving me alone in my room. I make sure to swallow down the chocolatey goodness before hurrying down the hallway in the opposite direction.

Though this building now stands as a sort of forced refuge for misplaced darklings, it was originally created to be a prison for darklings and monsters alike.

The creator had designed the whole thing to be as dull as possible. Bright white lights and white walls line every hallway. Elevator rides are silent, which is the best way to ride one. Rooms are dull and impossible to personalize.

My kind of place.

My pace slows as I lean forward and press the button to summon the elevator. Luckily, no others stand waiting or inside as it pings open. Stepping inside, I lean back against the far metal wall, always relieved that the machine was relatively new.

Nothing has settled into them yet.

I clench my teeth as the elevator gradually stops, opening to welcome another traveler. A woman stands waiting and freezes as soon as we catch each other's eyes. She takes a step back, her decision and reasoning evident on her face.

I roll my eyes as the doors slide shut, her disgusted face sinking into memory as I fold my arms over my chest. It doesn't matter what I do, people are always going to hate me simply for what I am.

We aren't even that different. See, lightlings often compare us darklings to monsters when we are more like the lightlings themselves. Monsters are of dark magic, created by some dark being at some point in time. A demon just had to create one blood sucker hundreds of years ago to make them a prominent problem today.

Darklings, on the other hand, are of dark energy which is naturally occurring. Lightlings are creatures of light energy which is also naturally occurring. We should be like two sides of a coin, different but equal.

Instead, they treat us as if we are more dangerous than actual monsters.

The elevator finally pings open on the ground floor, and I pause when I find it bustling with agents. The two agents assigned to me wave me forward and I dart after them, squeezing through bodies as I hurry after them. Most of the time I hate my small stature but days like these make it so much worse.

"Come on, boy," a harsh voice speaks out as someone grabs my arm and yanks me forward. I move to tear my limb out of his grasp before a sharp voice stops the both of us.

"Enough," one of the higher ups snaps and I am released. I stumble forward and send back a glare before facing the small and pudgy man. This guy is Ernie, one of the few bossmen than I absolutely loathe. He took one look at the worthless American dad trope and applied it to all facets of his life. He rides on the backs of better agents, making their accomplishments their own and treating nearly everyone, not just me, like garbage. I don't know how the N.A.S.O., the huge shifter agency, allows him to act the way he does even by their standards.

The fact that he had stopped them from yanking me around, however, means that something big has come along.

"Ryder Skye," Ernie spits out my name like a curse before he nods toward the door, "you know where to go. I'll be there in a moment."

I don't reply as I slide through the narrow door opening. As much as I want to, I refuse to glare back at the older man as I step into the morning sun. His large SUV stands parked along the street, running and ready to speed off as he likes to. Luckily for him, we live in the outskirts of the city so he can usually speed all he wants.

I climb into the backseat just as Ernie steps out of the building. Despite the cool air that surrounds us, he already has a layer of sweat covering his face.

"Sit back and relax," he says as he climbs into the front passenger's seat while another officer, one I didn't recognize, takes the driver's seat, "it's going to be a long drive."

Again, I don't reply as the car speeds away from the sidewalk. I lean my head against the cool window, hating the feeling of dread that washes over me. Something is happening, something big and I'm not sure I want to be a part of it.

What am I saying?

I know I don't.

Hours pass as we speed down a meandering road faster than humanly possible, one that takes us away from the city and away from the cool, green environment. Soon, a flat, brown, and barren landscape emerges.

Oh, great, the desert.

"We're two hours out," Ernie says as he tosses a tablet back to me. I catch it with a sigh before sliding my finger across the screen to unlock it. A fingerprint identification awaits me, and I do as it instructs.

"I don't know why we gave him the clearance," he mutters, complaining to the other agent who, like me, opts to remain silent.

I roll my eyes as I pull up the report. The first two pages are practically useless as most N.A.S.O. reports are. I get a whole history lesson, though this one was more important than most. The attack took place two nights ago inside of one of the last exclusive shifter communities in the United States. They used to be far more prominent back in the day when a group of warlocks started hunting pureblood children. Though the threat had long since been stifled, this community remains with one of the last teenage shifters of pureblood in the United States, if not the world.

Yes, shifters. Those annoying beings that can turn into animals and are somehow the "golden child" of the lightlings, though that may be a term they coined for themselves. The N.A.S.O., or North American Shifters Organization, is a shifter agency that deals with and protects shifters as a whole and their interests. I am kind of like their forced intern. I work for them, and they feed me.

Seems fair, right?

There are two victims. Austen Smith, the uncle, is just short of forty-five years old. Last night, he was attacked in his brother-in-law's house and pulled through the floorboards. Dark magic suspected, victim in critical condition in D.M.M.A. hospital.

The second, and the one deemed more important, was Theodore Emerson. He's fifteen, one of the youngest pureblooded shifters left, and was a straight shot to the academy if he had been able to pass the entrance exams. He was also attacked by an unknown assailant, dark magic affirmed by visiting D.M.M.A. agent. Unknown mark burned into his chest, victim in stable condition in D.M.M.A. hospital.

It must be quite dire for the N.A.S.O. to pull the D.M.M.A. in.

No one likes the D.M.M.A..

The D.M.M.A., Demon Monitoring and Managing Agency, has been around since medieval times. Back then, they did as their names suggests and dealt with an influx of demonic activity. Demonic activity that is rarely seen in modern times. Instead of becoming obsolete as they should have, they now work as a sort of government type agency that polices and claims to protect the supernatural population.

Key word: *claims*.

The D.M.M.A. is technically above the N.A.S.O., based on a treaty that was signed hundreds of years ago. Shifters around the old prison complain about it all the time, claiming that they got the bad end of the deal.

They have never, though, had to use the D.M.M.A. as an ally. How big would the fight have to be for them to run to the D.M.M.A. for help?

I let the tablet fall to my lap as I turn to gaze out the window. The bright sun is nearly blinding, the dull landscape offering no distraction from the work at hand. Finally, after what seems like hours, I can see us closing in on something in the distance.

Standing alone and sticking out like a pimple on otherwise clear skin, I can finally see the small community and its tall clay walls a few miles away. A soft murmur of excitement floods through the two agents in the front seats, an excitement I don't share.

As we grow near the iron gates, I can see the slight tint of fae runes carved into the walls. As we pass through, I can feel the power emanating off them as we drive deeper into the small town.

Though it is blocked from the outside world by towering walls, it looks just like any other small town in the middle of nowhere. A billboard welcomes you once you pass through the gates, boasting about the local football team. Jogging nobodies' wave as you pass by, grins plastered on their faces. Perfectly manicured and lush green lawns, despite the incredible dry climate, border the street with nearly identical two-storied houses, separated only by color.

We pull up to a house blocked off by police tape. N.A.S.O. officers are darting back and forth and yet no one dares to step foot in the building. I let out a sigh of relief as the SUV pulls to a stop.

They would have ruined it if they had gone in.

"You know what to do," Ernie orders, though I have already slipped out of the vehicle. I duck under the tap and ignore the stares that follow as I walk through the stone walkway and bound up the steps. I pass as I stand in the open doorway, a feeling of dread washing over me.

Whatever happened in here...it was no small feat.

Homes have memories, ones that linger long after mortal life. Some fade while others disappear completely. A few, however, of a certain *caliber* lay embedded in the walls, forever tainting its echo. These special few are never to be taken lightly. More times than not, they are horrific events that would haunt even the most seasoned veteran.

This is where I come in. My abilities, the reason I'm useful the N.A.S.O., is because I am what my boss calls a mind bender. I can read minds, alter thoughts, and access memories even hidden within inanimate

10

objects. There is no one quite like me which is why they stole me from my home when I was twelve and put me to work.

What fun.

The problem is, however, the more people who pass through, the more the memories tend to fade. Surprisingly, my boss had been smart enough to not allow anyone else into the house besides the medical team.

I step inside, the darkness weighing heavily in the emptiness. Homes aren't supposed to feel so empty. This isn't, however, a feeling that came after the attack. This house has never felt like a home…

Agents are moving around nosily outside, tugging on my concentration as I *mentally* reach out to figure out where the strongest memory lingers. I don't bother to flick on the light as I walk though, letting the house tell me where to go.

I am pulled toward the kitchen, the beckoning memories tugging me forward. Bright sunlight filters in through the blinds, sending cascading pillars of light draping across the red carpet and traveling across the dark ground.

Perfectly illuminating the large hole in the hardwood.

I kneel, hovering my hand over the hole. Deliberately, I press my palm over the sullied wood. I close my eyes as I open my mind, allowing whatever catches me to pull me in.

Almost immediately, as if the vision wanted to wait for dramatic effect, the events spring to life. The memories only ever appear visibly, never audibly, so it's always as if I'm watching a silent movie.

Before me, the hole fades away. The house springs to life, warm light stretching out across the once dark space. A pair of tapping feet replaces the hole, and paired with the bobbing head, I assume the man is listening to music. Chopped vegetables line the countertop and he stands stirring a bright red concoction in a pan on the stove top.

I assume this is the uncle.

Pushing myself to my feet, I turn toward to face the rest of the first floor. Sulking in the corner and sprawled out in a recliner, a teenager sits staring at a television set. He isn't watching it, though. He looks miserable, his entire face pointed downward. downward.

Theodore Emerson.

The uncle, Austen, is speaking, his entire demeanor changing as he shifts gears. The teenager mutters something in response, his lips unreadable as he dips his head even lower.

There is something incredibly familiar about him…

I wait for the inevitable bad event that always sparks the need for me. I turn away from the two and narrow my eyes as I spin around just in time to notice the shifting shadows that came to interrupt the chill family evening.

There are two distinct beings, ones I have only heard about in stories, twisting in and out of the dark shadows. They look human enough, except for the fact that they are devoid of any distinctive features. They have no face and smoke billows out of them, darkening everything around their feet. They crawl on all fours as they enter the kitchen, their limbs sticking out sharply as they moved. They are all smoke, twisting and pulling each other along.

Shadow demons, pets to much stronger masters.

As always, I fight the urge to warn the two. I know I'm watching the past and there is nothing I can do but…I always felt the need to try and stop it. There is nothing I can do but watch.

They don't see them until it's too late.

Austen is taken first. The creatures sink below the floors, disappearing from my sight. Dark hands stretch up through the wood directly below the shifter's feet. They hover over his legs before they dart out and latch onto his shins. He throws his head back as he is yanked down, his body falling through the wood as if it's water. I wince as he is finally released and the wood hardens around his legs.

I turn away from the man screaming in pain and anger as they make their move on the teenager. Most would have been running or screaming but he does neither. He just sits staring, his pale blue eyes wide as they twist around and crawl toward his rigid body. He is frozen, though I can't tell if it is simply from terror or by some effect coming off the shadow demons.

Again, I fight against the urge to call out to him.

One tackles him off the recliner, sending them both rolling onto the carpet. They tussle for a moment, the teenager finally seeming to realize the danger he is in. Before he can really do anything, though, the other warps around his legs and keeps in him place.

I step to the side and crane my neck, hoping for a better view. All I can see, all the memories allow, is his face twisting in agony as they do something to his chest.

The strange symbol in the report...

Something else nags at me, pulling my attention away from the teen. I turn just as someone new steps into view.

He looks far more human than the two currently tormenting the teen. With a mop of black hair and casual dress, he would have passed as human for anyone else. Instead, I catch his pitch-black eyes, seeing through his glamor instantly.

A warlock, a rather bold one at that.

How did he get through the runes that cover the community walls?

I follow his gaze and find a red-headed teenager hiding behind the railing of the stairway I haven't noticed before. Her bright eyes shine off the bright light as the warlock steps closer to her. I wait for her to run or even show an ounce of fear but, nothing.

No, she is waiting for him.

I groan as I pull away, the images slowly fading as darkness envelopes me once again. I pull my hand away from the broken wood before sinking back on my heels. I take a moment to bring myself back into my own head before pushing myself to my feet.

Unlike what I usually face, this brings more questions than answers.

2

The New Assignment

As I walk out, my eyes linger on the staircase and the image of the girl haunts my thoughts. Can she be the one who brought them here? Without help or any obvious disturbance, they wouldn't have made it through the runes.

"Finally," Ernie snaps as I step into the warm desert air. As always, his voice instantly annoys me as I bound down the porch steps to where he stands waiting on the lawn.

"It often takes a while," I remind him as we walk across the street, "your men can go in now and do their investigation."

"You don't give the orders around here," he snaps, my suggestion nagging at his ego. I roll my eyes as he steps away to give the order, not bothering to hide my annoyance. As much as it bothers the lower leveled idiots I usually deal with, I know the "big boss" cares very little for their complaints. As long as I get the job done, I'm in the clear.

I turn away as I head toward the line of SUVs. They are done with me so I get to it sit in the hot truck and finish my report until they are finished. As always, I consider wandering around the surrounding area, however, I doubt they'll want that either. I duck under the police tap before jogging over to the SUV I came in.

"There you are," a familiar voice stops me in my tracks. I turn the face the owner, plastering a fake smile over my lips. The man towers over me, his light brown hair gelled back. His piercing eyes seem to glare into my soul and I want nothing more to be free of his gaze.

Unlike the black combat clothes the other officers and agents have to wear, he sports a dark suit, one that even I can tell is expensive. A small owl pin sits tacked to his breast pocket alongside the one with a face of a wolf, two symbols broadcasting his allegiance to the two biggest supernatural agencies. Despite the fact that they are often at odds with each other, the D.M.M.A. and N.A.S.O. are technically allies. Due to his position, he had to play nice. He is the bridge between the two, having to deal with representatives from both.

"Senator, sir," Ernie comes up beside me, his cheeks puffing up as he offered the tall man a wide smile. He throws his hand out but Emerson makes no move to shake it. Ernie glances down at his outstretched hand before letting it drop to his side, "what brings you to this part of the world? I'm sure you're a busy man."

"Very but this takes precedence."

"Oh, well, I'm sure it told you-"

"It?" Emerson asks, clearly confused.

"Yeah," he gestures toward me, as if his meaning was obvious. Of course, it's obvious to me.

"It," Emerson repeats with a frown. He sighs as he pulls out his phone, "who is your direct supervisor?"

"Officer Tunchez, sir," he answers, his frown mimicking Emerson's, "is there a problem?"

"Yes," he nods, pausing for a moment to type furiously away at the small screen. After a brief silence, he slides his phone back into his pocket and continues, "you are no longer leading this case. I will be taking it over. There will also be a meeting discussing your future employment."

"Excuse me?"

"This *boy*," Emerson emphasizes his last word and places his hand on my shoulder, "has a name and he is a valuable resource. Exploiting him is one thing, disrespecting is another. Leave before I have you escorted to a holding cell."

"That went from zero to a hundred really quick," I comment as the man scurries away. The Senator seems to consider my words before looking down to face me.

"I do not tolerate such outward disrespect," he says, "especially in these circumstances. Now, tell me what you found out."

"They were attacked by two shadow demons and a warlock," I tell him, "though the demons did most of the work."

"A warlock? How'd he get through the runes?" he asked, folding his arms across his chest.

"I think the witch invited them in."

"The witch? Someone else was in there with them?" The Senator's eyes dart back and forth before landing back on me, "what did she look like? Why would you think she invited them?"

"She was watching it happen and…she didn't look scared or worried. She looked almost…excited. It was as if she expected it and was just waiting for something more. When she saw the warlock step in, her eyes widened but…she didn't look scared. More like…eager. As for her looks, her most distinctive feature is her bright, red hair."

"That doesn't make any sense," Emerson shakes his head, "she wouldn't do something like this."

"You know her?"

"I know all of them," he shrugs, "the boy is my son and she was his girlfriend."

"So, that's why you're here," I mutter as the realization hits me. That's who Theodore reminded me of.

"Yes. Are you all done in there?"

"I saw all I could."

"Good," he says before gesturing toward his house, "you'll be moving on to a new assignment."

"A new assignment, sir?" I ask with a frown. I have been on the same "assignment" since I came over to the United States. Why would it be changing?

"Was I not clear?" He asks, his eyes once again boring into mine. It isn't an accusation, like most. Instead, it seems like open curiosity.

"You were perfectly clear, sir," I respond with a shaky sigh, "I am just surprised, is all. I haven't changed assignments since I got here."

"Follow me," he orders without bothering to acknowledge my words. Emerson leads me back toward the house, holding the tape up for me to duck under. We walk past a perfectly manicured lawn. He bounds up the steps and into the open doorway, nearly disappearing into the darkness. I move to follow, passing by several officers leaving the building. Of course, I can *hear* their disdain for me as we move by each other.

I doubt, however, that it is because of Ernie. Everyone hates that guy, even his assistant.

Shifters tend to hate me. Well, most of them. There is Rodriguez and Emerson never seemed to mind me. The Senator sees me more as an inconvenience more times than not. He sort of inherited me after the past big boss died, leaving him stuck with a young darkling. Instead of sending me back or hiding me away like I expected, he set me to work to help where I can.

Now I'm here and now he needs my help, something that has never happened before.

I follow him through the house until he stops abruptly in front of a bookcase that stands beyond what the memories had allowed me to see. Emerson pulls out a book, one without a title, and the entire bookshelf moves to the side to reveal a staircase leading downward into darkness.

A true villain's lair.

He doesn't hesitate as he steps down, disappearing into the dark stairway, leaving me to stare fearfully after him. As much as I hate the feeling of weakness, I hate the thought of stepping underneath the earth even more. There is a darkling saying, one that details the danger of stepping in the darkness below.

Step away from the land of the ancients and face the monsters that came before. Hungry they are, awaiting new meat to wander ignorantly into their depths.

I shiver at the thought and force my feet forward, allowing the darkness to swallow me whole. Most darkling sayings and legends tend not to be true, at least, not true in modern times.

Sure, way back then they had to worry about getting trapped in caves.

This is just a basement.

Just a hidden, definitely normal, basement.

"Scared of the dark?" Emerson asks after I finally make it down there. His voice holds no jest, again just simple interest. That is what I usually get from him, an almost morbid curiosity.

"Nope," I tell him as I glance over the small room, "just wary of what lies within it."

"Aren't we all," he mutters as he steps toward dark archway, lit only by some kind of power lying with in…it is glowing.

A portal.

Another warning bell rings through my head but I shove it back and force myself to stand beside the shifter as he moves toward it. He leans over toward a shelf along the wall, pulling back an opaque jar. Reaching in, his hand escapes with a thick red substance coating his fingers. Emerson kneels down and spreads it across the bottom, whispering fae words under his breath. I stumble back as it springs to life, the spiraling colors stretching from the bottom to the top.

"This one is old," I mutter as I lay my hand against the cold, dark stone. Memories of older times flash in my mind, far too many to keep track of. I gasp as I struggle to keep up until Emerson's hand yanks mine away.

"I wouldn't delve too deeply into this one," he says, speaking softly, "too many have passed through this house. It has a long, and hard, history."

"Do all shifters have one of these?" I ask him as he gestures for me to walk through first. He pauses for a moment, as if considering the question, before letting out a sigh.

"No," he shakes his head, "this whole community was actually built around this one before portal travel outside of our realm was banned. Now, I can only use it to travel to sanctioned places and am the only one who has access. Few others, like the WWA academy, have their own portals that are regulated by the D.M.M.A.."

"Can you make it go to other places?"

"If I deemed it necessary," he says, his eyebrows popping up at my question.

"Just curious," I shrug before stepping through. When we were younger, my brother had always asked why to literally anything. I found it annoying as a child but, I now find it a rather useful. People are willing to answer almost anything, as if sharing their knowledge was pleasurable.

My nose is immediately bombarded with the strong stench of disinfectant. I squint against the bright fluorescents above me as the hallway slowly grows into focus. The walls are painted a stark white with matching tiles below. It takes a nurse hurrying out of the room before me to realize that we are in a hospital of some kind.

No, not just some hospital. The main D.M.M.A. hospital in New York.

Emerson appears next to me and, without a word to me, starts walking away. I move to follow after him before pausing to glance back behind me. A dark stone archway stands imbedded into the white walls, as if the whole building had been built around it. It stands out; however, it almost looks like a decoration choice.

I twist back forward and hurry after the older man just as he stops in front of a door at the end of the hall. Like the rest, there is no number to differentiate it from the rest but, he seems confident in his choice. He knocks on the door softly before pushing the door open and popping his head in. With a sigh, he opens the door wider and waves me in.

"As you know," he says, speaking softly as he closes the door behind us, "my son was attacked. They found him a few hours after his uncle had sunken through the floor boards. You said a warlock did that?"

"The shadow demons did," I correct him as I peer over at the unconscious boy laying unnaturally still in the hospital bed. Just as in the memory, he looks just like his father with his deeply tan skin, light and wavy brown hair, and almost identical face. Even laying down, however, I can tell that he is a good deal shorter and chunkier than his father.

"Have you known shadow demons to be so…"

"Bold?" I offer up the world. When he nods solemnly, his bright eyes shifting toward his son, I continue, "no, well, I've never known their *masters* to be so bold. They need a master to survive outside of hell and, as the legends go, someone far more powerful

22

than a mere warlock. Something bigger is behind this, I'm sure of it."

"Something bigger," he repeats just as his phone vibrates in his pocket. Emerson curses under his breath before pulling it out, "okay, I have to go. If he wakes up before I make it back, try and see if you can find out anything else."

"Understood," I nod as he hurries out of the room. The door slams with a strange finality and I turn back toward the other teen. I sit down in the cushioned chair beside the bed, enjoying the comfort for just a moment. Even without digging into his mind, I can feel how frazzled Theo's current state is. Even in his sleep, his mind is whirling.

I turn my focus away from the sleeping teen and lean back, hoping to relax in my few moments peace. This assignment, the new one, has something to do with Theodore and I doubt it is simply looking into his head.

I let my head fall back against the chair cushion, my eyes narrowing as I face the white ceiling. I shake my head at Emerson's questions and his expectation of my supernatural knowledge. Like everyone else, he thinks I know everything about the darker side of the supernatural. The truth is, however, that my knowledge is very limited. I know what little I learned when I was younger and there isn't exactly a place I can go to learn more here. Looking into the darker side is looked down here, making your actions something suspicious to investigate.

Everyone always gets angry when I admit it but, I'm just wasn't a kid who wanted to learn about such things. My brother is…was…the one who made it a point to learn all he could.

"Hello?" A raspy voice pulls me out of my thoughts. I bring my head down and meet his eyes, sighing when his widened.

He is quicker than most to notice my eyes. I used to hate them and their obviousness until I finally settled into their strangeness. My eyes are a deep violet, one you can't get from a simple genetic mutation. I have dark blood in me, one that has yet to be placed. No one knows exactly what I am.

All they know is that I'm of dark energy.

A darkling…something to fear.

"You're…"

"A darkling, yes," I answer before he can finish his question. We sit there in silence for a moment as I wait to see his full reaction. I have no basis of knowledge for this, as I don't usually sit beside hospital beds, but his mind…even when I'm not *looking*, I can usually tell what they're feeling and he, well, he doesn't feel angry or scared.

No, he's simply curious like his father.

"An actual darkling," he mutters, "I've never met one before."

"I don't doubt that," I say as I sit forward, "just know that I am not here to hurt you. I work with your father. He had to step out for a moment but, wanted to see if we could figure out exactly what happened."

He nods as he sits up, wincing as he does so. I make no move to stop him, allowing him to arrange himself as he sees fit. He grabs at his chest, seeming to realize something sits underneath the thin gown and turns questioning eyes toward me. Like his father, he shares the same impossibly bright blue eyes.

"What do you remember, Theodore?"

"P-please don't call me that," he stutters out before clearing his throat, "Theo, call me Theo."

"Done," I say.

"Thanks," he chuckles nervously as he rubs his legs above the blanket, "all I know is that we were attacked. I don't really remember details just…flashes and the feeling of something carving into my chest. That's what's on my chest, right? Bandages?"

"Yes, sir," I nod again, "you were attacked as was Austen."

"What about Jenny?" He asks, true fear extruding from his mind, "is she okay? I don't remember seeing her before…"

He carries off, not wanting to finish the thought.

"They haven't found her yet."

"What?"

"She's missing," I clarify, "and has been since that night. There are no clues to indicate who took her or where they disappeared to. Hence why I am here."

"She's gone," he mutters, "how can she just be gone?"

"That's what we are trying to figure out, Theo."

"I don't remember," he shakes his head, "I…I don't remember…I remember leaving her upstairs and I was watching a show as Austen made dinner. I heard this noise and I saw…I don't even know what I saw when everything went black."

A different feeling settles over him, one that is impossible to ignore.

25

"This isn't your fault," I speak up, "none of it was your fault. They're going to find Jenny and they're going figure out why they targeted you. They just need a little help first."

"How can I help? I hardly remember anything."

"That's why I'm here," I assure him, "my abilities allow me to see those memories of yours, even the ones trying to hide from view."

"Abilities?" He asks before he narrows his eyes at me, "you're going to read my mind or something?"

"Yes," I answer and his eyes widen slightly, "I am going to enter your mind and we're going to experience that memory together."

"Wait, really?"

"Yes."

"Okay," he nods, "anything to help Jenny."

"Alright, first-"

"This is now official D.M.M.A. business," a sharp, female voice cuts into our conversation just as the door flies open. I snap my head toward the noise and I inwardly groan as the woman steps in with the Senator trailing behind. Her bright, witchy eyes land on me and she folds her arms over her chest, "this is officially a D.M.M.A. case. We don't require your services. Please find your way out. I'm sure your supervisor will arrange transport."

"Leave," Emerson orders after I stay planted in the chair. Without a word, I stand and step past the two adults. Before the door closes, Emerson looks back and mouths the word *listen*.

3

D.M.M.A. vs. N.A.S.O.

"Church, I have this covered," Emerson's voice seems to echo as I watch the interaction from behind his eyes. He can't truly feel me there, especially since I'm not digging.

"Perhaps I would believe you if you didn't hire underage darklings," she snaps back, "I understand he was there when you got the job but that doesn't mean you have to use him, Emerson. He's fifteen! Would you like your son being used like this? They're the same age!"

"His abilities are beyond useful..."

"He's a child," she sighs, "and a darkling. There is bound to be an incident where someone ends up hurt. I'm surprised it hasn't happened yet."

"You doubt his intelligence and his self-control."

"I don't doubt him," she argues, "I doubt the will of your agents. You really think none of them would take the chance to hurt, if not kill, him if they had the chance? If they knew they could write it off as an accident?"

"Your hatred of shifters astounds me," he sighs with a shake of his head. As much as I'm sure he hates it, we all know her words are true. I've heard his officers threaten as much, and they meant it.

"My hatred for your kind has nothing to do with this. Did you learn nothing from Maybelle?"

Maybelle? What do they have to do with Maybelle?

"Obviously not," he sighs, "none of this matters. I am within the law when it comes to him. I am also within the law when I say that this is still my case."

"How so?"

"Your daughter may be involved," he explains, "but the victim is a shifter. According to our agreed upon rules, I am in charge as the leading member of the N.A.S.O.. I am entitled to your help but, I am not required to ask for it."

"My daughter-"

"Your daughter is a missing persons case that, as of now, stands separate from my son's. I'll give you what I can about her but, as of now, you need to leave."

"Charles," she snaps out. Their relationship is closer than I originally thought as I have never heard anyone use his first name.

"Shelly," he says, copying the warning in her voice.

"This conversation isn't over," she threatens, pointing her finger at his chest.

"I don't expect it to be," he answers simply as she stomps out of the room. I pull myself out of his head just as she steps out. Before heading down the hallway, she turns to me and gives me an almost apologetic look before hurrying away.

"Ryder," Emerson pokes his head out and waves me in. I nod as I follow after him as he leads the way back to the bed. Like last time, his phone buzzes in his pocket and he is torn away before his son can even say hello to him.

"Does that happen often?" I ask Theo as I take back my seat. Theo shrugs as he watches the door slam before shifting his focus to me.

"You're fifteen, too?"

"Yes."

"And you have a job?"

"Technically, I don't. I'm kind of under the category of unpaid intern."

"Ah," he nods as he absently pulls at a loose thread in the cotton blanket, "do we...do we do your thing now?"

"I think it would be best," I tell him, "you'll just gave to let me in."

"Let you in?"

"Just, don't fight me, okay? That will just make it harder," I tell him. He nods and leans back, squeezing his eyes shut as if waiting for it to hurt. I roll my eyes as I close mine as well.

His thoughts run rampant, calling out to me even before I truly reach out. I can hear the D.M.M.A. woman's shrill voice behind me, my name sitting on her tongue. I don't allow myself to be pulled away as I zero in on the thoughts that beckon to me, desperate for my attention...

Song lyrics, snapshots of some action movie, random math equations, and many more jumbled thoughts await me as enter his head. I struggle against the mass of information, completely hopeless to make sense of it all. It only, however, takes a minute for Theo to reign himself in and focus on the events that brought him here.

As sudden as the mess came, it clears up to reveal the living room we both know. I find myself standing on the hardwood of Theo's childhood home but, a far darker feeling has settled over this version of it.

"This used to be my safe place," Theo's voice echoes through the halls, "what is it now?"

"Just a house," I tell him, not bothering to linger on his pain, "we need to focus on that night specifically."

"I know," he nods, now standing beside me. He wears his hospital gown even in his mind's eye. Just like his body, he is broken and confused.

His memory slowly takes shape, shifting from the living room to one I haven't been in before. It is a bedroom, complete with a bed, a dresser, and a cluttered desk. It is easy to assume it belongs to Theo, my eyes finding the action movie poster tacked to the wall above the bed.

None of this matters, though. No, I zero in on the bright haired girl that sits sprawled out on the bed.

The girl from the memory...the one waiting for the warlock.

The witchy girlfriend.

"Look," her voice is muffled, "it isn't you...it's me...You have to understand, Theo, I've just felt like something is missing. I...I found someone who can fix that."

"Found someone," Theo repeats, a habit of his it seems. His past self comes into view with trembling lips.

"I know," she sighs dramatically, reminding me of those old soap operas they play in the cafeteria back at the refuge, "it's sudden and it isn't fair. But, don't you want me to be happy?"

Theo doesn't speak, his downturned face answer enough. She pushes herself up and saunters over to him, her face expressionless. She places her hand on his chin and forces him to look at her, she tells him, "he's really great. You'd like him."

"I'd like him?" He finally snaps to life, pushing her hand away from him, "you think I'd like the person you're cheating on me with?"

"It wasn't like we had an actual relationship, Theo. It was one of...convenience," she shrugs, "it was just something to do..."

"...You know," another voice speaks up as the memory fades, leading us back downstairs and into the kitchen, "I never liked her anyway."

"Liar," Theo mutters from the recliner, never looking up to face him, "why would she even come over if all she was going to do is break up with me? She could have called. She could have done it when her mother was still here waiting for her. I don't even want to see her, you know? I just want her gone."

"Everything will be fine," Austen says with a smile, humming softly as he cuts up vegetables, "time will show you. Besides, she'll be out of your hair as soon as I finish dinner, okay? I'll drop her off and we can go to the bowling alley or something."

"How do you know?" Theo asks, his voice barely above a whisper.

"How do I know what?"

"That everything will be fine?"

"I've lived a lot of years, Theo...a lot of years..."

The memory shifts slightly and I find myself beside Theo on the same chair as I had when I first saw him. Shame and guilt radiate through the memory, tainting any of the anger or sadness that he might have felt over his break up.

The creatures take his uncle, looking no more than shadows as he is dragged down. His agonized screams reverberate through my ears and I want nothing more than to pull back into myself. Instead, I force my eyes to face Theo.

Fear rises through the guilt, his frozen form an easy target for the two monsters. I hear his scream and feel the pain that still echoes through his body. I want to stumble away...I want to escape but...I have to see...

As everything goes black, I hear him...that warlock.

"Come on, fiery princess...let's take you to your new lover..."

I stumble away from Theo, my breathing coming out in heavy puffs as I struggle to reign in my thoughts to close myself off. Never before have I faced thoughts so distinct...so *real*. Slowly, but surely, I gain control of myself before a strong hand grabs my shoulder.

I jump and stumble away, spinning to face Emerson's gaze. He looks almost worried as he inspects me before moving on to check on his son.

"What happened?" He asks as I use the bed to keep my upright. I've never had this sort of reaction before but, then again, I've never felt the pain of their memories before.

How strange...

"Come with me," I mutter as I push myself away from the bed. Theo's voice calls after us as we step into the hall, neither of us turning to answer. Agent Church stands in the hallway, as if waiting to see if Emerson would mess up enough to allow her clearance.

He never will.

"The warlock spoke to the witch," I say after the door slides shut, "Theo didn't know because he doesn't understand daemonic but, I was right. The girl invited the warlock."

"What?" The agent, Church, asks, "there is no way."

"There is," I tell her, "he literarily says: Come on, fiery princess...let's take you to your new lover..."

"Am I just supposed to take your word for it?" She scoffs, "I know my daughter."

"But he can actually see what happened," Emerson speaks up, his voice softer than I've ever heard. It is strange watching him talk with an agent he genuinely cares and care for her he does. There is something there, present in both their minds, that neither dare to look into. He sighs before continuing, "an invitation was the only way for one of their kind to get through the runes unscathed. There was no indication that they had been broken."

"My daughter would never-"

"She did," I interrupt her, "that is a fact. However, something more is going on. She broke up with Theo, mentioning a want for more. A warlock shows up, mentioning a new lover. I mean, people have done less for love."

"You think something manipulated my daughter," she asks, "into giving up her boyfriend to a warlock and running off with him?"

"Yes. The warlock was probably just a means to an end. We all know warlocks never do any favors.

What if Theo was her form of payment to get her to her new man?"

"I mean," Church coughs out, "that would take a while, wouldn't it? To trick a girl into giving up her first boyfriend? I mean, she loved him."

"If it was a dark being, especially an older one, she would have found a way to hide it from you," Emerson grumbles. I wait for anger to override him, for him to lash out at her for the mistake her daughter made. Instead, he simply heaves out a sigh and turns to face me.

"You stay with him," he orders as he nods toward the door. He gestures between him and the D.M.M.A. agent before continuing, "we will see if we can figure out what we can about that symbol. Have you seen it yet? Do you have any idea what it means?"

"I haven't, but I'll take a look."

"Good," he nods, "we'll be back."

"What was that all about?" Theo asks as soon as I step back into the room. I sigh and move to plop back down on the chair beside him.

"I think it's better if you rest," I tell him. I should have said nothing; however, I hate lying. There is something about it, no matter how inconsequential, that twists my stomach.

"I think it's better if you tell me," he whines as he flops back against the pillows, "I hate being kept in the dark."

"I know," I tell him, trying to sound sympathetic, "but it isn't really my place to tell you. When your father gets back-"

"He'll tell me that I don't need to worry about it like he always does," he groans, "he never tells me anything."

"Can't be nice," I tell him, "would it make you feel better if I said I was usually in the same boat?"

"Not really," he says but chuckles. I smile slightly as I lean back, waiting as I always do on my higher-ups. I doubt my new assignment will only involve sitting with Theo while he recovers. What else would they need me for?

"But, hey," I say, leaning back forward, "that...symbol carved into your chest. Can I see it?"

"Why?"

"They think I might recognize it," I shrug, "so your dad asked me to look."

"Ugh, really?" He mutters as he pushes himself back up. Theo sits there for a moment before reaching behind himself. He groans as his movements stretch his chest and I shake my head as I stand up. With a quick pull, I undo the top knot of the series of strings keeping the gown up. His arms fall to his lap as I sit back down.

"Thanks."

"Sure," I shrug as he pulls it off his shoulders. A slab of bandages blocks it from view but Theo quickly rectifies that. With narrowed eyes, I follow the round shape as it curves and twists inside a circle. It isn't something I've seen before but, it looks vaguely familiar.

I know that language.

My heart drops at the realization and an overwhelming sense of dread washes over me. This language...it was daemonic, sure, but it isn't one that any run-of-the-mill demon would use. This was...this was far older and darker.

Used only by monsters of legend. Alter-demons, or so darkling historians believed. No one has been able to translate it. A shiver shakes its way down my back at the mere thought.

"What is it? What does it mean?" Theo's voice sounds far away as I push myself to my feet. Luckily, before I have to face his onslaught of questions, the door opens to reveal my boss looking more annoyed than ever.

"Son," he smiles slightly as he faces his son before he glances over at me. Emerson waves me out the door and slams the door shut behind him.

"You know what it is?"

"No," I shake my head, "no one does."

"What do you mean?"

"That language...it's in the book of the damned. It has never been translated...it shows only a basic similarity to the other daemonic dialects...it is said to have been used only by-"

"I know all about the book of the damned," Emerson nods, not letting me finish the sentence. Something new radiates off him...something close to *fear*.

"Whatever wants him," I tell him, "it isn't just some warlock."

"Well," Emerson says, his voice and demeanor shifting, "it is nothing you have to worry yourself about. At least, not for now."

"Yes, sir," I bow, slightly relieved that I am down with this mess, "shall I be on my way?"

"Unfortunately, no," he shakes his head as he stares hard at Theo's door, "I have another job for you. Your new assignment."

With that, he hands me a tablet much like the one I had in my hands when we were heading to the community. When it reaches my hand, the screen lights up. Theo's medical report flashes in front of me and I frown as I look back up at Emerson.

"What is this?"

"He's going to be your new assignment."

"My what?" I ask.

Before he can clarify, however, his phone rings and his focus is torn away from me...again. I watch as he stomps down the hallway, speaking quickly to whoever is at the other end.

With a groan, I step back into the room. Luckily, Theo's soft snores fill the small space. I'm not ready to answer his question as he, no doubt, has to be curious as why I ushered everyone else out. Instead of sitting beside him, I back up to one of the corners and let myself disappear into the background as a nurse pops in to check on the sleeping teen.

Random scenarios dance across my mind as I try to figure out exactly what being Theo's assignment actually meant. Surely, Emerson doesn't think my abilities can do anything more for him. Usually, I do my mind thing and I get ushered away.

Why is this time different?

4

Loud Thoughts and Sensitive Information

A soft knock at the door pulls me away from my worries. I glance away from the sleeping form as a nurse pops in and holds open the door to let a man in a wheelchair roll his way in.

I know this man.

Theo's uncle, Austen.

"Theo," he speaks, his voice barely above a whisper as he struggles forward. I resist the urge to dart forward and move the chair that stands in his way. Shifter's tend to not like me butting in, even if it is to make their lives easier.

"Austen?" Theo's groggy voice breaks as he shifts his head toward the older shifter. While they obviously aren't father and son, there is something similar about the two of them.

Perhaps the mother's brother?

Tears brim in Theo's eyes and I don't have to read his mind to know how much he cares for the man. I know Theo loves his father but the bond these two share is much stronger.

It is then that I truly notice his legs, well, the lack thereof. Two stumps linger where his knees are supposed to be. White bandages cover the stumps and

I wince as I unwillingly pictured him being dragged through the floor boards.

Poor guy…

"I'm…I'm sorry…" Theo cries out, his broken voice cutting into my want to ignore the conversation, "I should have done something…I could have…"

"Don't worry about me," Austen says with a warm smile, "I'll be fine. What about you, huh? How are you doing?"

"Surviving," he shrugs and winces, his hand rubbing at his still bare chest. Luckily, he had replaced the bandages before scratching at it, "I feel fine but…my chest."

"Don't mess with it," Austen reprimands him and yanks on a loose sleeve. Theo sighs and pulls the gown back over his shoulders, letting the man tie it back up in the back. Their conversation shifts past the events of the night before, moving on to more mundane matters. I can tell they're avoiding talking too much about it, especially steering clear from a certain red-haired witch.

This, however, is about to end. I can feel Emerson's impatience from down the hall. Even from here as he hurries back to the room, I can tell that he knows of the uncle's visit and he isn't too keen on the guy.

Emerson bursts through the door and outwardly sighs at the sight of the two. He hates small talk, especially when there are far more pressing things to discuss. He doesn't want to know how *well* everyone is as long as they're alive. No, he wants someone to blame…someone to *hurt*.

39

Emerson always thinks so *loud*. He makes it impossible to ignore, no matter how much I try. I can always tell where he is based solely on my inability to block it out. Every time I am with him, I am grateful that I don't work with him very often.

"As fun as this is," he says, finally voicing his thoughts. I shake my head as I stay planted where I am, watching as he marches over to the wheelchair and yanks it backward, "we need to discuss some rather *sensitive* information. When we are through, I'll have someone fetch you."

"You can't just dismiss me," Austen argues, locking the wheels and the chair screeches to a stop. He will have to practically carry him out now, "I'm not your employee."

"Sure," Emerson nods, "but this is *my* son and we are in the middle of a N.A.S.O. case. Unless you want to sit in a cell for interfering with official business, I would listen to me."

Austen curses under his breath, his eyes flashing bright for a moment. He doesn't, however, let himself shift. He instead opts to glare up at the old man, probably well aware of his new handicap. Austen rolls himself out with a heavy sigh. I step over and slide the door closed as he passes through before returning to my spot in the shadows.

"Dad!" Theo starts out but Emerson waves his comments away. He too glares at the older man but snaps his mouth shut. His father huffs out as he moves to sit down next to him in the cushioned chair.

"I'm sorry, son," Emerson's voice shifts away from that of a caring father to the serious agent, changing the whole atmosphere of the room, "but, we need to have a discussion."

"You're right," Theo nods, getting braver now, "like, how are you going to find Jenny? Why did Ryder have to pull you outside? What haven't you told me literally anything about this?"

"To answer your first question," Emerson gives me a sharp look before continuing, "we are working alongside the D.M.M.A. Witches have a knack for finding lost things and I'm sure it's just a matter of time before we find her."

"As for your second question, it was some rather sensitive information that we need to figure out before we tell anyone, let alone you. This isn't something that you need to worry about, though."

"What should I be worrying about?" Theo scoffs, glaring over at his father.

"Passing the exams," he says and Theo's face drops as he groans, "I've already talked to the academy. They've approved you for their summer program. You will take some remedial classes before retaking it before fall classes start. You and Ryder will be mostly alone, but it will be the safest place for you."

"He's coming with me?" Theo asks before I can speak, "I thought the school only allowed lightlings."

"They used to," he shrugs, "but they want to be more inclusive so it benefits the both of us."

"Sir," I say, "may I interject?"

"It won't change anything," Emerson states, "this is your new assignment. You are to look after my son."

"I'm sure my abilities can be used elsewhere," I try again.

"Unfortunately, no. You can sense danger coming faster than any of my agents, whether it be a physical or mental attack. You will also stand out far less than a pair of agents following him around."

"But…" Theo chokes out.

"No, son. This is final. You will go to the academy and you will be safe there. I will have no other complaints or comments about this from either of you, understand?"

"Yes, sir," we both say in unison as Emerson pulls out his phone and stands to leave. Without another word, he disappears into the hallway. Theo heaves out a sigh before falling back against the pillows.

"This sucks," he mutters as the door closes.

"Don't worry too much about it," I tell him, "you'll forget I'm there in no time. The others will learn to ignore me too."

"That doesn't sound fun for you."

"That's kind of my job," I shrug, moving to step back into the corner as I usually do but, alas, he won't let me.

"What exactly is your job?" Theo asks, "it can't be normal for the N.A.S.O. to hire a teenager."

"Yeah," I shrug, "they took me in because of my unique abilities."

"Mind reading is in high demand, huh?"

"Obviously."

"Do you like it?"

"Nope."

"How did you get into it, then?" he asks.

"I-" I open my mouth to answer when I'm interrupted by a nurse coming in to bombard him with questions. I let out a sigh of relief as I sulk back, happy to go unnoticed in the shadows. Theo's eyes, however, keep coming back to me as if his question still lingers. I groan inwardly, hoping that he'll drop it like everyone else would.

Why is he making conversation with me? A darkling?

Why does he care?

Darklings and lightlings together is never a good idea, especially if the past is anything to go on. Wars entangled our histories until, finally, the centuries long war was won in that cursed city.

Want to guess who won?

Once the nurses leave with a slam of the door, Theo sits up and immediately turns toward me. I bite my tongue as I wait for him to repeat his question.

He doesn't and opts for an easier one.

Thankfully.

"So, do you always work with my dad?"

"Almost never," I say, not bothering to move from my place on the wall, "I usually work with his inferiors."

"Is he nice?"

"Nicer than the rest."

"Cool," Theo nods but he doesn't sound convinced. Our experiences with the Senator are very different. He sees an absent, almost neglectful, father. I see one of the few shifters that don't spit at me as I pass.

I don't voice my thanks, though I'm grateful, as silence fills the room. Luckily, his mind is a lot less demanding than his father's, making it easy to ignore his thoughts.

The silence doesn't last long.

Soon, Emerson's strong mind is back, radiating with impatient anger.

"I am his father," Emerson's voice bleeds through the door as he argues with someone right outside Theo's room. The teen hangs his head as the argument continues, "and I will choose what is best for him. The academy is the safest place for him, you know that. There hasn't been a successful attack there in centuries and there has been no report for any outside incidents. The wards are stronger than even the D.M.M.A.'s."

"Let me go with him," the uncle's voice replies.

"No, you had your chance to protect him. Now, it's my turn."

"By entrusting him to a darkling *teenager*?"

I frown as he emphasized the word teenager instead of focusing on what everyone else notices first. *Darkling*...the word often comes off people's tongues like it leaves a bad taste in their mouths. Like Theo, there isn't a focus on his kind unlike everyone else outside of this family.

Like uncle, like nephew.

"I will protect him in whatever way I see fit," Emerson's voice comes out sounding more like a growl. I roll my eyes as I lean my head back against the wall.

What is he going to do?

Fight a newly legless patient?

A brief moment of silence follows before the door flies open and Theo's father enters alone. Theo waits a moment, his eyes on the open door before asking, "where's Austen?"

"He had other business to attend to," Emerson answers before clearing his throat. It is obvious that Theo doesn't believe the lie but he doesn't rectify that. Instead, he continues, "the hospital has cleared you to leave tomorrow. You will have a ride waiting for you tomorrow afternoon. Theo, you are to stay with Ryder at all times. If you try sneaking away from him, we will have words. Ryder, outside."

He doesn't give his son time question him as he headed for the door. I follow after him without a glance back at Theo's questioning gaze, avoiding his angry thoughts as he is once again left in the dark.

"Keep an eye on his mind whether he wants you to or not. We don't know what that mark is or what it can do. We can't have him going insane without some kind of warning," Emerson says as soon as the door closes behind us.

"Understood," I nod as he pulls out two smartphones. One already has a case and he hands it out to me first, "this is Theo's. We have a tracker in place as well as access to the camera. I hate having to spy on him but it's for his own good. Obviously, don't tell him."

"Got it," I say with a sickening feeling enveloping me. Even if it is for his safety, should they really be going that far?

"And this is yours," he hands me the other one, "it has two numbers programmed into it, mine and Theo's."

"Are you also going to be spying on me through this as well?" I ask him.

"No," he sighs, "I trust you enough and I'm sure we'll see enough of you through Theo's phone. I expect weekly updates, understand?"

"You got it, sir," I tell him, "will you be there to see us off?"

"Unfortunately, not," he sighs as he glances down the hallway, "take care of my son."

I watch him stomp down the hallway and turn out of sight. It makes sense now, I realize as I step back into the room. He doesn't want me there for Theo's physical protection. No, he wants me there to make sure his mental state isn't compromised.

After receiving his smartphone, Theo's eyes remain glued downward. I smile as it allows me to slip into the background, unheard and unseen as I usually do.

Thus, has been my life for the past three years. I was taught to sit there and take orders, ignoring my own inhibitions. I have no friends, no family, and nothing to call my own except for a charred book they let me keep after they yanked me from my…home.

Maybelle. Sure, it's a cursed place that most would do everything to avoid but, it's still my home. Three years ago, I watched my brother fall to his death because of a stupid mistake. Before I could even react, I was pull way and promised a life of purpose by Ernest O'Neil, the previous Senator for the N.A.S.O. for this sector of the United States. He believed me to be part of a prophecy. A *darkling* prophecy that isn't even acknowledged by said darklings. When he died, it came as a relief to many of his department.

Most deemed him insane.

His death occurred a few weeks after I had settled into the New York headquarters. Emerson took his place later, ignoring the old man's notes and completely destroying his research. I assumed he would do the same to me, however, Emerson turned out to be a smarter and rather kinder than even O'Neil.

At least Emerson gave me my own room and something to do besides sitting there and waiting for some big bad to happen that probably never would.

No, I had never truly had a problem with Emerson. The problems came from those he assigned me to.

My thoughts are interrupted by Theo's snores. His phone has fallen to the side and he still sits hunched over in a position that can't be comfortable. I plop down on the cushioned chair beside him, ready to let sleep take me away from the worries that occupy my busy mind.

It isn't long before Theo's rhythmic snores lure me to sleep.

***

"Good morning," a nurse pulls me out of a dreamless sleep. I sit there for a moment, glaring tiredly at the ceiling when I realize I'm not in my bed at the refuge. It takes me a moment to remember where I am and why. Theo is already awake, looking more energized from the night before. The bags under his eyes are less pronounced and he seems able to move without wincing from the injury to his chest. The nurse smiles at him as she checks the chart before saying, "so, Theodore, how are we feeling today?"

"It's Theo," he smiles up at her, "and I feel great."

"Perfect," she nods, "you should be all set to leave today if your father comes in to sign you out. We'll send you home with a few painkillers to make sure your chest doesn't bother you too much."

"Awesome," Theo replies. She gives him a nod before turning to leave the room without another comment. As she passes, her eyes linger on mine and I can't avoid feeling the slight fear that sparks in her mind.

Typical.

"Are you as bored as I am?" Theo asks with a groan as he falls back down on his pillows. I shrug as I uncurl myself and push myself to my feet. Stretching my tired body, I raise my hands above my head and lean to the side.

"So," Theo says, seeming desperate to fill the silence, "it isn't fun to work with my dad?"

"First off, I don't with your dad. I work for him. Second off, my job is not at all exciting or fun."

"Does he ever let you do anything fun?"

"Like what?" I ask, "there isn't much I can do. I don't exactly get paid and there isn't a lot of darkling-inclusive entertainment in the N.A.S.O.- run refuge. What about you? Does he let you do anything or is that really up to Austen?"

"Well," Theo frowns as he tilts his head, "I don't know how much is my father and how much is Austen, I guess. He had never really been all that involved in my life, anyway. I guess that's why he thinks I always need babysat."

"What do you mean?"

"I mean," he nods as he gestures toward me, "you are basically babysitting me from now on even though we're the same age. Austen was forced to babysit me even though I'm fifteen. Do you know how stupid it is to need a babysitter when you're this old? I can handle myself."

"Can you, though?" I ask, gesturing toward his chest.

"In normal circumstances," he shrugs, taking no offence, "yes and...and my uncle would still have his legs. If he hadn't had to stay with me..."

"You don't know what would have happened if you had been all alone," I sigh as I lean forward. I don't mention the fact that the outcome would have probably been the same, "look, you can't change what happened, okay? There is no point in playing the 'what if' game. It'll only hurt more."

"I know but," Theo's voice shakes as he looks away, trying to hide the tears that fall past his eyes. I look away, trying to give him as much privacy as I can in the small space before he speaks up again, "I just can't shake this feeling of guilt. I mean, I watched him get dragged down. How could I just sit there and do nothing? I could have done something..."

"What could you have done?"

"I could have shifted...I could have fended them off until help came..."

"What you faced, Theo," I explain as I lean forward, "were shadow demons. Do you have any idea what they are?"

"Demons that are shadows?"

"I-well, yes," I nod with a grin, "I guess. There are very few things that truly hurt them. There wasn't a weapon in your house that would have caused any damage. There was truly nothing you could have done to help your uncle."

"That doesn't make me feel better."

"I know. Nothing will."

"Knock, knock," a nurse, the same one as before, pops her head in before pushing the door fully open. She has two duffel bags in her arms, both falling to the ground as she steps fully into the room.

"What can we do for you?" Theo asks, a smile stretching its way across his face.

"Your father has signed you out. There's a ride waiting to take you to your destination.

"Wait, like, right now?"

"Right now."

5

The Academy's Summer Program

A woman waits for us in the lobby. She is an owl shifter, if her strangely wide eyes are anything to go off of. She has a serious face, one that is emphasized by the deep wrinkles that look as if they were carved into her tan skin. Intelligence sits behind her spectacles, hiding away in her brown irises.

"I'm Mrs. Sagle," she introduces herself with a grainy voice that matches her face, "and I will be in charge of you while you attend the academy. Any questions, concerns, or comments will be directed to me, understand? No other teacher or administrator, besides the super, has been debriefed on this situation. We want to keep it as quiet as we can in order to properly protect Theo."

"I understand," I nod and Theo mutters the same.

"Good," Mrs. Sagle says, her face breaking into a grin, "now, Theo. Your father has told me a lot about you and a lot about your failing exam grade."

"Yay," he mutters.

"Don't worry," she winks, "we'll have you ready to test by August. I have yet to have a student fail under me."

"I may be your first," he jokes as she turns her focus toward me. There's an easiness about her, and her mind, that throws me off. She is serious, but kind, asking her questions with zero expectations to where we should or should not be at.

One of the best kinds out there, if you ask me.

"Have you had any schooling?" Mrs. Sagle asks, her eyes staring into mine. If I were to stand under anyone else's gaze, I would have been uncomfortable. Instead, I feel at ease as I search for the best way to answer.

"I went through a few programs as per Senator Emerson's requirements," I tell her, remembering the few remedial classes I had taken a year prior, "however, I doubt it is up to your expectations."

"Agreed," she nods, looking over at the both of us, "Theo, your scores leave much to be desired but, so do most of our homeschooled students. You two won't be alone for the summer however, you two will be the only ones working strictly under me. I, and only I, will be instructing you. Everyone else will be assigned to a group of other teachers."

I zone out as their conversation continues, turning my focus to the bag that rests on my shoulder. We only know whose who's because of the tags tacked to the straps. I hypothesize what lays within mine, wanting nothing more than to open it. My curiosity mixes with slight embarrassment when I consider the possibility that Emerson had someone go to my room to collect my things.

I have nothing to hide, as I don't have much, except for that charred book and a few souvenirs I had snuck back from my outings. They are stupid and hold no value except that there is something comforting about having something to call my own.

Even if it is a foot keychain from a town I will never visit again.

"Ready?" Theo's voice pulls me away from the back and I turn back to see both looking my way with curious eyes. I clear my throat and nod, following after them as they lead the way out of the hospital and into the large parking lot.

It is a solid fifteen minutes before we find our transport in the annoyingly large parking lot. It takes another five for Mrs. Sagle to converse with the man waiting outside about where exactly we are going.

It's a dark taxicab, not one you'd normally see out and about. When I climb in, I am hit with the stench of cigarettes and cheap cologne. Theo's nose furrows as he climbs in behind me, reminding me of shifter's advanced senses from their animals.

Poor guy.

There is no cab driver, something I notice once I get used to the smell. At first, I assume the guy she was talking to is our driver. Instead, he walks away and leaves us alone in the car. Perhaps Mrs. Sagle is driving us? Leaning forward, I see no steering wheel or anything else that can replace such a feature. All that sits on the dashboard are switches and knobs for the radio.

Oh, no.

"Alright," Mrs. Sagle says as she climbs into the front seat. She twists around and gives us both a smile, "we're going to head to the W.W.A. station. It should only be about thirty minutes and from there we'll get transport to the academy itself. Any questions?"

"No, ma'am," we say in unison; however, one lingers on the tip of my tongue. I don't let myself ask it as she twists herself back around and presses the single red button that replaces the steering wheel.

"Is this what I think it is?" Theo whispers just as the car shoots forward. I gasp as I hang onto the door, the speed impossible to decipher. Theo seems to be having the same reaction as me as his hand latches onto the only other thing to hang onto…me.

Yay.

The outside passes by in a blur and my stomach lurches as I feel the car twist and turn through the city. The city…are we even in New York anymore?

Just like it started, it stops just as suddenly. Both mine and Theo's body snaps forward into the seatbelts but Mrs. Sagle seems unbothered as she climbs out of the car with little effort.

"That was awesome," Theo grins as he releases me, "I've only ever heard about these. The perfect mixture of magic and technology, used to make the world a better place."

"By creating super-fast cars," I comment as I unbuckle the seatbelt and climb out, my knees shaking as I squint against the bright sun. We are no longer in the city, as I suspected, and instead standing in the middle of rolling, treeless hills supporting miles and miles of farmland. I can't even fathom the distance we traveled, let alone where in the country we now stand.

"Come, now," Mrs. Sagle calls out as she makes her way into the wheat field that lined the road. Both Theo and I share a look before following her, neither of us questioning her confident stride.

It doesn't take long for me to realize that the field is just a front. Fae words leave Mrs. Sagle's lips, the spell illuminating what truly stands before us.

A tall building stretches into the clear sky. The deep wood and old architecture hints at its old age as does the old W.W.A. seal that decorates the large front doors. It is an older one, one that has since been discontinued.

Like the D.M.M.A., they have an obsession with owls.

"She's fast for an old lady," Theo comments as he gestures toward her. She's already disappearing into the doors. Theo groans as we pick up our pace, "where did that come from? Shouldn't we have seen that from the road?"

"Really?" I ask as I glance back, "you live in a world of magic but can't recognize a spell being cast?"

"A spell?" He tilts his head, "that's what I was hearing?"

"Yes," I nod as we step toward it, "you live a rather sheltered life, don't you?"

"I guess."

"Hence why he needs two months to catch up," Sagle's voice cuts us off as we step inside, the cool air a nice contrast to the warmth that coated us outside. A gasp leaves both mine and Theo's lips as we turn to face what stands in front of us.

I hate the fact that today is a day of surprises and overwhelming instances.

The back wall of the building is curved in a half circle. Like the old portal Emerson brought me through, there are several bright doorways lining the wall. Dark stone frames the bright swirls of color and words are etched at the very top.

Places...they are the schools that lay scattered around the world.

Fascinating.

I have always known about the large number of supernatural schools around the world but, I never knew that they are all connected to the W.W.A. The WWA standing for White Witches Academy. Of course, they accept more than just witches in today's world. It made sense to spread its wings to encompass all supernatural beings sometime in the late seventies.

I follow after them as she leads us to the doorway labeled "Washington". She hands over a few papers to the man standing beside it, every portal has one, before turning to face me and Theo.

"Ever portal traveled before?" She asks.

"Very recently," I reply as Theo shakes his head back and forth.

"Okay," she grins, "it is as easy as walking. You'll feel a little tickle in your stomach but it's like going over a bump a little too fast in your car. Nothing too crazy, okay? Just, keep your eyes open, understand?"

"Yes, ma'am," he nods as she steps through. I gesture for him to follow, watching as he disappears into the mess of colors. I take a deep breath and step through, ignoring the nagging feeling that something is about to go terribly wrong.

As I step through, I realize that I do exactly what she said not to. I stumble forward, my stomach twisting as I bump into Theo. He doesn't seem to mind too much as he just glances back with a raised eyebrow before turning back to Mrs. Sagle. She is talking but her voice is lost to my ears as I face the large room we stumbled into.

Like the building before, this one looks like it was built in the 19th century. A large marble staircase occupies the long wall, curving upward toward the second floor. Directly across from me stands a lounge area with long couches and a receptionist sitting behind a desk, typing away at a computer. A computer that looks very out of place in this old building and old-fashioned décor.

Heat warms my back and I glance back to find myself standing in front of a large fireplace with green flames crackling. The portal frame is etched into the dark marble, almost indistinguishable. Bookcases line the walls on either side with couches spread out around it. A large painting stands above it, showcasing the stoic face of a man that everyone, darkling and lightling alike, knows well.

Charles Maybelle.

Creator of the W.W.A.

Founder of Maybelle.

Maybelle, aptly named after her creator. Maybelle…my home. Like everything else he touched, the island city was created to be something *good*. The city had originally been created to be a safe haven for all supernatural beings whether light or dark. When he died, however, his replacements didn't share his same sentiments.

He was seen as a hero by the darklings, acting as the sole lightling that would stand for them when times get dark. I doubt, however, that any darkling ever truly knew him. I often find that most lightlings, if not all, hold some sort of hatred for darklings no matter how hard they try to hide or move past it. Even Austen had a lingering distrust for me.

Everyone except Theo. Perhaps his sheltered life offers him a fresh outlook that isn't muddied by those older than him.

I definitely have my own preconceived notions of my own about lightlings, especially shifters. However, that may only be because they are who I am stuck with. I find them to be a proud bunch, ones that hate being wrong and hold an arrogant rivalry with any other species or association.

Why do you think there is a N.A.S.O.? The D.M.M.A. is protection enough.

The lightlings see Charles Maybelle as a naïve dreamer, one to be looked up to but not one to be like. They teach his ideals like they are dreams that were crushed by the darkling populace.

"Know him?" Mrs. Sagle asks, catching me staring.

"Doesn't everybody?" I reply.

"Nope," Theo says, popping the 'p'.

"Of course not," she mutters, "did they teach you anything?"

"Apparently not," Theo says, his shoulders sagging as she rolls her eyes. She lets out a huff and starts toward the receptionist desk. Theo groans as he follows her, his embarrassment radiating off his mind.

"So," she stops and spins around as we come up to the desk, "I was originally going to give you your tour, however, I thought it would be more authentic to have an upper classman show you around as they do in the fall. Like you, she has to stay over the summer. She will mostly be in my class as well so you will see a lot of each other. Chrissy, can you send Stella out?"

The receptionist nods without looking up from her computer or stopping her furious typing. Behind the desk is a closed door with a plaque plastered in the middle. Names with their adjacent jobs list down it with their corresponding room numbers. It makes it easy to guess where the door leads. To the side of the desk and out in the open, a hallway leads deeper into the building.

A girl steps into the main room from said hallway with a wide grin on her lips. She is pale with thick makeup coating her face. Her lips are painted black with her eyelids matching, standing in sharp contrast to her bright red eyes. Her dark hair stops at her shoulders, but only half of it. The other side is shaved off and I can just make out white rune markings lining her hairline.

Rune marks?

Warning pings ring off in my head as I glance over at Theo, who seems entranced by her appearance. I can't deny that she is beautiful…in a dangerous sort of way. I can't, however, allow myself to get wrapped up in the mystery of her. Her eyes are red but the only creatures with red eyes are dark elves and vampyrs, both of which are an impossibility. The runes and their placement, however, hints at an appearance spell…one that can hide the attributes that will have otherwise made her species obvious.

Why would she hide herself?

"This is Stella, your tour guide. Stella, this is Ryder and Theo," Mrs. Sagle bows slightly, "I will fetch you two in the morning."

59

"Thank you," Stella calls out, her voice like bells as she gives the older lady a wave. She spins toward us, pulling a gasp from my lips as she grins at us.

Come on, Ryder, she's not even that attractive.

"Whoa," she says as our eyes meet, sucking in a breath before stepping closer to me, "you're a darkling."

"Yes," I cough out before composing myself, "and you are not who you claim to be."

"Yeah," she giggles as she gestures to her face, "I may have a slight obsession with vampyrs since *Twilight*. My eyes are contacts, and the runes are to help me appear paler."

Ah, so it isn't make-up.

It's an illusion.

Something, though, still feels off.

"That's fun," Theo says with a wide grin though the look in his eyes as he glances my way is anything but nice. I roll my eyes as Stella looks back and forth between us before clearing her throat.

I don't care about being rude if it meant I can do my job.

"Alright," she says, "do we want inside or outside first?"

"Outside," Theo answers. She nods as she leads the way to the large door. I stay a few steps behind, letting him ask his million questions as we step out into the bright sunlight. I bask in the warmth for a solid ten seconds before bounding down the steps to follow after them.

The blue sky stretches out above us, the view only interrupted by the large expanse of trees that surround the grounds. The perfectly manicured lawn stops abruptly at the tree line with wildflowers and other natural life taking seed under the cover trees beyond.

The building itself is a huge, red-bricked mansion. It is four stories, each floor distinguishable by the lines of windows that interrupt the red. There is a single tower on the left side, sporting windows only at the top level. Small buildings, made of the same red brick, lay scattered around the grounds with stone trails connecting them all.

"These are the classrooms," she explains as we pass by, gesturing toward them and sending her many bracelets clinking together on her wrist. Besides her head, they are the only other unique thing about her. She wears a plain blue polo shirt that has her name stitched into it with khaki pants and a pair of dark dress shoes.

Probably a uniform.

"The building we started off in houses the students, staff, the cafeteria, offices, and so on. Behind the building is for our leisure. There's a basketball hoop, a tennis court, and some hoops set up high to replicate some game from a fantasy novel about witches. There aren't any games during the summer but, you could try out when fall comes. I don't usually mess around too much back there."

"Cool," Theo says, and their conversation continues but I find something else to hold my attention.

A single dirt trail sneaks away from the others and disappears into the dense wood. Almost immediately, I want to explore it. Something resides in there, something that I need to find...

Everything grows out of focus...only the trail remains in my sight. Something lingers in those shadows. Something that wants-no, *needs*-

"Yo," Theo's voice pulls me back to reality. Blinking wildly for a moment, my dazed mind slowly clears as my world grows back into focus. I stare hard at the trees, desperate to figure out what caused such a strong reaction from a single glance.

"Oh," Stella says, her voice dropping, "we don't mess with that trail."

"Why?" I ask.

"It's off limits for one," she shrugs, "but, there are so many stories about kids disappearing into the woods and never coming out."

"Creepy," Theo mutters as I glance back at the trees, my mind reeling as I struggle to figure out what had a hold of me.

What lingers in there and what does it want with me? Were the kids who disappeared under the same influence?

I'm not dumb enough to play into my curiosity. Instead, I simply make a mental note to avoid it.

Hopefully, Theo does the same.

6

The Tower

The staircase Stella leads to sits at the very end of the second floor. It spirals upward, disappearing into the darkness up above. It doesn't stop at any other floors, only leading to what stands ahead. The metal railing is faded, and the steps look less than safe. Theo grins as he peers upward, apparently not getting the same sense of wariness that I feel.

"A lot of the rooms are being remodeled for fall semester, so you'll be moved once they are finished. If you need anything else, I'm in room three hundred and two."

"It's perfect," he lets out a little giggle as he starts up the spiral staircase, hurrying up like a child. I roll my eyes as I turn toward Stella, raising an eyebrow as she watches him rush upward with a grin.

"Um," she says as she turns her eyes toward me, "it's the door at the very top. I mean, it's obvious because it's the only door. The uniforms and schedules will be waiting up there for you. Do you need me to walk you up?"

"No," I tell her and her head drops a little as if she's disappointed. My heart pangs at the thought but I shake the feeling away before I continue, "seems pretty straightforward. Thank you, though."

"Anytime," she nods, grinning as she takes a step back into the hallway. I watch her leave before making my own way up the stairs. There is something about her…something that I can't place.

She doesn't *feel* dangerous…just different…

I just don't know if she is a good or bad thing.

The room itself is rather large. Two twin beds sit at opposite sides of the round room, each accompanied by a small dresser and a desk. The only light comes from the many windows and the chandelier that is little more than a glorified nightlight.

I claim the bed closest to the door, tossing my duffle bag onto it before Theo can make a move toward it. He sighs as he takes the other one, falling back against the bed. Luckily, we have our own bathroom.

I turn my back to him as I open my bag, my curiosity finally being appeased as I pull the zipper down. A shaky breath leaves my lips as I slowly pull out the few pieces of clothing I have. Surprisingly, even my trinkets made the cut.

Sitting below everything, sits the book.

Emerson really did go through my room and send all my belongings, no matter how trivial, with me.

With a sigh, I run my fingers over the charred cover. It holds memories of home, sparking flashes of simpler times as it always does.

Maybelle…

Auntie Rosa…

My late brother…

I shake the image of his face out of my head as I drop it back into the bag. Pushing the bag to the side, I move to toward the dresser to organize the few pieces of clothing I owned. A few pairs of the school uniform, blue polos and khakis, already sit folded neatly in the drawers. I shove my own clothes in with them before plopping back down on the bed.

I watch stupidly as my bag teeters on the edge of the bed before flipping toward the floor, as if in slow motion. The few contents of the bag fly out and there is Theo, darting forward to help gather the few items before I can even get up.

I sigh as I kneel to help but most lay back in the bag before I can. A small sigh leaves my lips as I see the book sitting half open, showcasing the faded pages. Without comment, Theo carefully grabs it and hands it over to me.

"Is that everything?" He asks before his eyes narrow at something under the bed. Theo drops to all fours and reaches down underneath the wooden frame. He comes out with a small slip of paper. At first, I think it is something left behind by previous students but…no, it isn't paper.

It's a picture.

My picture that I had stashed in the book, something I have had no intention of ever showing anyone.

Great.

"Nope, forgot this," Theo grins as he moves to hand it over to me. He pauses for a moment as he glances down at the picture, "aw, they're cute. Who are they? Brothers?"

"They…" I sigh as I pull the picture out of his hand. As much as I want to tell him to mind his business, I can't. The innocence on his face, much like that of a puppy, and the open curiosity on his mind make it impossible to be even somewhat snippy with him.

Of course, that would be far easier than explaining the two smiling kids in the picture. Both have blond hair and equally pale faces. They are identical twins but, that changes about five years after the picture is taken. A smile stretches across my face before I can stop it and I look up to face the expectant gaze that waits patiently for my answer.

"Oh, well, that was me and my twin brother when we were five. That's the only picture there is of us."

"Wait," Theo says, glancing back at the picture in my hands, "how? I mean, I'm not trying to be rude but...you're so tan...like, tanner than me! How do you go from that pale to this tan? The sun can't do that, can it?"

"I know. We were born identical," I shrug, "but we aren't anymore."

"How?"

"Well," I say, pausing as I try to figure out the point of telling the story. We aren't together to be friends. This is a job. I need to treat it as such but...what harm can it do? I give up trying to reason with myself and continue, "I mess with a warlock, and she cursed me."

"Cursed you?"

"Yeah," I say, "cursed me to look like this instead."

"Oh," he frowns as he looks me up and down, "you'd think they'd make you look, I don't know, like, bad?"

"I know," I nod, "but I was also ten. I don't think they wanted to damage me too much."

"Oh, fun," he laughs, "messing with warlocks when you were ten. That's insane. You've lived a much more exciting life than I."

"Probably."

"What's his name? Is he also working for my father?"

"His name was Jasper and no. He died a couple years back."

"Oh, I'm so sorry."

"It's life," I say and silence envelopes the room. I can tell, without peeking inside his head, that he wants to ask more questions but, thankfully, he bites his tongue. Most shifters wouldn't even be curious but, alas, if I have learned anything about Theo since I met him, I know he doesn't fit my expectations. It is so strange being with someone, especially a shifter, who actually cares about something that has nothing to do with his life.

I'm still trying to figure out if that is a good thing.

Theo steps away and plops down on his bed before pulling out his phone. Once he is properly distracted, I grab the book. I shake the thought of Jasper's face out of my head as I force myself to focus on the pages themselves. Most of them are too faded and damaged to read. There is only one page, the only reason I keep the book, that I can decipher.

It is only legible because my brother, when I was home, would keep tracing over the sprawled handwriting so the words can never be lost.

The prophecy.

I slide the picture into the back cover before flipping to the page that I have been religiously reading since I was twelve as it is the only real connection I have to my old life. I trace my fingers over my brother's handwriting, never truly reading the worlds I had memorized some time ago.

"Creatures of old will rise again," I whisper as I picture my brother's excited face when he had first found it when we were ten. Everyone knew the story, but no one had found the book of prophecies...it was the only one that was still readable when we found it after the fire. Jasper took it as a sign; I took it as purely coincidental.

"To wreak havoc on the realm of man. Only children to man, six of strange blood will stand against the darkness."

There is a reason why even darklings believe that this prophecy is nonsense besides the fact that it was uttered by some unknown hag. Most prophecies would end there as a vague idea; one that left the words up to interpretation. There used to be people who dedicated their lives to interpreting prophecies.

The Prophecy of the Six, however, is different. The rest is strangely specific, calling out the six "children" the world needs to fight against whatever is coming. There is no need for interpretation...no need for disagreement but, that is what came from it. Everyone, including darklings themselves, think it's fake. It is too long and too detailed...a hoax.

Jasper had believed in it but, he had always been a gullible child.

Emerson's boss believed in it but, he was a rather gullible adult.

Theo's giggles erupt as he shifts in his bed, sending a tinge of fear through me that he may have heard me. His mind, however, is too occupied with the flashing screen to pay me any attention.

I'm instantly reminded of how out of place I am here. Everyone moves at a fast pace, stuck in their own little worlds without a care of what is happening around them. No one ever seems to linger on one thought or one *feeling* for too long before something new comes to grasp their attention.

My life used to be a lot simpler.

I shake thoughts of home from my head as I slide the book into my dresser. My brother is dead. My home is a desolate place. I have nothing left for me there and yet...here I am wanting to go back.

"So," Theo speaks up, rolling to sit up as he lets his phone slide onto his bed, "I know my father said he sent you with me for my protection and, don't get me wrong, your powers are cool and all, but what can you do against a warlock?"

"Believe it or not," I tell him as I sit up, "I can do more than read minds, but I am more of an alarm in this case. I can sense danger a lot faster than you can even smell it. I can hold my own in a fight until help arrives. None of that, however, matters. Nothing is going to happen. The academy is the most secure place in the United States, Theo. You have nothing to worry about."

Of course, that nagging feeling I've had since the portal settles deeper into my gut as I assure him. Something is going to go wrong; a conclusion that cements itself deeper and deeper the longer we're here.

I can't stop the nagging feeling that it has something to do with the trail and that damned prophecy.

That stupid prophecy that tore me from my home.

That stupid prophecy that will probably never come to pass.

That stupid prophecy that killed my brother.

That stupid prophecy that calls for a pureblooded shifter and one of ancient blood...ancient blood that has always lingered over my head since I can remember.

I close my eyes and let out a shaky breath as I push the memory as far back as I can. I hate that today has been such a spiral...that his *face* keeps popping up in my mind.

I need to get ahold of myself.

"Ryder?"

"What's up?"

"Can we set up some ground rules for the mind reading thing?"

"What did you have in mind?" I ask, grateful for the distraction.

"I don't know," he shrugs, "I just...don't want to worry about what I'm thinking all the time, you know?"

"Well," I nod, "here are the rules I have for myself. I never dig unless I get permission, like I did with your memories, and I'll do my best to avoid your thoughts unless the situation calls for it."

"Your best?"

"Yeah, I'm usually pretty good at shutting everyone's thoughts out but my own, however, sometimes my focus breaks."

"You can always hear them?"

"It's like when you're in a crowd. You can vaguely hear everyone's voices, but you zone it out, right? Half the time we don't even notice or latch onto the words. You zone it out until you accidentally zone into it and now you can't zone it back out...it's a constant struggle."

"That sounds exhausting."

"It is, but it makes me valuable."

"I'm not sure that's a good thing," Theo says, his words hanging over the room for a moment before he continues, "what do you mean about the situation?"

"Oh, your father wants me to keep an eye on your mental state," I explain, "he wants to make sure the warlock didn't do something that would lead to your mind being compromised."

"Oh, like possession?"

"Something like that."

Like before, he seems satisfied to leave the rest alone as he nods and falls back against his bed to mess with his phone. I sigh as I lean back against the wall the bed is pushed against and fold my arms across my chest.

This was going to be one boring assignment.

7

Mrs. Sagle's Lessons

Nothing seems familiar to the shifter. Mrs. Sagle is currently working on the basics of a healing potion, one that will be beneficial for *every* being to know. Theo can't seem to wrap his head around mixing simple ingredients and bringing them to a boil. He keeps grabbing the wrong amounts or even the wrong species of plant.

That can, however, just be an indication at his cooking skills.

"I'm sorry," Theo groans for the hundredth time as he messes up yet another potion. I sit on Mrs. Sagle's desk as she leans over Theo's, glaring into the mini cauldron. I try to hide my smile that seems permanently set upon my lips as I face his inability to work under the gaze of the teacher. There is something amusing about his almost adult sized body yet childlike face.

Luckily for me, I have learned most of these basic potions before I even came to the States.

"It isn't funny," he complains as he notices my smile. He, however, has a grin of his own as Mrs. Sagle gets ride of his concoction. I keep my mouth shut as she turns to look at the one that sits on my desk. She too gets rid of it before pointing at the seat. Sliding off her desk, I scurry over to sit in my own.

"You are on book study duty. Study the potions and their ingredients. Tomorrow, I want to see one properly made. Ryder, since you have gotten a hang of it, why don't you show him how it's done when he gets sick of the book."

"Yes, ma'am," I bow my head slightly. Theo gives a mock salute, and she simply rolls her eyes in response. She moves on to help the few other students also participating in the summer program. Two sit huddled in the corner with their phones hiding in their laps. I watch with a grin as Mrs. Sagle walks up to them, both seeing her too late. After she magically makes their phones disappear, she sends them stumbling out before turning toward the only other student in the room.

Stella.

As if she feels my gaze, she looks up. Her fake red eyes bore into mine, leaving me stuck. I want to look away and I keep telling myself that there is nothing particularly interesting about her, but instead I stay as I am and wait for her to look away first.

She doesn't.

"Hey," Mrs. Sagle's sharp voice and a well-placed book smack to the back of my head pulls me out of it, "like I said, help him since you're so confident in your abilities."

"On it," I mutter as Theo reaches out and pulls our desks together with a screech. She places a pile of worksheets in front of us before tapping on them with two fingers.

"All of this needs to be done before you two leave today, understand?" She speaks. After we nod, she sits at her desk and seems content to stay that way for the rest of the afternoon.

As soon as we move to get to work the door bursts open and a group of ten kids or so slide in and scatter to fill open desks. Mrs. Sagle stands to call order to the room just as another adult glides in.

Unlike Mrs. Sagle, the newcomer doesn't look like a teacher. She wears a faded pair of overalls with a button up fleece underneath. Her boots are covered in dark mud that travels up to her knees. Her blond hair is tied up in a loose bun and her bangs frame her smiling face. Her bright green eyes hint at her being a witch, though the color is common even in humans.

"Good morning," she says, the sugary-sweet tone in her voice immediately gains my suspicion as she continues, "and I am sorry for the mess, Mrs. Sagle. I was just showing the students around the jungle gym behind the main building. It's a little more intense than the ones they remember from elementary school."

"As long as it gets cleaned," the older lady says with a tone like venom, "I don't mind. You are, however, interrupting an important lesson. Does this interruption have a purpose?"

"Of course, it does," Mrs. Katherine says with the same sugary voice, "as it always does. I just wanted to stop by and welcome you all to our great school and introduce you to the rest of the students staying with us over the summer."

Mrs. Sagle sighs as the younger woman pauses as if knowing what is coming next.

"And though *we*," Mrs. Katherine gestures to the students who had entered with her, "are here to enhance our knowledge and perhaps test out of our current grade while you are working to re-take the test that gets you here in the first place...I just want to let you know that we are here together. Though you are separated now, you will join back up with your classmates come fall. How exciting is that?"

Her students cheer.

Obviously, we do not and neither does Mrs. Sagle.

This doesn't seem to bother Mrs. Katherine. She seems to enjoy it as she grins wide before saying, "I doubt; however, you'll be able to truly appreciate our great school and this great opportunity we are giving you without a little history. Does anyone know when the WWA first opened their doors?"

"1825," I answer, "but that was the very first one in the city of Maybelle. This one opened...I want to say 1956?"

"Look at you," Mrs. Katherine smiles, "someone has done their homework. The founder, Charles Maybelle, wanted to help young lightlings learn how to control their abilities without the threat of humankind lingering over them. Today, we strive to do more. Not only will you learn to fully embrace your abilities but also learn how to survive and thrive in the world beyond us. We give you a look into different cultures, worlds, and even a new insight that came through the same portal most of you did."

"Oh no," Theo mutters beside me as she raises her arm and gestures toward where I sit. Everyone turns to stare and I immediately want to sink into the shadows. Even Theo slouches in his seat as everyone turns to stare.

"Ryder Skye," she sings out, "our first *darkling* student."

Awkward silence.

"Now," she continues, "we are to treat him with all the respect and welcome as we do for the rest of these students, understand?"

Giggles sound from her students as they mutter in agreement. Unlike Theo, I know what their agreements mean. Mrs. Katherine had only said what she did to appease Mrs. Sagle. Everyone knows that, especially the kids.

I can feel their opinions of me already forming before I can stop myself, each and every one of them negative. Most plan to avoid me, others had a sort of morbid curiosity that begs them to befriend me, while a few even plot ways to get me kicked out.

"If I hear of anyone treating him badly," she shrugs, her words as meaningless as her bun, "we will have a talk later."

"Yes, ma'am," unenthusiastic voices ring out as her smile, though I haven't thought it possible, grows even wider as she turns to Mrs. Sagle.

"Now, I know you are helping our students in need," she drawls out, "but, is there any way they can be released early to attend the mixer I have set up? I just think it will be *so* good for them."

"How can I refuse?" Mrs. Sagle asks through clenched teeth with a smile that looks more like a sneer.

Theo grins slightly as we both stand. I gather our books and papers as he moves to follow after the rest of the students. He seems far too excited to be mingling with other shifters, despite what they just said in front of us.

76

"Have a good night, ma'am," I bow to Mrs. Sagle. Before she can speak, I grin and continue, "I will make sure he finishes everything before tomorrow morning."

"Good," she nods and grins down at me, "and take care of him, okay? He's too naïve for his own good."

"I know."

She nods as I hurry away, my eyes finding Theo in the crowd of shifter boys. The girls, there are three of them, avoid Stella like the plague as she walks by herself. She glances back and meets my eyes, stopping and waiting for me to catch up.

"He makes you carry his stuff for him?" She asks, glancing down at the books in my hands. I chuckle, just barely stopping myself from making a joke about babysitting. Instead, I opt for what I feel is a more acceptable answer.

"I think he was wanting to 'forget it'," I tell her, using air quotes as best I can with the books in my arms as I say forget, "so he would have an excuse not to do it."

"Ah, smart guy," she nods with a grin.

"Perhaps."

"Are you staying at the mixer?"

"I have to."

"Why?"

"I'd feel bad about leaving him alone," I answer, saving myself from having to tell the truth. It feels too easy to talk to her...too easy to fall in line with her and act like we can possibly be friends, "they're acting all friendly now but...what that lady was saying?"

"I know," she groans as we walk up the steps. I pull open the door for her and step in behind her, scanning my eyes over the large room. There are food and drinks and probably everything a teenager can want when it comes to games in the little lounge area by the fireplace. All of the other shifters are here but no Theo.

"Where is he?" I mutter, my eyes narrowing as I look through the crowd again.

"Maybe he decided it wasn't as fun as he thought," she shrugs, "more for us, right?"

"Yeah," I say as she moves toward the food table. I hurry toward the stairs as I stretch out my mind, my heart skipping a beat as my mind goes through the worst-case scenarios. Thankfully, I find him rather quickly.

"Hey," I say as I burst into our room and slide the books onto my desk. He looks up from his own plate of food to offer me one that is stacked high with a few bits of everything from the food table. Freezing, I stare at it for a moment before grabbing it, "what happened? You seemed pretty excited to hang out with those guys."

As much as I hate to admit it, I was looking forward to hanging out with Stella. There is something about her that I want to figure out, if only for Theo's safety. I definitely do not want to admit that my curiosity and her strange magnetism are getting the better of me.

Nope, definitely not.

"I was," he nods before scooping up a spoonful of mashed potatoes, "but only because I have been looking forward to coming here since I was a kid.

I have never spent much time around kids like me and I thought it would be easy to make friends when I got here. I never thought about how I was getting here."

"Ah," I say as I take a seat at the edge of his bed.

"They were acting just as I imagined they would," Theo chuckles bitterly, "acting as if they wanted to be my friends. They asked me like two questions about me before all they wanted to talk about was you. It's like they only thing they think is cool about me is you and you don't matter when…"

His voice cuts off and all I want to do is apologize. As much as I understand Emerson forcing this on him, I know I'm going to hinder him in more ways than socially.

Instead, I nod and move to sit at my own desk.

"Ryder, look," I hear him let out a heavy sigh as I set my plate down next to the books, "I'm sorry. I didn't-"

"I should be apologizing to you," I tell him, "I'm going to be a big reason why people won't want to hang out with you. You don't have to explain yourself."

"But I do," he says. I hope my back is enough halter any conversation, but he seems content to speak as if to no one, "you do matter, obviously, but I didn't mean it that way. I just meant-"

"I know," I say to stop his stammering, "I know what you meant, okay?"

"Because mindreading?"

"Because," I finally turn toward him, "even though we haven't known each other for very long, I know you aren't a malicious or mean person. Even to darklings which is the most surprising thing about you. I understand that you're angry because I wasn't supposed to be a factor in your schooling. For that, I apologize but your father really is the one to blame."

"Yeah, I definitely don't blame you," he shrugs, before smiling over at me, "so, we're good, right?"

"We always were," I tell him as I scoop up some of my own food, "thanks for this, by the way."

"Of course," he smiles, "I was there so…"

Silence falls over us as he trails off, but I can still see Theo fidgeting. Something else is bothering him but, I'm not going to ask. If he wants to tell me, he will. I turn my attention to my food just as he starts to speak with a small voice, "can I tell you something? And you promise not to laugh?"

"Of course," I tell him as I look back up at him with what I hope to be a reassuring smile. I'm not used to being around other teens, let alone someone who legitimately needs to talk.

"To be honest," he says, his eyes on his hands as they keep opening and closing around each other, "I, uh, kind of expected them to look down on my but not because of you."

"Okay," I nod, "so, why?"

"I don't know. I know I'm not like any of them," he shrugs and at first I think it's because of his lack of supernatural knowledge until he says, "I don't know myself like they do. I haven't even…I…"

"You haven't shifted yet," I finish for him, unable to hide my shock. His face contorts in shame as he turns away from me, his self-hatred radiating off his mind.

He is fifteen years old. Most shifters have their first shifts when they are between eight and ten years old if not sooner. I have never heard of anyone shifting for the first time in their teens.

Emerson much hate that.

"Do you know why?" I ask him, setting my half-eaten plate down, "like, can you even shift?"

"Can you imagine how embarrassing that would be?" Theo chuckles, "if one of the last actually pureblooded shifters couldn't shift? No, I can but, I can't. The therapist my dad made me see says I'm mentally blocking myself. She said something about trauma from something that happened when I was a kid...something I don't even remember."

Before I can ask him to elaborate, a knock sounds at our door. Theo jumps up before I can and yanks it open. He steps aside and lets Stella into the room. She spots me and lets out a sigh as she sets her plate on my desk.

"Why did you just ditch me?" She asks as she fills her mouth with a handful of chips, "I got extra food and everything."

"Uh..." I start but struggle to come up with an excuse.

"He saw me disappear and wanted to make sure none of those idiots downstairs did anything. He's a good guy."

"What?" I mutter as he gives me a wink and pushes himself off my bed.

"Cool," she smiles before jabbing her thumb toward the door, "I just wanted to make sure everything was good. Um, I should go. They don't like girls in rooms with boys."

"Okay!" Theo grins as he waves goodbye. Her eyes linger on me for a second too long before she disappears into the hallway, slamming the door after her.

"Dude! She likes you!" He says with a giggle.

"What? No, she's only known me for a few days."

"She came looking for you and only you. If she didn't care, she wouldn't have walked up all those stairs."

"She doesn't like me. She's just curious."

"Sure. There's a very easy way for you to find out."

"I'm not reading her mind."

***

Long after the room has grown silent, Theo's soft snores being the only interruption, I lay awake. His confession still lingers in my mind, something that confuses me. He is a job, not a friend, and yet here I am worried about how they are going to treat him if they find out he hasn't shifted yet. That, of course, brings forth another question.

How can you spark a shift?

Before I can dwell on my question for too long, a shining light catches my attention. I snap my head up, glaring at one of the windows. Whoever prepared the room before we came, never considered the need for shades. The moonlight keeps the room lit up and impossible to darken.

I keep my eye on the window as I lay my head back down against the pillows. The light flashes again as I roll to my feet and scurry over to the window. I keep my eye on Theo and his soft snores as I step past him, not wanting to wake him.

I lean forward and peer downwards through the window, my eyes narrowing at the trees. The moonlight keeps the grounds lit up as well and there isn't a living soul from what I can see.

Just like before, something in me clicks. Everything around me blurs and all I can see is the forest. There is something there...a figure encased in light.

Who are they?

What do they want with me?

"Ryder?" Theo's sleepy voice pulls me away from it. I blink as I step away from the window, my neck aching from the position I was just in.

"Sorry," I mutter as I head back to my own bed, offering no explanation.

8

Storytime

No one except for the select few ever ventured past the long wire that outlined the safety zone. Parties of trained men and wishful trainees go out every so often, bringing back supplies left over by the war and rescuing those who dared to live beyond the safety of Dante's reach.

None of them went out alone but, then again, neither did I.

My brother was trailing behind me, keeping his eyes on more things than I could. He was trained for it...trained to face danger at a moment's notice. I, on the other hand, worked more as a diplomat who's only goal was to keep the peace between the two warring groups in the cursed city.

I hated it.

"You still haven't told me where we are going," he spoke up, his voice echoing off the rotting buildings around us.

"I told you," I smiled as the **building** came into sight.

That was it.

That was how I was going to prove I could be more than a glorified peacekeeper.

I finally force myself awake, the haunting memory slowing fading as my eyes adjust to the darkness around me. My dresser, scattered desk, and Theo's soft snores slowly bring my back to the dorm room we share. I sit up and wipe the sleep from my eyes, my hands shaking as the memory threatens to resurface.

With a groan, I glance over at the sleeping shifter and marvel at how easy it is for him to sleep. I shake my head as I roll out of bed, hissing out a breath as my bare feet touch the tile below.

I always hate the feeling that always follows that dream. Right after I got to the states, I had latched onto it in a desperate attempt to keep my brother forever present in my mind. I despised the thought that I would forget his face some time in the future, despite the fact that I had the only picture of us.

Now, it is simply a reminder of my mistakes.

It has been some time since I had that dream until we arrived here. Now, every night I face it and hope to wake up before it ends. It has been a week of sleepless nights and getting to know the campus with the people who come with it.

I pull on a pair of sweatpants and a t-shirt before yanking on my tennis shoes. Pausing to make sure the shifter is still sleeping soundly, I slowly sneak out the door and bound down the spiral staircase.

The week might have been fine if it wasn't for the few interactions that we had with Mrs. Katherine's "gifted" students. The worst is Arnold, a cocky bear shifter who takes every opportunity to slam into my shoulder. Luckily, every muttered insult is pointed at *me* but that can't make it any easier for Theo. He wants a normal school year, a *good* one, and instead he gets stuck with me.

The mostly empty lobby welcomes me as I hurry down the large staircase. A couple of upper classmen, Katherine's kids, sit sprawled out on the couches, dissolving the majestic look of the place as they snore loudly into the quiet air.

Part of me questions why they aren't in bed. The other part reminds me that I probably don't want to know.

Quietly, as not to disturb them, I dart across the long floor and slow only as I reach the door. I glance back as I pull it open, wincing as the wood creaks before slipping past it. With a soft slam, the door slides closed behind me and I face the empty lawn.

The cool air works wonders to calm my frenzied mind as I stretch my tired body. I make sure to keep my mind open to Theo. He isn't awake but instead trapped in a strange dream about Mrs. Sagle.

I don't look too deeply into it.

As I jog down the trail, I make sure to keep my eyes away from the trees. Every night, I see the same figure in light and that same obsessive feeling washes over me. I'm not one to give into temptation, not since I left Maybelle, and I'm not about to play into this one.

This is how my mornings usually play out. I wake up at some ungodly hour without the ability to fall back asleep. I run myself until I am exhausted enough to catch a few more hours of sleep before Theo's alarm yanks me out of it.

He always wants to go to breakfast early, claiming that he doesn't want to get stuck in line when we both know it's because of the other students. It's a lot easier to avoid the stares and comments if we beat everyone there because we only interact with them during mealtimes.

I'm not going to matter in a week when we move on to shifter studies. We are going to have to join up with them for a few days to go over the whole shifting process. Everyone is required to *shift* into their other forms, something Theo can't do.

I stumble to a stop as the thought lingers in my head. Theo has gone through so much, should he really go through that embarrassment?

There is nothing I can do about that; I remind myself as I jog down the trail. He would have had to face it alone if I wasn't here. It isn't something that can be helped. I groan as I stumble to a stop again, not able to stop the argument in my head.

As much as I want to convince myself that this is only a job, I know Theo has managed to worm his way past my attempt at indifference in the short time we've known each other.

Come on, Ryder, it has barely been over a week.

He isn't a friend.

Ignoring my own reasoning, I turn around and jog back toward the building. Stumbling up the steps, I freeze as the hairs on the back of my neck stand up. As always, I feel someone watching me, but I refuse to turn around. Instead, I shake away the feeling and pull the door open.

The students are still snoring as I hurry through the dark space. I step behind the receptionist's computer and power it on, hoping the series of numbers taped to the keyboard is the password.

Luckily, they are.

It is light outside by the time by the time I head toward the stairs with a stack of papers in my hands. I can already hear Theo's music blasting halfway up the spiral staircase.

I step into the room to find the bed empty and the shower running. I slide the pages onto his desk before moving to get ready for the day. By the time he comes out, I have already made my bed and move on to my shoes. He mutters a greeting, as the morning is the only time he isn't talkative, and I turn away as he gets dressed.

"What's this?" Theo asks.

"I know it's not any of my business," I shrug as I pack my books into the small backpack they provided, "but, I couldn't sleep last night so I took the liberty of looking up some ways to get past your shifting slump."

"Really?" His face lights up and I frown as he continues, "dude, thank you. I have always been too scared to talk to anyone about this and my dad didn't want anyone else to know. Have any of these worked?"

"Yes," I shrug, "there has been substantial studies showing them working on much younger targets than you but, it's worth a try, right?"

"Right," Theo grins as he slides the papers into his drawer, "thank you."

"Sure," I nod as he pulls on his shoes.

"Did you think I wasn't going to like it? You looked a little scared for a moment."

"I wasn't sure you'd enjoy me butting in like that."

"Eh," he grins before elbowing me, "we're in this together, right? Might as well help each other out."

"Right," I say as I follow him out the door.

"I meant to ask you yesterday," he says as we make our way down our spiral staircase, "do they update you at all about the case? About Jenny?"

"No," I tell him as we head into the cafeteria and make a beeline for the near empty breakfast line, "I am as out of the loop as you are. I can call for you, but I doubt I'd get any information."

"No," Theo shakes his head with a sigh, "I know how my dad is. I don't want you getting on his bad side by asking too many questions."

"Thanks."

"Can you do me a favor, though?" He asks as we load up our trays.

"Go for it."

"Can you not just follow me around like you have been? I'm not my father and I don't need someone trailing behind me. I'd much rather you walk beside me like a normal teenager and as if we're actually friends. I mean, I see you as a friend. You're a lot cooler than any of these other guys."

"Sure," I say as I follow him to the nearest table. We sit across from each other and he immediately digs in, cutting off any further conversation before he swallows.

"Good," Theo says with a mouthful of food before silence falls over us. I pick at mine until Theo's back goes rigid. His spoon falls from his hand as snickering sounds from behind me. I glance back and glare at the group of shifters that sit a few tables away. They don't even try to hide their jeering faces.

I turn to offer to take care of them, but Theo shakes his head, seeming to already know what I was going to say. He keeps his gaze on the group behind us, staring hard as if trying to breathe life into the phrase, 'if looks could kill'.

Finally, Theo finishes and we move to dump our trays. We discard our trays and leave the building, opting to hang outside for the thirty minutes until class instead of inside with those idiots.

As we walk, I again find myself looking toward the trail despite my attempts to avoid looking that way. It was a lot easier to ignore when the night sky hid everything. As I have before, I can feel myself getting pulled toward it. Everything grows out of focus and my breath hitches in my throat as a familiar blond-haired boy appears just within the tree line.

Jasper...just as he was when I last saw him...

"Let's get moving," someone grumbles behind me, pulling me out of my thoughts as someone slams their shoulder into my back. I stumble forward as the world grows back into focus. Theo catches me as I finally reel myself in and nudges me out of the way as he steps forward to face a shifter much larger than he.

Arnold, the big, burly bear. Even without his eyes, I can tell he is something huge even by shifter standards. He is tall and wideset, with thick muscles covering his body. His brown hair is long and scruffy, sticking up all over the place as he towers over Theo.

"Really?" Arnold scoffs with a wide smile, his teeth sharpening slightly as he sneers down at Theo, "you wanna play? Let's see who wins, okay? A little doggie or a grizzly?"

"Oh," Theo grins back, looking just as confident as the other guy. Such bravado, "you have no idea what you're dealing with."

It is then that I realize that Theo has every right to be confident in his shifter abilities. He is, after all, one of the last truly pure-blooded shifters in this realm. He is more than likely going to be bigger and far stronger than anyone here will ever be.

Now, if only Theo can actually use his abilities to shift.

"Enough," I say and grab Theo's shoulder, "class is about to start."

I have spent way too long trapped by that trail.

"Oh, yeah," Arnold laughs and spins around in a slow circle as if to appease the small crowd that has gathered around, "let your little darkling *pet* drag you away. How pathetic."

I don't mean to punch him. I am usually pretty good about not letting my anger get the better of me, however, it is as if my arm has a mind of its own. I watch my arm shoot out like a snake, catching the bigger teen off guard. My fist sends him stumbling to the ground at Theo's feet with the latter's laughter following close behind. Pain erupts through my fist as Arnold immediately scrambles up, his round face squished up in anger.

"What's going on here?" Mrs. Sagle's voice saves the day, stopping any repercussions. I grin slightly as he growls at me before looking over my shoulder to glare at the older lady. I can almost see his brain ticking as he mentally tries to weigh the risk of fighting in her sight.

"Nothing, ma'am," I answer for him, "we were just having a friendly argument."

"Is that so?" Mrs. Katherine walks up, almost out of nowhere, eyes darting back and forth between us. Arnold clears his throat as he smiles, one that looks more like a grimace, and turns toward his teacher.

No one mentions the red spot forming on his jaw.

"Yes, just a friendly argument."

"Good," she snaps before glancing around at the crowd, "get to class. All of you!"

"You're dead," Arnold whispers as he slams his shoulder into mine as he walks past. I step back and nod for Theo to go ahead as I watch the 'smarter' crowd head to their building. Theo is wearing a stupid grin as he sits down beside me.

"That was awesome," Theo whispers as he twists around toward me in his seat, "you just...nice. I wanted to but I knew we'd get in trouble but you just...dude, you're far braver than me."

"It's my job to protect you," I shrug, ignoring the strange sense of pride that rose with his words, "whether it be from a warlock or an idiot shifter."

"I'd be careful if I were you," Stella says, sitting down behind Theo, "Arnold is going to retaliate and the school isn't going to do anything about it."

"Why not?" He asks.

"He doesn't usually get punished for anything. He's the Supers son so we all assume that's the reason why. She can't be blind and neither can Mrs. Katherine. He's a jerk to everyone, even sent some kid to the infirmary last week. They know what's happening but they just ignore it. Awesome punch, by the way."

"So, he's allowed to mess with us but we'll get in trouble for sticking up for ourselves?" Theo points out.

"That's usually how it goes," she answers.

"Don't mind him," I tell him, "he'll have to come through me."

"You really think you can take him? He's a bear, Ryder. They are notoriously to meanest, and strongest, animal form."

"I have my own tricks up my sleeve," I remind him. He catches my meaning and nods, his eyebrows furrowing as he opens his book.

"I have your back too," Stella offers, "you two seem a lot better than the rest of these guys."

"Cool," Theo grins just Mrs. Sagle steps up to our group of desks.

"So good to see you joining a group," she says as she nods at Stella, "now, we are moving to more advanced potion. As with before, you are going to study them before we actually get into creating them."

I let my focus wander away as she continues and I find myself looking out the window. Again, I see Jasper's pale face peeking out from the shadows of the dark trees, standing on the trail and beckoning me forward.

Again, Jasper holds the same form as he had when I last saw him. He shares the same chubby cheeks I used to have before I thinned out. Now that I'm closer, however, I can see the dark red splotches in his hair and clothes as well as the odd shape of his legs.

I know he is an apparition, a vision of some kind. What I don't know is if he is some sort of hallucination because of memories resurfacing or if something outside of my own mind is causing me to see such a terrible sight.

What wants me in those trees?

How does it know who I am?

***

It is dark outside by the time we make it back into the room. Theo babbles on about a good dinner while I fall back against the bed, completely exhausted, and wait for him to tire out as well.

He doesn't but, at least his conversation veers away from the cafeteria's pizza.

Instead, he comes up with a detailed schedule for his days to incorporate the shifting strategies I had printed for him. Of course, it all has to occur in the early mornings and late afternoons when we're alone without a chance of being seen by nosey onlookers.

I play along, shaking my head when I see fit though I don't truly hear his words. Once he is content with his plan, he didn't really need my input, he jots down his notes before getting ready for the night. I let out a sigh of relief as he disappears into the bathroom, glancing at the window overlooking the trees.

Before I can linger on my half-made plan, Theo is settling into his bed. As always, it doesn't take too long before his snores fill the room. With a sigh, and desperately trying not to second guess myself, I throw my blanket off and swing my legs off the bed.

I am already dressed with a stolen steak knife stuffed in my hoodie pocket, angled painfully as I bend forward to pull on my shoes. There is something hiding in those trees, something that stands as a danger to everyone here. I have to make sure that no one, especially Theo, gets hurt.

Jeez, Ryder, when did you get so righteous?

I can't, however, claim that curiosity has nothing to do with me sneaking down the spiral staircase. After all, it had been curiosity and pride that led me to being trapped here in the first place. If I hadn't snuck away when I was twelve, I would still be home and my brother would still be alive.

Shaking the thought out of my head, I tiptoe onto the second floor. As usual, there are several kids lazing about but no one turns my way as I hurry through the lobby.

I slip through the door and the cool night air chases away any thoughts of sleep from my mind. Turning toward the trees, a shiver shakes through me as Jasper's young, curious face appears just within the darkness. He seems to be glowing, highlighted by some unearthly light.

I know it isn't my brother. I have no doubt that something bad lays hidden beyond this apparition…something that no doubt loves to swallow whatever idiot tempts it.

Today, I am that idiot.

9

Mystery Solved

I stand alone just outside the tree line of the forest that has been taunting me ever since I got here. There is something so satisfying about the thought of finally getting to see why.

The trail beckons to me as it always does, somehow appearing right in front of me. Fear bubbles in my throat, instantly reminding me of my brother and his inability to have fear. I have always been jealous, but never jealous enough to face what truly scares me.

Today is the day, I suppose.

I raise my hand, mentally thanking my darkling blood as the spell falls easily past my lips. Thanks to the dark energy running through my veins, I have the ability to master spells. I am never allowed to truly look into expanding on my knowledge of said spells, however, there is one that I had mastered before I left Maybelle.

I smile, as I always do, as a small ball of light slowly stretches out between my fingers. It always looks like it should burn my skin but it's harmless, doing nothing but lighting the way.

Before I can step into the trees and follow the ghost of my past, a hand grabs my shoulder. I freeze for a moment before spinning around, swinging my fist with me.

My fist connects with Theo's nose, sending him stumbling back with a gush of dark red following after. I immediately hurry forward as he holds his nose, my light emphasizing the tears in his eyes.

"What are you doing out here?" I ask him, glancing back at the trees. Empty...I sigh before turning back to Theo, "I didn't mean to punch you. I'm so sorry..."

"S' cool," he mutters as he grabs his T shirt and pulls it up to combat the nosebleed, "I should have said something. What are you doing out here?"

"Nothing," I snap reflectively, hating how dismissive I sound.

"Dude, I'm not stupid. You wouldn't come out here and stare at the trees for nothing. Going in?"

"Yes," I admit with a groan, "but you shouldn't be out here. It's...dangerous."

"The only thing that has hurt me since we got here," he replies, his smile visible through his shirt, "is you."

"Theo-"

"What's the phrase?" He says as he steps past me and onto the trail, "friends will keep you out of trouble but best friends will be right there with you."

"We are not best friends."

"I don't know," he answers, his voice growing farther away. I groan as I hurry after him, "I think this makes us besties, you know? The phrase says so."

I don't reply, as I know I won't get anywhere, and step into line beside him. Luckily, the trail is just wide enough for us to walk side by side.

I stumble to a stop as the realization hits me. I *see* Theo stop beside me. I *hear* him question me but...I feel nothing.

How can I just feel nothing? No matter how hard I have tried to suppress my powers throughout my life, I can *always* feel people. I couldn't always feel their thoughts but I could *feel* them there.

Nothing...this silence...it's *deafening*.

Something, or someone, is blocking me.

Nothing has ever been able to do it so completely before.

"What's up?" Theo's voice cuts into my concentration as he too stares hard at the trees.

"We're done here," I say, deciding it better to leave instead of investigate with a shifter I am bound to protect. Instead of following after me, however, Theo stays put, his back goes rigid as he stands as still as a statue. With a sigh, I step forward and grab his arm. He doesn't move, his eyes staring blankly forward.

"Theo," I say, speaking louder as I wave my free hand in his face. My heart drops as he steps forward.

"Theo!" I yell as I tighten my grip on his arm and yank back. His elbow shoots out and slams into my face, sending me back. My feet catch on the rough undergrowth, sending me falling to the ground. By the time I scramble back up to my feet, he has already disappeared into the darkness.

"Theo!" I call out and dart forward, stumbling down the trail that gets more and more rough the farther along I go. I stumble to a stop as my lungs start burning, despite the fact that I have only run forward a few yards.

What is happening?

Something is wrong.

Something is *very* wrong.

"Indeed," a harsh voice echoes through the trees. Yet another shiver shakes its way through me as I spin around, trying to place a face to that horrid voice. Though my mental abilities aren't working, I can still feel the dark power radiating off whatever being hides somewhere near me.

"Theo!" I yell again without acknowledging the speaker. I pray to whatever creator is out there that it is just a hallucination, just like I hope Jasper was.

I am already justifying it in my head. Someone could have easily slipped a potion into my dinner which, as sad as it was, is a just conclusion. It isn't a secret that most, if not all, want me gone. We had just gone over potions with Mrs. Sagle and we, though we never made them, have talked about several basic memory potions that didn't take a genius to concoct and that is just our class. I'm sure Mrs. Katherine went into more detail. I also know, either way, that a few more advanced, through still intermediate, potions sit deeper in the book. It would only take replacing a single ingredient to turn any one of those nasty.

I can't *see* anything. There is no physical proof that anything is standing out there. Beyond the weakening light of my spell, nothing moves because nothing is there.

It's probably just Arnold getting his revenge.

See, Ryder? I tell myself, everything is fine.

"Sill boy," the voice speaks again, sending a jolt through me, "you don't get it, do you? The true power you hold?"

"Theo!" I call out, again ignoring the voice. You aren't supposed to acknowledge hallucinations, right?

"Ah!" I yelp out as my body flies back. Before I slam into the ground, something grabs me by the throat and yanks me up into the air.

"Underneath the earthen soil, ancients will rise to reclaim what was lost," he spits though I still can't see my attacker. Only darkness stands in front of me though I can still feel a solid hand on my throat, "sound familiar?"

"What?"

"You are the key to our prophecy," his voice lowers to a whisper, "we will meet again…"

"Ryder!" Theo's voice cuts through the darkness, chasing away the shadows. I fall, slamming into something soft before trying to scramble to my feet, tangling up in…are those blankets?

My bed…the dresser…my organized desk…a worried shifter standing above me…

It was just a nightmare?

"You good?" He asks, his eyes widening for a moment before his hand goes to his neck. Even with just the moonlight shining the way, I can see the fear on his face, "what…who did that to you?"

"Did what?" I ask, reaching for my own. Theo pulls out his phone and hands it out to me. I sigh as I look at myself in his camera app before lifting my head up.

Dark bruises are already forming on my neck, obvious fingerprints standing out against my dark skin. It wasn't a nightmare.

No, it was a message.

I untangle myself and roll off the bed, my heart dropping as I see my mud-covered feet. I stumble toward my dresser and yank at one of the knobs, accidently pulling the entire drawer out of its place. I let it fall to the ground with an echoing crack before kneeling down and tossing the few pieces of clothing to the side.

Nothing.

Where is it?

"You didn't touch anything of mine, did you?" I ask Theo, hoping he'd say yes.

"No."

"Do you have your phone?"

"Obviously," he says as he dug around in his pockets. He tilts his head to the side as he moves to search his bed, yanking the pillows and blankets free, "I just had it."

"I'm sure it just fell," I mutter, despite knowing his is gone too. Whatever grabbed me in the woods was here too.

"So," I conclude, "someone, or something, was in our room."

"Excuse me?"

"I just…Theo, something is out there and we need to talk to your father."

"How do we do that?" He asks, "our phones are gone."

"True," I say as I flip on the light switch. The moon had been enough to work off of but now, well, now I need the fake fluorescent light or at least the bare minimum that the chandelier provides. We have spell and potion books, I know there is a way to send a message a magical way.

"Ryder!" Theo yelps out as he stumbles into me. I turn around and let out a gasp of my own.

Etched into the walls were the words:

Creatures of old will rise again,
To wreak havoc on the realm of man,
Underneath the Earthen soil,
Ancients will rise to reclaim what was lost.

"What the is that?" Theo asks, half whispering and half yelling, "when did that happen? Someone was in here…while we were…while we were sleeping?"

"Seems like it," I answer, trying not to let my sarcasm bleed through. Of course, he isn't worried what the words mean…what they confirm…

"The words…" Theo mutters as he steps up to them. He runs his hand down the torn wallpaper, tracing over the bottom line, "I've heard them before. Do you know where they're from?"

"They're from an old darkling prophecy. How do you know about it?"

"My mother," he chuckles before his voice broke, "I…she used to read it to me when I was younger. That was so long ago…why would it be showing up here?"

"That is what we need to answer," I nod, "but, why take our phones?"

"Do you think it was someone here at the school? A student who wants to scare us enough to leave?" Theo asks.

"This wasn't anyone here," I shake my head, "students wouldn't be dumb enough to leave such a physical mark."

"Who was it then?" he asks.

"I would guess," I tell him as I step closer to the wall, "that it has something to do with that warlock attack. We need to see if we can send a message another way. The less people we involve in this, the better."

"We aren't telling anyone," Theo chokes out.

"What?" I ask as I turn toward him. A groan leaves my lips as I face a small photograph tacked to our door. On it is a smiling face of a young girl, around our age, with bright red hair. It is a school photo, or so I assumed, but red blotches coated the edges.

The young witch from Theo's memories, the one who invited the warlock.

"Is that…" Theo's voice drops off as he pulls the picture off the wall before pulling it up to his nose to smell it, "blood."

"What does it say on the back?" I ask, narrowing my eyes at the dark writing. Theo's breathing shakes as he slowly flips it over.

"Just as you'll be alone when the darkness invades," he reads aloud, "you'll be alone in this endeavor."

"So, we can't tell anyone," I comment, "because they have her. She being Jenny, correct?"

"Y…yes. What did it mean that we'll be alone when darkness invades?"

"I have a theory," I tell him as I plop down on his bed, "one that I'd rather not think about but, I suppose, we have to. Do you know the full prophecy?"

"I mean," he says, glancing back at the words carved into our wall, "I don't remember. I didn't even know I knew some of it until I saw it there."

"Okay," I nod, "here is the whole thing: Creatures of old will rise again, to wreak havoc on the realm of man, underneath the Earthen soil, ancients will rise to reclaim what was lost. Only children to man, six of strange blood to stand against the darkness. One with the mark of a dragon, One with skin of stone, One with pure blood running through his veins, One with a heart of gold, One with a control over life and death, One of ancient blood. All from different worlds, must stop demons who escaped the underworld, they join forces to stop the demon lord, Hell's gate no longer being ignored, Love or hate, the world will fall if they fail."

"I don't know what any of that means."

"Yeah," I shrug, "most darklings don't even believe in it."

"Why not?"

"It's different from the ones that came before," I inform him, "most of the prophecies we had were said thousands of years ago and came from respected members of the darkling community. The last one came to pass like, two hundred years ago, I think. This was stated twenty years ago by some rotten witch hag that was a nuisance to her own community."

"Okay…"

"And this one is far more detailed than any of the previous ones," I tell him as I jump up and hurry to look around for the book I keep close. Pulling it out from under my pillow, I shove it into his arms, "this is a book of all the darkling prophecies that had ever been in existence. You will see, even though most of them are faded, are little more than a single stanza. All of them have been vague and only fully realized until they fell into full effect. This one? It's way too specific."

"So, this," he points from the book to the picture, "is the same darkness?"

"Yes," I shrug, "almost certainly."

"Do you believe in the prophecy?" Theo asks, his voice soft as he flips through the book.

"I mean," I gesture around us, "leaning more toward the affirmative, especially after this. I was taken away from my home for this prophecy. It's kind hard not to believe in it."

"So, what part of you?" He asks.

"'One with ancient blood', believed to be born from an ancient monster of some sort, I guess. That's what they told me."

"Oh, fun."

"I just can't wrap my head around you," I tell him, folding my arms as I start pacing around the room, "I've never heard of a shifter, except for Senator Jepson, even entertaining the thought of a darkling prophecy, let alone reading it to your only child."

"You don't know everything about shifters."

"I know enough," I remind him, "after being spit on by each one I walk by, after being looked down on because of something I can't control, by…"

"Got it," Theo shakes his head, "I get it. Shifters are the worst."

"Not all of them," I shrug, "but I can't think of a single one that would engage in such a dark fantasy except for the one that brought me here."

"Archibald Jepsen," Theo nods as he leans forward, "that was my father's old boss. He brought you here?"

"Yes."

"That was my mom's father," Theo tells me, his voice growing quiet. There is a thought lingering behind his eyes, one I dare not look into, "I never met him but my mom adored him."

"So, your mom told you the prophecy," I frown, "but did she believe in it? Is there a reason she told you?"

"I honestly don't know," he says helplessly. He stands too, running his hands through his hair and tugging at it as he walks to the window, "this prophecy...you...everything...what does it have to do with me?"

"Isn't it obvious?" I ask, "One with pure blood running through his veins...you're a part of the prophecy as much as I am. That might explain why your mother told you the prophecy and why your dad never let you meet your grandfather. It would finally give the warlock a reason for marking you. We have to call your dad."

"No way," Theo shakes his head and jumps up to block the door, "they have Jenny."

"Right," I let out a groan, "that kind of makes my job harder."

"When you woke up," Theo says, "you had bruises on your throat and mud on your feet. Where did you go? Did that have to do with this?

"A dark being grabbed me and told me that I was the key to the prophecy," I shrug, "nothing too crazy, right?"

"It is insane. What are we going to do?"

"I guess wait until they message us again? If we can't tell anyone…"

"You're kidding."

"They want something. They will tell us what it is eventually. Either way, we need to get some sleep. I heard class is going to suck tomorrow."

"How can you worry about class?"

"What else can we do at this moment?" I ask him, "we can't call your father. We can't fight this thing. All we can do is move on for now until something else comes up. Also, Theo, what happens if you skip class or drop lower than a 'C' here?"

"Parents are called."

"Do you really want your dad coming out here and potentially putting Jenny in danger?"

"I-"

"No, you don't. Go to sleep, Theo, you don't work well tired."

"I'm not done talking about this!"

"I am," I snap back. He opens his mouth to argue but there must have been something about my face that makes him sigh and turn toward his bed. Theo plops down on his bed, leaving me in silence. Like most nights, surprisingly, his snores taking over the room soon after.

10

Brave Little Boy

Theo doesn't speak to me in the morning. He doesn't comment when one of Arnold's friends faceplants in the mud. Instead, his blue eyes stay forward as we make our way to our class. Mrs. Sagle is already welcoming the other students and Stella sits where we usually do, a wide smile widening on her face as she sees us.

Theo walks past her, choosing to go sit in the corner instead. I roll my eyes as I sit in my usual seat, not bothering to look his way as I pull out my books.

"Everything okay?" Stella asks as she moves to take Theo's regular spot beside me.

"Yeah," I shrug, "we're good."

"You two don't look good," Mrs. Sagle speaks up as she steps up to us, "what's going on?"

"Nothing big," I lie as I lean forward, "I accidentally dropped his phone and it cracked. He's furious at me especially since he's not going to be able to get a replacement until Christmas vacation."

"Ah," she sighs, "you should have been more careful."

"I know."

Content with my answer, she steps away. The assignment is on the board and I flip to the page just as Stella leans over toward me and says, "I call bull. What happened?"

"It's none of your business," I whisper back.

"Ouch," she mutters and falls against the back of the chair. I glare down at my book as I try to figure out what to say to her. I hate the thought of being a jerk but, at the same time, I know it isn't something I should be focusing on.

I, again, make the mistake of glancing out the window. Jasper stands there, as always, grinning before nodding toward the shadows around him.

Another encounter...

My arm shoots up and Mrs. Sagle releases me to the bathroom. I can feel both Theo's and Stella's eyes on me as I hurry out but I don't look back. I glance back at the windows to make sure no one is watching after me before jogging to the trail that twists into the trees. With a deep breath, I follow the trail and ignore the rising feeling of panic the deeper I go.

It's different this time. I'm not getting sucked in and I can *feel* everything around me. The animals darting through the undergrowth, the students somewhere behind me in the classrooms...It almost feels like a normal forest.

Except I also feel *it*...a dark presence unlike anything I have ever felt before.

Is that what grabbed me?

"Brave little boy," the voice whispers, his voice again coming from all around me. I gulp down my fear and try to calm my breathing before he continues, "daring to come visit me...most would have ignored my threat."

"What do you want?" I ask, keeping my eyes on a nearby tree. It is something to focus on...something to distract myself from the being and the fear that accompanies it.

"I want what I was promised," he tells me, "a boy to do what needs to be done. You will travel to Maybelle and you will do as you're told."

"If I say no?" I ask him.

"Everyone you ever loved will be dead and delivered at your feet," he promises, "before I finally kill you."

"I-"

"Here comes your friend," he giggles, "I wonder how they'll *taste*."

"Ryder," Stella hisses, appearing beside me. The dark being, and the feeling, is gone, leaving me to face her, "what are you doing out here? You know you're not supposed to out here."

"I'm aware," I sigh as I start walking back toward the opening. She grabs my arm and I stumble back a step, turning to raise an eyebrow at her.

"Look, you need to be careful," she tells me, "I know you probably think it's a stupid fear but, Arnold isn't someone you want to mess with. He'll hurt you and his mother will find some way to justify it. You really don't want to be wandering into dark spaces alone."

I nod and hold back a chuckle as I follow her up the trail. Little did she know, that bear is minor compared to what I now have to face. I would take Arnold any day.

When we make it back to the classroom, I frown when I find it empty. The sun hangs low in the sky and I realize that I had been in those trees for most of the day when it only felt like fifteen minutes.

"Where's Theo?" I ask her as we start toward the building.

"Last I saw him, he was following Mrs. Katherine's group around the building."

"Why is he entertaining that group?" I mutter as we both make our way toward the back end of the mansion. Like she had told us on our tour, there are several areas for outside activities. I don't spend much time looking at them, though, because I can already see the group of shifters surrounding what looks like a rock wall.

There is Theo, halfway up the wall without the safety harness that hangs off the side. Why wouldn't he be wearing it?

As we make our way over, I narrow my eyes when he doesn't make any advancements upward. The crowd is cheering him on from below, their screams and laughter matching their moving bodies. Their excitement isn't going to last long. Theo is sacred, I only have to see his shaking hands to notice this, and when he's scared, he freezes.

He's stuck up there in front of a crowd that will love to see him fail.

"Theo!" Stella calls out as she pushes through the crowd, "what are you doing?"

"Leave him be!" Arnold's voice cuts through the noise, "he volunteered!"

If Theo were to fall from that height, I suspect he'd break a leg or at least sprain something. The wall stretches unbelievably high into the sky, higher than any I've ever seen before. Why wouldn't there be an adult out here monitoring this?

111

I glance over at Arnold, who is standing almost directly under Theo, and let out a sigh. Is this payback for what I did? Why would he be after Theo?

"Should I go grab a teacher?" Stella asks as I make it up to her.

"No," I say, "Theo got himself into this mess. He can deal with it."

As those words leave my mouth, Theo loses his grip. I step forward as he falls though I know there is nothing I can do to stop his decent. I can already watch as the crowd starts to laugh as he nears the ground, the terror evident on his face.

That's when Stella shows me who, or what rather, she really is.

Her arm darts out, a twisted piece of dark wood appearing in her hand. Words, *dark* words, fall past her lips. A dark blue spark erupts past the tip of her wand and splashes against the patch of grass below his falling body.

A giant, warped flower stretches up before he can hit the ground. His body hits the giant bud, breaking his fall before crumbling to the ground and out of existence.

A stunned silence falls over the group and Stella lowers her arm, the wand disappearing back into her sleeve. No one else seems to notice her actions nor do they even spare a glance in our direction.

They stand transfixed, watching as Theo stumbles to his feet with red cheeks before his eyes land on me and Stella. He veers off, hurrying through the crowd and toward the building. Stella and I share a look before we both push our way through the crowd and rush after him.

"We are going to have a chat," I tell her as I hold the door open. She doesn't respond as she rushes ahead of me. I follow after, glancing back to see if anyone else decided to follow.

Luckily, no one does.

"Theo," Stella says as she bursts into our room. He is lying face down on his bed and doesn't even acknowledge us as I kick the door closed, "what were you thinking? You could have really hurt yourself."

"He wasn't," I answer for him. Theo groans in response and rolls over to glare at me.

"I just wanted to feel normal," he grumbles, "and I don't feel normal with you."

"Fair," I reply as I sit down on my bed. Stella follows after, sitting beside me with her eyes on her feet. I bet she's wondering when this conversation is going to turn toward her, "but that doesn't mean you should put yourself in danger."

"They said everyone does it!"

"They don't like you, Theo," Stella says, "they are never going to like you because you associate with Ryder. That is how it's going to be even if you stop being friends with him."

"It isn't even about them," he mutters as he sits up. I sigh with him as I lean back, "I just…"

It is then that Stella's eyes land on the words carved into our wall. I frown as her eyes widen and she stands up to trace her fingers over them just as Theo had the night before. We watch her, waiting for her reaction as she turns back toward us.

"Why do you have part of the prophecy of the six carved into your wall?" She chokes out.

"How do you know the name of a darkling prophecy?" I ask in response, "it isn't something that lightlings tend to talk about."

"And how did you make that flower?" Theo asks as well, posing a question I too need an answer for, "I saw it coming from you, the magic…it was dark magic, wasn't it? It didn't look like any magic I have ever seen before."

"Why is this being turned me?" She asks as she points at the wall, "you have words carved into your wall!"

"Because you can use dark magic," I tell her, standing as I move to block the door, "which means you are not the light witch you claim to be. You are something on the darkling side, one who immediately befriended us since we got here. You know of the prophecy, one that isn't taught here or literally anywhere else. A little suspicious, isn't it?"

"Or you're a little paranoid," she retorts.

"Look," Theo says, rubbing his face with a groan before continuing, "we've kind of been through a lot so we have to be a little paranoid. I was attacked by a warlock before we got here and Ryder is here to stop that from happening again. He's just making sure I'm not in danger and I'm sorry for making that harder today."

"Ugh," she groans, "fine! You're right. You've always been right."

"About what?" I ask, though I know the answer.

"I'm not this," she gestures toward herself.

"Obviously," I mutter before I can stop myself.

"Yes, obviously," she groans, "the reason why I befriended you two so quickly is because I have finally found someone I can relate to."

"A darkling," Theo confirms.

"Yes," she sighs, "can I use your bathroom real quick?"

"Sure," Theo answers before I can. He turns toward me and closes his eyes as if preparing himself for what he is about to say. I raise an eyebrow, mentally preparing myself as well, "look, Ryder, I wasn't meaning anything bad about you when I said I didn't feel normal with you."

"I know, Theo," I chuckle, "you need to stop apologizing for speaking the truth. There is nothing normal about me or about this situation. I wasn't offended in the least. What did bother me, though, is the fact that you decided to endanger yourself the moment I left you alone."

"I know," he nods, "I just...I know they are jerks and I shouldn't care but there has always been a part of me that just wanted to fit in with them, you know? If I can't fit in with these guys, how am I going to fit in with the rest of the students when fall comes, especially when nothing we've tried works to help me shift?"

"I don't know but..."

The bathroom opens, halting any conversation as Stella, a new version of her, steps out.

I can't stop the gasp from leaving my lips. She is just as pretty as she was before, however, she looks more at home with herself. There was always something about her that just wasn't right but now...she *feels* like her.

115

Her features have sharpened, with her round cheeks hidden away. The red eyes that first caught my eyes look more natural against her pale sea green skin, the whites of her eyes looking more red than white as well. Her hair is the same except for a dark green tint, though she is missing the white runes that once decorated her hairline.

"Whoa," Theo chokes out, a small smile stretching out.

"A dark elf," I nod, "the magic makes sense now. Your kind is known for your nature manipulation magic."

"Yes," she smiles slightly, "we are. I'm not the best at it but I'm trying. Mrs. Sagle knows and she's been working on it with me so when I use my magic it isn't so obvious. As you can see, I haven't made much progress."

"Why do you hide yourself?" Theo asks, his voice low, "you look great."

"Don't be so naïve, Theo," she chuckles as she plops down next to me, "people aren't nice to darklings especially ones as obvious as me. Things seem fine now but when the actual school year comes, they aren't so nice. My dad thought it would be better if I look more…well, normal. That's why I know the prophecy. That's why I was hiding what I was, okay?"

"I believe you," I nod and Theo mutters the same. She folds her arms and lets out a shaky breath before nodding at the damaged wall.

"Can I get some answers now? It's only fair, right?" She asks.

"Our situation is a little different," I inform her.

"What could it hurt, Ryder?" Theo asks, "it's not like she's going to tell anyone."

"Did you forget the warning?" I remind him.

"Obviously," he shrugs, "but how will they know?"

"Theo-"

"Seriously, though," he says, "it or they or whatever, only talks to you in the trees, right? Or in your dreams? They've only came in here when we've both been checked out. Maybe she can help us figure out what everything means. She already knows the prophecy! Three heads are better than one."

"Think about Jenny, Theo," I warn him, "do you really what to test his patience?"

"We don't even know who he is!"

"So, there's a whole conversation about me is happening without," Stella says as she lets out a sigh, "I think we're all deep enough to let me know what is happening."

"No," I tell her as I point toward the door, "thank you for showing us who you really are but we have to have a little private chat. We'll see you in the morning."

"That's not fair!" She complains but still does as I ask. She glances back at the both of us before disappearing into the dark stairway. I follow and close the door as she leaves, frowning as I turn back toward Theo.

"What's wrong with you?" I ask him, "why do you think we should tell her? We could not only be endangering Jenny but Stella too by involving her in this."

"Ryder," Theo responds, "we have no idea what we're doing."

"I told you that we just needed to wait. I...spoke with him again."

"Really? What did he say?"

"Maybelle. He said that I have to go to Maybelle."

"Just you?"

"He only ever says me. Never has he even mentioned you or multiple people following through with his plan. Theo, I don't think this is the warlock that marked you. I think it's something a lot worse."

11

Friends again?

The next day is gloomy and dark, in both mood and in nature. Everything seems to be bogging Theo down and there isn't anything I can do to help him. As we move through the day, the other students are especially icy since the events of the day before. That, however, is an improvement over my expectations.

Arnold especially avoids us when we pass by him on the way to breakfast.

Stella too is nowhere to be seen, though I try not to think about that. We didn't tell her, obviously, so she has to be fine. There would be no reason for him to touch her.

"So, friends again?" Mrs. Sagle asks as we wait for class to officially get started.

"For now," I say, grinning as I glance over at the shifter. He doesn't acknowledge my joke as he flips absently through the book, waiting as everyone else is in a zombie-like state. I sigh as I too flip through the book, hoping this isn't how it's going to be for the rest of our time together.

I have to go to Maybelle. The dark guy said nothing about Theo. That can't be an accident, right? Theo can call his father after I leave and get an

119

alternative safety measure. Will he be watching Theo after I disappear?

"Alrighty, class," Mrs. Sagle calls out, "let's get started."

The class passes by annoyingly slow. I can't stop myself from eyeing the clock every few minutes, praying for it to be lunch time to finally stop pretending to pay attention.

Unfortunately, Mrs. Sagle notices this and doesn't let me leave with the rest of the students. I glance at Theo, who waits right outside the door as I step up to her desk.

"What can I do for you, ma'am?" I ask her.

"Do you have anything to tell me?" She asks, "not as your teacher but as someone who reports to the N.A.S.O.?"

"No, ma'am," I tell her, hoping I'm convincing, "we just…did you hear about the incident yesterday?"

"I did," she sighs, "Theo should know better."

"He does now."

"Good."

"Is there anything else?"

"I suppose not," she leans forward and pulls down her glasses to look me in the eye, "I trust that you will let me know if anything happens that I should know about."

"Yes, ma'am," I bow slightly before turning toward the door. Theo falls in line beside me and we don't speak as we go to get our food.

"What did she ask you?" He asks, finally breaking the silence.

"Nothing, really," I reply and he falls silent again, the only sound coming from him crunching on celery sticks. I struggle to think of something to say, however, nothing enters my mind. Instead, I focus on the food in front of me, hating the unusual silence.

"So, what's the plan?" Theo asks, finally bringing up what is on his mind once we make it back to our room, "I mean, you said the guy just wants you? You can't just go to Maybelle, not by yourself."

"Are you suggesting that I bring you along?" I ask him as I sit down on the bed and glare at the ceiling. It is a relief to know that whatever this is isn't after Theo himself. If I can get away with only me having to face whatever it is he wants, I would be golden. Something tells me, however, that it won't be that easy.

"Yes...no...maybe?" Theo groans out, "I don't know. I don't want you going alone. If any of the rumors are true, that place is way dangerous. You could die."

"Or Jenny could," I mutter, lifting my head to meet his eyes, "make your choice."

"That isn't fair."

"Being fair doesn't matter," I tell him, "but being realistic does."

"Ryder..."

"Theo, I'm tired. It has been a long day. Can we continue this in the morning?"

"Fine."

I sigh in relief as the room grows quiet. Theo isn't asleep, his snores have yet to take over the room, but I let my own eyes close and welcome whatever comes after it.

I really wish I didn't.

The large broken skyscraper, standing alone against giant piles of debris, stands ominously before me. The negative feeling is relatively new. When I was that age, I had been ecstatic to see it. I was so confident in my plan that I failed to follow the very basic protocol that I now live by.

Always feel for other people lingering around.

"*Ryder!*" Jasper hissed as he yanked me back behind a building, "*are you joking? This is what you thought we should do? We're going to get killed. If we don't die from them, Auntie Rosa and Dante will finish the job.*"

"*Oh, come on,*" I shrugged him off as he peered around the wall we hid behind. *The small valley sat below me with the single skyscraper sticking up over the debris. The tracker, a giant and very terrifying mix of magic and technology, charging station was empty, meaning they were already spread out across the city. There was no sign of anyone in the building itself. The D.M.M.A. hadn't been to Maybelle for six months and I doubted today would be the day they finally come back to visit.*

"*Jaz, no one is here.*"

"*That doesn't make me feel any better. Just because they aren't here now doesn't mean they can't show up later.*"

"*We'll get out before anyone even realized we were there,*" I said, "*everything will be fine, okay? I promise.*"

"*This on you if it goes bad.*"

"*Deal.*"

We hurried toward the front door and I was grinning the entire way. I had been looking forward to that small mission for months. I grinned back at Jasper, just as his body slammed into mine. We rolled to the ground just as a spray of darts slammed into the ground beside us. I rolled onto my back and saw suited men coming out from behind several piles of debris.

Darts?

"*Told you!*" *Jasper yelled at me as he yanked me to my feet and pulled me into the building. I didn't argue as I let my brother drag me through the building. The men were following after, entering through the doorway just as Jasper and I started up the stairs. Jasper never once looked back as he hurried upward.*

Jasper cursed as we made it to the fifth floor, only to find the rest of the staircase to be blocked. I pulled my hand out of his brother's as we hurried forward. We both zeroed in on the door at the very end of the hallway.

"*So, what now?*" *I asked as Jasper closed the door, "what are we supposed to do now?*"

"*I don't know,*" *Jasper shrugged and spun toward me with fury in his eyes, "how about you tell me because you were the one with the plan!*"

"*I've been watching this place for months,*" *Ryder snaps, freezing as I heard voices in the hallway. Jasper groaned as he spun around before hurrying toward the desk that stood against the wall of windows that stood strangely intact. He started to push it forward and I moved toward the bookshelf, hoping to knock it forward and block the door from opening before he could block it with the weight of the desk.*

Just as I wrapped my hand around the rough wood, the door behind me exploded.

The force slammed me into the bookshelf and I slid to the ground, covering my head as wood shards rained down on me. I sat there for a moment, disoriented as my ears rang and my vision swam. I crawled away from the gaping hole, searching for my brother. He was no longer standing, hidden somewhere among the mess...or so I thought until I saw the shattered windows.

"*Jasper?*" *I called out as I stumbled to my feet, my voice sounding strangely muffled. I scrambled to the desk and pulled myself forward, my heart hammering in my chest as I peered around it. Tears slipped past my eyes when I found nothing waiting for me except for broken glass. I glanced around the room one more time before stepping toward the glassless windows.*

"No, no, no," I cried out as I fell to my knees. I could feel the glass cutting me through my jeans but I couldn't feel the pain as I grabbed the metal bearing and peered over the edge.

I let out a sob as I saw my brother's broken body lying on the cement below, his legs twisting unnaturally around him.

"No," I sobbed as a pair of arms yanked me away from the edge.

Instead of facing the familiar man that I always did when I had this dream, a dark being stands above me as the rest of the dream fades away. Again, I see no features, just a humanoid shadow hanging onto my body as he watches my reaction.

"You cause destruction wherever you go, don't you?" The horrid voice laughs, "first, you get your brother killed and now...well, now you're getting that innocent little shifter killed."

"What?" I cough out as I struggle against his hold, "why? We didn't do anything! We told no one!"

"Someone knows," he sighs, feigning disappointment, "and now someone has to pay."

I scramble up in bed, sweat coating my body as I struggle to comprehend where I lay. Bed...bed...dresser...windows...I groan and fall back, glancing over at Theo's bed before my heart drops.

Theo's gone.

"No!" I cry out as I dart over to his side, listening for the bathroom as I glance at the window. Below, Theo stands right outside the trail, looking up at me with a blank look on his face. He turns toward the trees and steps inside. I dart away from the window and hurry down the staircase, not bothering to sneak away as my heart hammers in my chest before I make it to the main floor.

My body slams into someone else's and I roll away, intent to keep moving until a familiar voice calls my name.

Stella.

Anger seizes me and I spin around to face her. Her makeup is smudged with tear streaks and she doesn't turn away as I step toward her. Before I can decide against it, I grab her shoulders and push her up against the wall. She doesn't flinch as I glare at her, my words leaving my lips in a whisper, "you heard, didn't you? You stayed back and eavesdropped."

"I'm sorry," she cries out and drops her head, "I didn't hear a lot-"

"You heard enough!"

"I know," she nods, "I...I had this terrible dream and..."

"Of course you did," I groan out as I release her. I hurry down the marble staircase, darting out of the front door and into the cold air. Stella is following after me, her shoes clacking against the stone path, but I don't look back.

Without pausing, I burst into the trees and follow the trail, ignoring Stella's surprised gasp as I do so.

Still, though, she follows.

"Theo!" I call out as the trail curves to the right. I stumble to a stop, my breathing heavy as I face Theo's back. He turns around, his expression no longer blank as he looks around.

"Ryder?" He asks, his voice shaking, "what…what happened? Why are we out here? I don't even remember getting up…"

"Everything is fine," I tell him as I step forward, "just…come with me. We need to get out of the trees."

He nods as he steps forward and my hands shake as a shadowy form appears behind him. I don't speak or react as a large, dark hand wraps around him and pulls him off his feet.

"Let's consider this an added incentive," he hisses out as he raises Theo higher, "and you can even bring your little elf friend along too. You'll find him in the same cursed city you came from."

"Wait!" I call out as he throws Theo back, disappearing as his body hits the shadows. The dark being dissolves, leaving us with an empty trail that twists out of view.

He's gone…

"I'm sorry," Stella sobs out and I only groan in response as I dart forward. I reach out, the dark being and the shifter nowhere within my range.

"What is going on? What are you two doing out of bed?" I spin around to face a teacher I have never encountered before. I groan as Stella tries to stammer out a response but is unsuccessful.

"Office! Now!"

Stella and I share a look before we follow after. Before we make it to the building, I grab her hand and make the connection easier before I mentally link with her mind.

Look, I know this is weird but just let me do the talking. It's going to be confusing for you but just follow along.

I pull out of her head and she nods visibly as he leads the way past the receptionist desk and toward a door labeled 'Principal Katherine'. He pushes it open and gestures for us to sit on the two chairs waiting for us. Katherine sits down and I lean against the nearby wall as we wait for the empty desk before us to be filled.

I feel her coming before she enters and I sigh in relief as I plant in the basic thought as she yanks the door open. She plops down behind her desk, covered in a pink robe with curlers in her hair.

"What were you three thinking?" She scolds us as she rubs her forehead, "going out into the woods, not only that, but at night? They're forbidden and you all know that."

After she is met with silence, she demands, "Am I going to get an answer or no?"

"Look, Theo has been having a rough time," I tell her, gesturing toward the illusion sitting in the empty chair, "he wanted to do something a little more exciting that sitting through boring classes and getting picked on by other students. You know about that, right? In fact, if my suspicions are correct, I'd say you encourage it. We just wanted a break from all that. It's just a walk in the woods. What harm can come from it unless you're keeping something dangerous in there?"

"We don't have to explain anything to you," she snaps, "rules are rules."

"I'm sure the N.A.S.O.," I lean forward, "would love to know how you treat your struggling shifter students, especially his father. I'm sure they're also going to be as curious as I am as to why the forest is off limits without even a sign to warn kids away. A simple fence would work wonders."

"I..."

"I know the N.A.S.O. or the D.M.M.A. hasn't been briefed about the dangers lingering in the trees," I wave her comments away, "but I don't want to report you as much as you don't want me to. You are going to let this go and we will be on our way."

"I can't just let this go," she sighs, giving in, "it has already been reported. What I can do is give you a detention without a call home. I can downplay its importance and say you've learned your lesson."

"Perfect," I nod as I gesture for Stella to leave. As I shut the door behind me, I pull myself out of her mind and walk beside Stella as we head up the stairs.

"How did that guy even know?" She complains.

"He probably heard us talking," I reply as I turn toward the door that leads to my room. Exhaustion and emptiness threaten my anger, pulling at my eyelids as I force my feet forward.

"What are we going to do?" She cries out, pulling on my arm. I yank my hand out of her grasp as I turn toward her.

"There is no 'we', Stella," I mutter, "I need to figure out how to save him. You've done enough."

"I don't accept that," she argues as she follows me up my staircase, "I want...no, I need to fix this. I can help you get to Maybelle."

"How?" I spin toward her, standing above her because of the stairs, "how can you possibly know how to get to Maybelle?"

"I mom used to live there," she tells me, "I know how to get through the barrier."

12

Maybelle

We're alone in my room, the darkness lit up only by the moonlight as Stella flips through a large binder sitting in her lap. She's sitting on my bed as I pace the room, my mind whirling at the thought that someone knows how to escape the island and are hiding that information from everyone else who are trapped there.

That isn't very fair.

"I've never done it by myself before," she explains, "but I'm sure we can figure it out. I only wish I knew someone in Maybelle. Maybe then I could have asked someone to look out for them."

"I know people in Maybelle," I say, "you can send a message out that far?"

"Yes," she shrugs, "well, sort of. Do you know where they are? We can send it to a place."

"I know where they should be."

"Perfect. Everything works out," she mutters as she jumps up with the binder. I lean down as she holds it out, and there is a list of instructions sketched out with ingredients beside it, "this is what we need to send a message over to Maybelle. Getting there is a little harder because we need a portal that isn't connected to the school. An older one...I know where one is but, it is quite hard to get there."

"You know how to work them?" I ask her.

"Yes."

"Even the ones attached to the school?"

"Yes," she nods, "but they will only lead to specific locations."

"I know where one is," I tell her, "it's super old but, it might be a stretch."

"The one I know of is in Greece. There's no direct way there."

"Mine is easier," I reply as she leads the way back downstairs, "we just need some ingredients. I have them in my room."

I nod as I follow her, my heart pounding as I think about how Theo is going to fare in Maybelle. As positive as I want to be, I know how likely he is to survive. If the monsters don't get to him first, the darklings will kill him without a second thought.

No matter how hard I try to convince myself otherwise, Theo is more than just a job. He's a friend that will cause me personal turmoil if he gets hurt in that wretched city. We are going to save him, even if I have to die trying before I can even think to follow whatever demands that *thing* has.

It is a weird thought, after all...having a friend I'm willing to die for after so long...it comes with a strange sense of belonging that lingers off both Theo and Stella, one that leaves a painful emptiness knowing where he has gone.

"I'm going to get the ingredients," she says as we stop outside her door, "stay out here. I don't think my roommate will appreciate you coming in there. Try to figure out where they'll be so we can be ready to pass on the message."

"Of course," I nod as she disappears into the dark room. I already know where we're sending the message. Dante, my late twin's mentor, uses it as a home base of sorts. He had created an almost normal home before I left. He will probably be the best darkling to run into because he has no true qualms with lightlings. All he wants is to survive and keep his people alive. That is all based on how I remember it, though it may have changed.

Nothing stays the same in Maybelle.

My biggest worry is Marcus. Like Dante, he is a vampyr who rules over a small group of darklings. I know pop culture has blurred the difference between blood suckers and vampyrs, one being a bloodsucking demon spawn while the other simply lives off blood instead of meat itself. Both Dante and Marcus have every ability to live peacefully, however, the former loves bloodshed. I have never met him; however, I grew up hearing horror stories starring him.

If Theo ends up in Marcus's turf or if he has finally taken Dante down…I shiver at the thought as Stella comes out of her room with a filled duffle bag.

"Okay, I went ahead and packed everything we can potentially need for our little trip. We have to leave tonight or risk them finding out about our missing friend. They send healers whenever a student is sick to make sure they're not just trying to skip."

"Fun," I mutter as I follow her down the stairs. She leads the way to the fireplace and drops her bag before kneeing down to dig through it. She holds her hand out and hands me a cloth bag, the crunchy material feeling weird in my hands.

"What's this?"

"Soil from Maybelle," she answers, "that's all we need for the spell to find a connection."

"Okay," I nod, "why do you have it?"

"My father has a lot," she shrugs, "he made sure I was able to contact my mother before she died. Now, I have it for a reminder of her. Came in use, huh?"

"Do we need anything else?" I ask, unsure of how to react to her response. What am I supposed to say to that?

"A fire," she gestures forward. I keep my eyes peeled as she lets out a shaky breath. Fae words leave her lips and I glance over at the fire as she tosses a handful of dirt in. The green flames flash blue and Stella gestures him forward.

"Think about where you want to send it," she tells me, "but it has to have a fireplace."

"Okay," Ryder sighs as he looks into the green flames. He can...he can see it. The familiar library that I always found my brother in. The dusty table, the armchair my brother had always loved...and a dark silhouette standing in one of the aisles.

Hopefully it is someone who can help.

"Hi, there," I say, waving before realizing that whoever stands beyond probably can't see me. I do see him turn toward my voice, though, which is refreshing, "I'm looking for Dante, if you could pass the message along. I'm Ryder, he should remember me, and I have a friend who traveled to Maybelle by accident. We're coming but could you please go find him and keep him alive until I get there? You'll know him when you see him. He won't be blending in. Bright blue eyes, average height, a shifter…I'll explain everything when I get there. Thank you."

The fire splutters and, for the first time since I got here, goes out. The lobby grows dark, darker than I have ever seen it. My heart skips a beat as her hand slides into mine as she pulls him back toward the stairs.

"Go pack clothes and whatever else you need," she says, "I'll go to Mrs. Sagle's classroom. She has a bunch of pre-made potions and ingredients we can use."

"Okay," I reply as I hurry back up to my room. With the bag Emerson had given me, I shove the clothes into it before pulling my book from underneath my bag. I have nothing else of use but I pause as I pass by my desk.

Sure, I already know a lot but a potions book can't be a bad idea.

I shove the textbook into the bag before bounding back down the stairs. She is waiting for me at the bottom of the staircase with a bag of her own. She hooks her hand through mine before leading me back toward the fireplace.

"You know how to get to that old portal?"

"Yes."

"Okay," she nods as she pulls back some red-looking sand, much like Emerson had when we were leaving his house, before spreading it along the protruding archway before whispering.

Just like with the other one, I gasp as the spiraling colors stretch out and fill in the space. Stella pulls her bag over her shoulder, the clanking glass impossible to ignore.

"Are you sure about this?" I ask her, "there's no going back after we step through."

"You still need me for two more portals," she shrugs, "you need me."

She waves me forward and I close my eyes as we walk through together, her arm hooking through mine before the cool, whirling wind takes over.

When I open my eyes again, we are standing in the small station with the line of other portals. All of them, however, are powered down. We step through and she whispers a word I can't decipher before the light leaves it.

"Ryder," she says and I pull her behind me as two guards step up to us. Their bright lights flash forward, nearly blinding me. I ignore their orders and take a deep breath, raising my hands as I mentally reach out.

"Sleep," I order and their eyes go wide for a moment as my mental command takes hold before they both slump forward. Stella doesn't say a word as I release her and step up to the guard. I dig around in the closest one's pocket before pulling out a pair of car keys.

"We're stealing a car, now?" She asks as we hurry toward the door.

"Bigger picture, Stella," I reply as I kick open the door, "bigger picture."

We find the parking lot around the back, almost completely hidden in the field. It's a small car, complete with a tiny back that barely fits our bags. I pause as I move to put my hands on the steering wheel and groan when I realize that it doesn't have one.

It's one of those magic cars.

"I got it," Stella giggles as she grabs the keys from me and we climb out to switch seats, "where are we going?"

"The D.M.M.A. hospital in New York City."

"Okay," she says. I close my eyes and hang onto the seat as it shoots forward, trying desperately to ignore the feeling of panic rising in my gut. It feels like hours as the car twists and turns at impossible speeds.

This isn't worth it.

"Ryder," Stella's soft voice forces me to open my eyes and I sigh in relief when I find us already sitting in the parking garage that I had been in a few weeks ago.

Whoa, it feels like so long ago.

"So," she says as we grab our bags and step out of the car, "what's the plan?"

"Stay behind me and don't say a word."

She mimics zipping her mouth shut and we head toward the two sliding glass doors that will let us into the first level of the hospital. This was going to be a little trickier than simply tricking Mrs. Katherine. Hopefully, I only have to mess with the front desk.

Right before I step through the glass doors, I enter the older woman's mind as she sits alone behind the desk. Luckily, no one else stands in the lobby as I walk up to the desk.

"Good morning," I say in a conjured-up image of Emerson, making the lady sit up straight as she faces me, "there's a patient here I need to interview on the second floor. Any way you can ring me up?"

"Of course, sir," she stammers out, "I do just need to see identification-"

"Ma'am," I shake my head, trying to embody the well-known shifter, "you know who I am. This is a time sensitive manner and I am already late. You can check my identification and my clearance when I come back down. I don't want to make a report about the D.M.M.A.'s lack of urgency."

"Fine," she mutters as she presses a button on her desk. The elevators at the end of the hall ding open, "just make sure you stop by the desk."

"Thank you," I nod as I speed walk to the open doorway, letting out a sigh of relief when we step inside. Facing the lobby as the doors close, I see Emerson himself stepping up to the counter and the flustered girl pointing toward the now closed metal doors.

"We need to hurry," I mutter as I press my hand against the bright number two.

"Why?" Stella asks, speaking for the first time.

"That man is who I pretended to be."

"Oh, fun," she groans as the door pings open to the second floor. Luckily, no one is there to meet us as I pull her through the hallway. If I remember right, the portal should be...

"Here," I say as I point the weirdly dark archway in the middle of a white hallway. She nods as she kneels down and gets to work, leaving me to look for any upcoming danger.

Just as the portal powers up, a familiar voice shouts my name. I wince I turn to face my boss, his face red with anger as he zeroes in on the portal.

"What is going on?" He asks, waving for the guards behind him to stop.

"You have to trust me, sir," I tell him, "I'm doing this for your son."

Emerson's face shifts from anger to concern as he glances back at the guards behind him. With a loud grown, he says, "fine. You know what will happen to you if you're lying to me."

"Yes, sir," I grin as I step through, pleasantly surprised that I didn't have to do more to convince him. I stumble into the darkness, a pair of arms catching me before I can fall.

We've made it to Emerson's secret room.

"Are you ready for this?" Stella asks as she leans down to spread her own concoction on the portal frame.

"As ready as Theo was," I retort as it spurts to life. This portal is different than the others. The others had bright spiraling colors but this one...this one has little sparks of darkness interspersed.

She grabs my hand and gives it a squeeze before pulling me through.

Theodore Emerson
Pureblood Shifter
Hater of Bullies and Rom-Coms
Lover of Friends and Good Times

13

The Dead Twin

"Silly *pet," a dark voice shakes me to my core. There is no placing it...no way to tell exactly where it's coming from. Darkness surrounds me, leaving me nothing but the voice to remind me that I'm still alive. Though it had long since grown quiet, the voice still reverberates through my skull.*

"H...hello?" I cough out, my voice shaking as I struggle to get the words out.

"You are a rather spineless one, aren't you?" He speaks out, laughing as a rough hand yanks my face upward. In the darkness, I can see two glowing orbs.

"Couldn't protect your mother," he hisses out, throwing me back, "too pathetic to shift...even your uncle being pulled apart wasn't enough for you to grow a pair. Not even your own girlfriend wants you...she too sees what I see...that you're nothing but a feeble little pup who can't even help himself."

"Where is she?" I scream out, my heart jolting as he mentions her.

"Oh, Maybelle will have fun with you."

"M...Maybelle?"

He only laughs and throws me back, sending me twirling away from his dark presence. I scream, or try to, but the sound is muffled as I fly backward...

Bright light sits beyond my eyelids, the heat warming my skin. I lay there for a moment more before forcing my eyes open. A clear blue sky welcomes me, a little tinge of red resting in the east. Little bits of white float into my vision, looking like…snow? Rolling to my side, I realize that I am no longer in the forest beyond the academy jurisdiction.

I scramble backward, my palms scraping against rough stone as I look around wildly, desperate to find something familiar. Staring numbly at the broken streets around me, I try to comprehend where exactly I am.

It's unlike anything I have ever seen.

It's like something out of a horror movie.

Large cracks snake out across the asphalt, stretching up and through some of the townhouse walls. Potholes interrupt the cracks, ones that look more like footsteps of some gigantic creature. The buildings are old and worn with shattered windows and colorless bricks. A layer of ashy grime coats everything around me, even my clothes.

It's not snow falling, the thought sparking in my head as I reach my hand out, it's ash.

"Ryder!" I call out, my voice echoing through the empty streets. Nothing calls back, the silence nearly deafening.

I gulp as the ground below me rumbles and rumbles again. It feels like footsteps, though I don't want to think about the size of whatever is causing it. I let out a shaky breath as terror seizes my body, freezing my limbs before I can even think to move.

I should be running or hiding or doing *something* but instead…instead I am just standing here, unable to move or even look back at what is about to destroy me. I should be ready to fight instead of freezing up just like I did when that warlock attacked and took out my uncle's legs.

"You should probably run," a voice speaks up from somewhere above me, snapping me out of my shock momentarily. I glanced up at the windows, searching for the form until I finally find him sitting on the room. His legs are kicking out below him, much like that of a child, as if he isn't hanging three stories above the ground. He tilts his head and leans forward before speaking again, "don't you feel it coming? You can't escape it once it sees you."

"Once what sees me?" I ask as his head nods toward something behind me. He shakes his head and, before I can respond, pushes himself off the roof. I stumble back with a scream as he falls through the air, slowing just moments before he would have slammed into the sidewalk. Instead, he lands softly on his feet before slowly stepping onto the street.

Dude, he can fly…

He doesn't look like I'd expect someone to living in a city like this. Though his blond hair is clean, it's cut unevenly and falls just past his eyes. He looks more like he's dressed for a middle school dance with his white button up and dark pants. He does, though, wear a dark trench coat that looks more shadow than fabric…

…Cool.

"Before that sees you," he gestures behind me, pulling my attention back to the danger at hand. After I spin around to face whatever monstrosity awaits me, my breath catches in my throat as I struggle to fathom what exactly *it* is.

It stands nearly as tall as the buildings around it and it's relatively humanoid but it's anything but living. Like out of a science fiction horror movie, gears and a thick layer of goo-like skin covers the giant robot. Instead of hands, thick, black cords stretch out from its arms, twitching and stretching as it steps closer to us.

Just like when I watched the shadow demons tear at Austen, I watch this huge thing lift its arm and I do nothing. I don't even move. My legs turn into cement as my mind begs for me to move. In my heart, I know I am dead. It's as if my body has already given up on me...

"You're hopeless," the other guy mutters as he waves his hand as if swatting a fly. Only, there is no fly. Instead, my body flies to the side just as the cords slam into the place I once stood. My back slams into the wall just as the robot turns its attention toward the blondie, stretching the cords out to meet him.

I watch in horror as he doesn't move, allowing them to stretch closer and closer. Before the cords can wrap themselves around him, however, a flash of light shines from his hands and pieces of cord fly away from him. It takes me a minute to realize that he now holds a blade in each hand, ones that easily cut through the advancing menaces.

My horror soon turns to awe as he dodges past the remaining strands before running up the robot's arm. Once he reaches its shoulder, however, a cord wraps around his ankle and yanks him back. His body flies through the air but he swings his arm, sending a twinkling blade through the air. It impales itself between the two red lights that resemble eyes, the robot standing stock still for a moment before the large metal beast starts leaning to the side.

The guy swings himself downward and slices through the cord attached to him as his body starts to fall with it. Ignoring the rules of gravity, he freezes in the air for a moment as he twists back around before dropping to the ground and landing on his feet. He lifts his hand toward the robot and I jump as his blade tears out of the artificial flesh and into his waiting hand.

"Dude," I chuckle as I step back out into the road, "that was-"

Something wraps around my ankle before I can finish, tearing me back. My body flops forward, my head slamming against the asphalt below as I am yanked back into darkness...

***

A groan leaves my lips as I try to roll over, momentarily forgetting the fact that I'm not safely tucked away in bed. Cords tighten around me as I try to move and I struggle to breathe as they tighten around my chest. I'm still moving, the binds pulling me deeper and deeper into the blackness that surrounds me. I want to scream but I can't take a deep enough breath, my exhales coming out in small huffs as I struggle against an opponent I can't see.

At least now it isn't just my body stopping me from saving myself.

The ground me below me disappears and a scream finally escapes my lips. I hang there, wrapped up in the cords, suspended just long enough to see what awaits me below.

A conveyor belt slowly chugs along, bringing forward car pieces and other discernible garbage toward a large incinerator at the end of it. Other groups of cords hang around me, each dropping their loads down below. To my left, a tuft of blond hair is tangled up in the cords as well and part of me hopes that is the blondie from before.

He'll know what to do.

I scream again, a very manly one, as I free fall into the hot air. My body recoils off something hard, sending me rolling across the belt. I groan as I push myself to sit up, holding my shoulder as I slowly move with the belt toward the large red fire at the end of it. I let out a shaky breath as I force myself to my feet and try to find a way out.

The sides of the belt are perfectly smooth and impossible to climb. The other option is to go against the movement, however, when I stumble in that direction, though, that too won't work. A large turned over semi-truck blocks the way. I can see the wall behind it and the tiny space that allows the belt through from beyond, one impossible to climb under. I turn back toward the fire, tears forming in my eyes as I turn to face what will inevitably kill me.

There is no escape, my body tenses up as that realization settles deeply into my entire body.

"Don't tell me you already gave up," a vaguely familiar voice speaks up from behind me. I spin around with a grin to find the blondie standing on the semi's side. Though his face is smudged with dirt and his once clean button up looks more brown than white,

146

he doesn't seem fazed in the slightest. He simply reaches a hand down toward me and I rush forward to grab it. Surprisingly, he pulls me up with very little effort on my part. I open my mouth to comment on it when I see something dark darting back and forth between pieces of debris.

"Oh," he says with a shrug as he climbs off the metal shell of a vehicle, "don't worry about him. That's just Bean."

"Bean?" I cough out as I follow the steps he takes to get down. The creature looks up and I realize I'm looking at the form of a dog, one that I imagined myself looking like if I could figure out how to shift. We stare at each other for a moment, its bright red eyes boring into mine before it darts away and runs through a wall. Before I can react, the blondie is dragging me forward. I move with him as best I can, however, his almost inhuman pace gets the better of me.

We make it to the wall that blocks our way, the conveyor belt feeding through a tiny space neither of us can fit through. He releases my arm and doesn't slow his pace as he nears the wall. I stop as he yanks up his hood and passes through in a blast of shadows, just like the shadow dog.

How am I supposed to do that?

"Um," I mutter aloud as I turn around, desperate to find another way through. Bean is standing behind me, watching me with a tilted head. Without warning, he charges forward and slams into my body. I stumble back against his weight, the shadows enveloping me until I fall to the ground. As soon as they dissipate, I roll to my feet and gasp when I find that I too have made it to the other side when I see an empty belt. Bean is gone and there is the blondie, making his way toward the ladder that leads to the platform above without a glance in my direction.

"Hey," I call after him as I hurry toward it. He doesn't answer as he disappears over the ledge. I hurry to catch him, sending throbbing pains through my hurt shoulder as I too climb over the ledge. With a sigh of relief, I take his offered hand and he helps me to my feet before turning toward a metal staircase that leads down toward an open doorway. I call out again, "hey, wait up!"

He only stops after we make it out the door and by then my attention is grabbed by something else. A gasp leaves my lips as I face the large expanse of blue, the soft waves beating relentlessly against the sandy shore that sits beyond the tall chain link fence and sharp incline.

Despite the horror of my situation, I want nothing more than to climb the fence and march down that hill. I've only ever seen the beach through a television screen.

"Beautiful, right?" He says, interrupting the calming beat of the waves. He steps up beside me and watches them for a moment before glancing down at the old-fashioned watch wrapped around his wrist, "unfortunately, it's extremely dangerous to go down there. Come on, we don't have any time left to waste."

"Time?" I ask as he turns to start heading toward the large hole in the fence. I follow after him and climb through before facing a long line of large warehouses that look identical to the one we just came out of, except many have collapsed inward.

"Yeah," he answers without looking back, "you don't want to be out after the sun sets."

"Why not?"

"Isn't it obvious?" He asks without looking back, "monsters thrive in the moonlight, especially here."

"Where's here?" I ask, though I already know the answer.

"The cursed city of flames," he says, his voice low, "or, you may know it as Maybelle."

My heart drops after he confirms it. There's something horrifying about having it audibly confirmed. Maybelle, the city people only mention in whispers. It is like a secret, one everyone is afraid to acknowledge and here I am, standing in it.

Just as that dark guy said…

"I don't see any flames," I comment as I follow after him.

"Nearly half the city is engulfed in eternal flames thanks to the D.M.M.A. playing with technology and magic," he says, "just not this half. You are lucky you landed on this side."

"Cool," I mutter as I keep my eyes peeled for the mentioned monsters. After the warehouses, we step onto a large parking lot that stretches into a shipyard. There is only one ship in the dock, one of those large cargo ships sticking halfway into the water. The blondie leads the way away from the water and up a slight incline. Beyond that stands a series of small buildings, each boasting supplies you can only want when you're around the beach. Of course, all of them look utterly destroyed just like everything else.

I freeze as shadows shift inside one of the buildings.

Monsters in the dark...

"What's up?" He asks, pausing and turning back toward me. Now that I'm not in imminent danger, I can actually see that there is something strangely familiar about him. He is annoyingly tall and paler than anyone I've seen except for Stella. Three scars run across the left side of his face and...

His eyes are a deep violet, though they hold a slight blueish tinge. A color I've only seen once, actually, *twice* before.

"Oh, shoot," the words slip out of my mouth and his eyebrows furrow as he glances around us before coming back to me, "I know you...you're James...no, Jay? Jacob? Jasper? Yes, you're Jasper!"

An eyebrow hikes up and his eyes narrow, glowing slightly as he steps forward. I gulp when I realize that Ryder's eyes do the same thing when he's using his abilities. Something unseen wraps around my body and I fly back before slamming against the nearest wall. Jasper walks up to me with a glare before casually swinging out his arms and catching his blades as they fly out of his sleeves.

"You have five seconds to tell me who you are and how you know my name," Jasper warns, lifting his blades toward me and waving them around slightly before continuing, "before I use these on you."

"This is insanely awesome," I mutter as I eye his sharp steel, "I...I'm Theo. You're Ryder's brother, right?"

"Ryder," Jasper scoffs as he tilts his head to the side. He squeezes the hilts of his blades and his hold on me tightens, "he's dead. Try again."

"I know this is insane," I inform him, "and he thinks you're dead too. He works for my father now."

"He's alive?" His voice cracks as his hold breaks, leaving me to fall on the ground. Luckily, I'm not too far off it so I land on my feet without too much of an issue. Jasper steps away from me, his head tilted upward toward the sky.

"Yeah," I answer him, searching my mind for a way to prove it, "he, ah, has this picture of the two of you when you were really young. You look like the picture but he doesn't. He said he had a bad experience with a warlock?"

"Ha," Jasper chuckles, "he taunted a warlock when we were kids. He's lucky he got off so easily; most wouldn't have been so nice...Look, if you say he's alive and I find out your lying...you're going to wish I never saved you. Hope kills people here."

"You are free and welcome to kill me," I assure him, "because I'm not."

"Ryder is alive," he mutters, a frown stretching across his pale face. He turns toward me and opens his mouth right as a loud siren breaks the silence around us.

Like one of those tornado sirens I've only heard in movies.

"What is that?" I ask as he lets out a groan. He doesn't answer as he grabs my arm and pulls me toward the nearest building. He kicks down the door with one swift movement before pushing me into the musty darkness. He swings out his blades and darts around the building, moving quickly through the large room we stepped into and disappearing into a narrow doorway.

It looks like an old clothing store. Faded signs showcase bikini sales and there is a pile of foul-smelling swimsuits in the corner. The sound of a growl outside sends me stumbling back as fear, once again as it grips me.

"We're clear in here," Jasper says, coming up from behind me. I yelp as I spin toward him, my heart jumping in my chest as I turn to face him, "but we can't stay out here. Come on."

"You still haven't told me what's going on," I tell him once I calm myself down. I follow him deeper into the building until he points toward a staircase leading downward.

"We both have our questions," he replies as he hurries down the stairs before me and disappears into the shadows, "but time isn't our friend right now. When that siren rings, that means it's time to hide. It's set to warn us at sunset. We'll have to wait until morning to leave."

He whispers a spell I only know from Ryder and light erupts from his hand. He leads me into a small storage space filled with old, deteriorating boxes. With a wave of his hand, a pile moves and blocks the doorway as he sits down on a pile of old newspapers. Pulling out a small rod from within his coat, he places his light on the tip and stabs it into one of the nearby boxes and lighting up the room.

I stand there for a moment, awkwardly looking down on Ryder's brother. Finally, I let myself relax enough to follow his lead and take a seat on the hard ground. I lean back against one of the piles and count to ten, hoping against hope that it is enough to calm the constant fear that threatens to overcome me.

I glance over at Jasper, ready to ask my questions when I realize he's asleep. He's hunched over with closed eyes, his breathing slow and steady. My mouth falls open in shock and I can't help but think of how bad things have to have been to be able to fall asleep at such a time.

With a sigh, I fold my arms across my chest and glare up at the dirty ceiling above me. The floor above us shifts, sending a cloud of dirt downward.

Something's up there and the only person actually capable of fighting is asleep.

14

Vampyrs vs Bloodsuckers

The boards above us keep groaning, almost as if whoever is up there is looking for something. I gulp as they slowly move closer to the stairs, my hands shaking as I glance back over at the other sitting with closed eyes. How can he sit there and rest when danger is just up a few stairs?

I clench my fists as a chill runs through me as laughter chirps from somewhere above. The footsteps stop and I let out a breath when they move back toward the front. As soon as I do, the footsteps pause and move back toward the staircase except this time, with more purpose.

When I look back down, Jasper is already standing with his blades out. His head is tilted upward toward the ceiling, his violet eyes narrow as he steps toward the blocked doorway.

They are at the top of the stairs.

"Hide," Jasper orders, nodding toward the scattered stacks in the corner. I nod as I duck into the shadows, holding my breath as I squat down. Luckily, I can see the doorway through a small space between two stacks of smelly boxes.

Jasper slowly waves his hand to the side, sending the stack out of the way before darting up the stairs. A moment later, his body flies back down in a flash. He crashes into a pile of boxes, disappearing into a flurry of debris as the boxes crumble. The little light of his goes out, draping the room back into darkness. I hold my breath as laughter again sounds from above before the steps creak as someone, or something, makes their way down the stairs.

"Mr. Skye," a voice sings as a flashlight beam passes over my hiding place. The light lands on the crushed pile, Jasper's legs poking out as the figure steps closer to his still body, "what are you doing so far from home? Did Dante's little pet wander off?"

"Marcus," Jasper says, sitting up in the muck. He looks amused with a small smile stretching across his face despite the trail of blood leaking from his head and down his face. He pushes himself to his feet and continues in a chipper voice, "tired of sleeping around with monsters?"

"Actually," Marcus sighs, "I'm looking around because we got a little message saying that a shifter had found his way into the city. When my...*friends* confirmed there was an abnormality with the border in this area, well, I had to check it out. You haven't seen a lightling anywhere, have you?"

"I'm just looking around for supplies," Jasper shrugs, angling himself so that he stands between the man and where I hide, "I lost track of time and popped in here to wait the night out."

"Around the docks?" Marcus chuckles, "we both know you aren't dumb enough for that. I thought we were friends, Jasper, and friends don't lie to each other."

"More like desperate enough," Jasper replies with a shrug, never dropping the chipper tone, "you don't really leave much for us. As for our friendship, I'll melt in Hell before being even slightly amiable with you."

"Quite an image," Marcus says, "but we both know why you are really here. I can smell him and you know that. Why do we have to bounce around like this? Just hand him over and we won't have an issue."

"Yeah," he smiles, "I knew that. I was just giving you a chance to back out. How many times have we fought, Marcus? How many times have you won?"

"Hm, your arrogance will be the end of you, boy," Marcus spits out, his voice dropping, "you seem to forget the sun was up when we last fought."

"The moon isn't going to help you," Jasper grins.

"Just give me the shifter!"

"Can't do that," Jasper retorts as he points his blades toward the dark figure. Moving unbelievably fast, Marcus leaps forward. I jump up as Jasper lunges to the side, swinging his blade out. A yelp echoes out as fabric rips, a splash of red breaks through the falling beam of the flashlight.

All I can see is a dark pair of boots heading toward me. I stumble back, fear once again seizing me before Jasper pulls me out of my hiding place and pushes me toward the doorway.

Charging toward it, I ignore the growling body on the ground and take the stairs two at a time. Jasper is right behind me, his hand grabbing a fistful of fabric as we make it back on the first floor. He yanks my shirt to the side, pulling me toward the doorway leading out to the moonlit street.

"Come on," Jasper mutters as he releases me, breaking into a full sprint as we charge down the broken road. Again, his inhuman speed is impossible to keep up with. The only thing that keeps me on my feet is Jasper always catching me right before I stumble.

I know my father would be embarrassed by me.

I don't have time to feel the same way.

"Jasper!" I call out as the ground shakes below me. He glances back, something I am too afraid to do, and he sighs before pushing me to the side. A large, stone fist slams into the ground as I stumble into a nearby wall. Jasper dives out of the way just as a foot stomps down beside it.

"Holy…" my voice carries off as Jasper turns to face a large, stone giant. I've only seen them in pictures. Though not as tall as the robot thing from earlier, it still towers above Jasper as he turns to face it. It's round and moss grows over all the nether regions as it raises a large tree trunk in its hand. It swings it toward Jasper but he slides out of the way.

"So many distractions," Marcus speaks up from behind me, stepping out of the shadows. I snap my head toward him and step back. He grins as he waves a hand at me, his smiling face shooting fear down my spine.

His eyes don't have whites, instead a deep red with a dark circle as an iris.

Blood sucker…no, *vampyr*.

"What do you want with me?" I stutter out as I stumble back. He tilts his head and grins, revealing the two incisors that every television vampire has.

157

"I want you, my dear boy," he says, "you came through…just like the witch. She is such a fun plaything…will you be fun too?"

"Jenny?" I cough out as I step toward him, my fear disappearing as anger replaces it, "what did you do to her?"

"Oh, nothing she didn't want," he waves his hand out before stepping closer, "you'll see…he shows us all what real power feels like."

"Nope," Jasper says, sending Marcus flying into the air as he runs up to me, "don't stop to listen to him."

"He has Jenny!"

"I don't know who that is!"

I allow him to pull me along despite my wish to demand details from that vampyr man. We run for what seems like hours, dodging past monsters I can't place and darting down alleyways with the only sound coming from distant roars and our own footsteps.

Jasper doesn't let us stop moving until we are deeper in the city and I can just start to see the colors of the sunrise. He finally slows and yanks me to a stop as we step up to a manhole. Jasper pulls the top off and gestures for me to climb down.

"Into the sewer? Wouldn't that be worse than out here?" I ask as I step onto the first step of the rusted ladder.

"I've kept you alive this long, haven't I?" Jasper asks as I climb deeper. He moves to climb down behind me when a large stone hand wraps around him. His eyes go wide and I move to climb back up to help as he disappears from view. The manhole cover flies back into place, leaving me in complete darkness.

"Jasper!" I call out, climbing back up and pushing up against the metal. When it doesn't budge, I let out a groan and do the only thing I can.

I climb down.

Cool water soaks through my shoes but, luckily, there isn't the expected stench. To my right, bars block my way and I sigh in relief as I turn to my left and find open space. Spreading my hands out and running them over the cruddy walls beside me, I walk forward with slow, careful steps.

I turn a corner and sigh in relief when I find a metal door. A torch sits beside it, lighting the way as I stumble forward. Pausing before grabbing the handle, I take a deep breath and pull the door open to reveal a lit up, meandering hallway.

"Hello?" I call out as I step into it, warm musty air hitting me as the door slams shut behind me. Jumping, I spin around to face no one before glaring at the old wood. It is scary enough down here without having to worry about someone coming up behind me.

"Okay," I sigh out as I turn back around just as a large black bag is pulled above my head. Stumbling back, I fall against the rough fabric as it wraps around my entire body. Voices surround me but no word is distinguishable through the thick material. Before I can even complain, they're pulling me around without a thought of the hard, sharp stone below me.

"Hey!" I scream out, fighting against the bag. Here I don't freeze, though, as it is far less scary being pulled around in this bag than facing a giant robot or a warlock. This is solid; this is relatively normal. I can focus on the feel of the fabric and the steady pace of the steps of my assailants.

I can focus.

"Okay," I mutter as I try to reach my hands up toward the opening. I don't have a plan, just a thought of getting out. Perhaps I can catch them by surprise...

I yelp out as the bag swings up and off the ground. The brief reprieve from the rough ground is met with my hurt shoulder slamming into a something hard. The top of the bag goes slack as I fall to the ground, wincing as the sharp sound of screeching metal echoes off my skull.

I lay there for a moment, hating myself for wandering into this situation. With a groan, I crawl toward the opening, pulling the fabric up over my head and clenching my teeth as my hands find metal bars. The cage is suspended, hanging fifty feet off the ground below. It swings slightly as I shift my weight, turning back toward where they threw me through.

As I do so, the cage moves, sliding away from the thin walkway. A figure disappears into the shadows and I call after him as the cage jolts to a stop, sending me falling against the metal. It swings back and forth for a moment before slowly coming to a standstill.

I gulp as I look down, looking past the little square holes below me. Torches dot the large space and I can see people hanging out, ignoring me and my yells. Other cages hang around me, most empty. The others I don't linger on, not interested in seeing what awaits me if I stay here for too long.

"Hello!" I scream out and only my voice answering me as it echoes through the large space.

15

A Failed Murder Attempt and Two Thrown Shoes

"You can't just keep him a cage," a familiar voice argues from somewhere nearby, pulling me out of a fitful sleep. I wince as I move my body, narrowing my eyes at the walkway I had been thrown from yesterday. I can see two figures, standing just outside the light of the torch.

It is weird to see actual wooden torches.

I feel like I'm in a medieval movie.

"Jasper," a deep voice says, "he's a lightling. Remember what happened with the last one that just appeared here?"

"He hasn't done anything but almost get himself killed," the teenager argues, "he isn't guilty because of what those like him have done. You should know that. You should also know that I can't stand here and let you continue this. Get him down or I will. We can interrogate him once he's comfortable and taken care of."

"You aren't in control here," the deeper voice groans but, nevertheless, the cage starts moving toward them, "and you left, remember? I shouldn't even be engaging in this conversation."

"And yet here we are," Jasper says as the gate stops in front of him. He pulls the gate open, the

161

screeching metal ringing in my ears as I pull myself to my feet. Jasper offers up a hand and I ignore it, instead opting to hug his thin body as I let out a shaky sigh of relief.

"Thank you," I mutter as I pull away, Jasper pulling me away from the edge. He nods before turning to glare at the other man. I follow his gaze and narrow my eyes at the other figure. Like Marcus, he's another vampyr wearing a suit that doesn't fit what's around him. He's bald with dark brown skin and a frown on his thick lips. He watches me, his eyes darting back to Jasper before he lets out a sigh.

"I won't apologize," he grumbles, "for trying to protect my people."

"We didn't ask for one," Jasper replies, "in fact, we'll be on our way. Thank you, Dante, for taking such good care of him."

"I don't think so."

"Why is that?"

"Everyone knows he's here," Dante explains, "they're going to want him taken care of after the fiasco with the girl."

"This girl," I speak up, "she showed up a few weeks ago, right? Tall, red hair, fair skin?"

"A friend of yours?" Dante asks before raising an eyebrow at Jasper as if to say, 'I told you so'.

"Yes," I answer, "an ex actually. A warlock attacked my home and took her with him. I need to bring her home."

With that, both Jasper and Dante let out a chuckle. I glance between the both of them before Jasper clears his throat, "I don't think she'll go with you, bud."

162

"What do you mean?"

"Oh, boy," Dante sighs as he starts walking down the hallway, "perhaps he isn't like her."

"Come on," Jasper says, nodding toward him. I bite my lip as I follow Dante, the other teen following up behind me, "why don't you tell me this whole story with you and the warlock and how my brother is involved with you?"

"It's kind of complicated."

"I don't care how complicated you think it is," he mutters, "give me the quick version."

"A few weeks ago," I tell him, "I was attacked and marked by a warlock. I really wasn't given a lot of information on it. No one even knows what the mark means. Ryder came to see if he could spot anything in my memories. Afterward, he came with me to the W.W.A. academy where this thing carved a prophecy into our wall and taped a bloody picture of Jenny on the wall. He said Ryder had to come to Maybelle and not tell anyone. I...I kind of tried to tell someone. I think that's why he threw me here."

"He?"

"I don't know," I shudder at the thought of him, "I just saw him once and he was all shadow. His voice came from everywhere and I...I opened my eyes, and I was on that street where you found me. Why were you there in the first place? I couldn't have just been lucky."

"You know how Marcus brought up an abnormality in the border?" Jasper asks as we come up to a staircase meandering downward.

"Yes."

"We can sense them too," he explains, "but, we usually operate in the daytime while he likes to move with the moon."

"Why?"

"Monsters are more powerful with the night," Jasper shrugs, "don't ask me how. I don't know the science or the magic behind it. I just know that is the fact of the matter. Marcus aligns himself with monsters, so he moves only when his friends do."

"Fun. Now, about Jenny...you've seen her? You can...can you help me get to her?"

"We don't get too many visitors here in Maybelle so it would be hard to go unnoticed. Especially when said person didn't exactly keep their visit discreet. She's alive, she's probably fine, and I have an idea of where she is, though I won't help you get there. You seem like a fine enough guy, Theo, and I would just forget about her. It'll be better for everyone. You should just focus on how you're getting home."

"What?" I ask, my voice barely loud enough for myself to here, let alone him. I clear my throat to repeat my question, but he is already answering.

"Look, Theo, going after her is a suicide mission. She showed up out of nowhere and, like you, I found her. I brought her to Dante and he kept her safe, like he does with every lost soul. Want to know what she did to repay us for our niceness?"

"She isn't a bad person. She'd never hurt anyone."

"Oh, but that's exactly what she did. Dante and his people were held up in the old college. They had a barrier that kept the monsters out and they could live a relatively safe life. Your girlfriend comes along and finds a way to slip Marcus and his monsters past it. Hundreds suffered, over fifty died; fifteen at the hands of your girl. She has been terrorizing everyone who isn't in Marcus's little gang ever since. Theo, she aligned herself with the most dangerous darkling in this city."

"She…"

"Whoever you knew," he sighs as we step into a large opening, the opening I saw from the cage above, "I don't think she exists anymore."

"She wouldn't," I shake my head. Memories of her giggling face bombard my mind as I try to picture her doing something so terrible. She couldn't have done it, right? She doesn't have it in her…

"She would and she did," he replied, "I've seen too many of my people die because of her to sugarcoat it."

"I can't…I can't believe that."

"I'm sorry," Jasper says, his voice growing soft as he places a hand on my shoulder, "I don't know how it feels to have someone you love turn out so wicked."

"You're lying," I snap, "there's no way. She wouldn't-"

"I'm not going to argue with you," he frowns, "and I have no reason to lie to you. You have been safely tucked away while we have been dealing with her. I wish I was lying, Theo."

"I…I can't just forget about her."

"I can't help you get her. I'm not willing to risk my life for you to try and convince her to change. Maybe, though, I can get an audience with her. One from a distance but that would only be if Marcus agrees."

"What would make him agree?"

"I don't know…probably supplies. We'd have to see if Dante has enough to spare."

Silence falls over us as Dante leads the way past groups of people sitting round tables, every single one watching as we pass by. We pass through until we find another walkway that leads to a more secluded rooms carved out of the stone. Dante pauses and gestures for us to walk through. There are two piles of fabric on the ground, a bare resemblance of a bed.

"Jasper, I know this isn't your home," he says, "but you vouched for him. You will keep him in line as long as he's here."

"Understood."

"Theo," Dante sighs, "I'll send someone by to deal with your shoulder. Behave, please. We've lost enough because we trusted your kind."

I nod as he disappears into the darkness, the only light coming from the small torch sitting in the hallway. Jasper sits down on one of the piles, completely unbothered by the lack of comfort. I sit down on my own, pulling my knees up to my chin as I peer over at the teen.

"Thank you," I speak up, breaking the silence that had taken us over, "and…not just for helping with Jenny. I would have died multiple times if it wasn't for you, or I'd still be in that cage or…"

"Yeah, probably," Jasper nods with a grin, "but, no need to thank me. It's kind of my job around here."

"What is?"

"Saving those who can't save themselves."

"But," I say, "you're like...fifteen, right? How is this your job?"

"Age doesn't matter here," Jasper shrugs before frowning, "in not-disgusting aspects. Sure, I'm fifteen but I'm a lot more capable than most of the adults here."

"Because of your powers?"

"Because of my powers."

"Whoa," I mutter, instantly reminded of Ryder. Just like him, Jasper is used for his abilities. At least Ryder isn't used by his own people.

"So," Theo coughs out, "what now?"

"I need a nap," he shrugs, "and you need a healer. Let me sleep for a few hours and after we can talk about how we're contacting Marcus. I highly suggest, though, that you don't leave this room without me."

"Why not?"

"So, I can protect you," he answers, "God knows you can't protect yourself."

"What do you mean by that?"

"Out there, Theo, you didn't run, you didn't fight. You froze. We can't do that here. That is how people die. Even here where it's relatively safe, you need to be on your guard, especially as a lightling. Sure, Dante has the final say but the others probably voted for your death."

"So, someone might try to kill me if I wander around?"

"Yes."

"Fun."

"But this is better than being outside."

I don't reply as I lean back against the wall. Jasper lays back and glares up at the ceiling as I try to make sense of everything, though I don't think I can. Jenny is a bad guy, even if I don't want to believe it. Even if Jasper had a reason to lie, I doubt he can fake the pain and anger I saw in his eyes.

"Shifter," a raspy voice spoke up from the doorway after Jasper's breathing becomes steady, "you require assistance?"

"Yes, ma'am," I reply as I push myself to my feet. A short, stout man steps into the room and my cheeks immediately feel hot, "I-I'm so sorry. I just…I haven't seen a male healer before."

"It isn't my choice of profession," he laughs as he walks over to me, "I'm just one of the few that have the abilities for it. Now, what hurts?"

"My shoulder," I tell him, grabbing the aching side. He nods as he steps up to me, running his hand down my shoulder to my elbow.

"Looks like you pulled something," he mutters as he digs around in a small bag tied to his belt, "and I have quite the fix."

"Get out of here, Felix," Jasper speaks up, a shoe flying through the room and knocking the small bottle out of the small man's hand. It crashes into the ground, spilling the red liquid onto the dark stone. Once it spreads out, it starts to smoke and sizzle. I grab my throat in horror as I stumble away from the man.

"Watch yourself, *lightling*," with that, he spits at me before spinning on his heels. Before he can leave, however, Jasper's other shoe hits his head, sending him stumbling into the wall. He doesn't look back, instead wobbling faster down into the darkness.

"And this is why I left," Jasper grumbles as he falls back against his pile.

"Because they try to kill outsiders?"

"Because they have no faith in anyone," he says, "not even those trying to save them."

"So, they haven't been too nice to you either," I comment as I move to sit back down.

"Nah," he laughs, the bitter sound echoing off the walls, "I'm almost as big of an outsider as you."

"How so?"

"I scare them. My abilities are too much for them."

"Ah," I nod as I keep my eyes on the ceiling, my mind wandering toward Ryder and if he felt the same alienation as his brother.

"Jasper," a choked voice speaks up from the doorway and he groans as he rolls over so that his back faces the woman that had just stepped into the room. I frown as I sit up, raising an eye at the woman as she steps into the torch light.

She is only slightly taller than the man that had just tried to kill me and a great deal thinner, only skin and bones. Her thinning brown hair is wild and brittle, sticking up and tangled as if she refuses to take any care of it. Dark veins travel up her neck and down any skin that isn't covered by the bright red, though very dirty, robe she wore. A rotten smell comes off her, one that is difficult to ignore as she steps closer to me.

"Hey," I speak up, "are you the actual healer?"

"Yes," she nods, bowing slightly, "most around here call me Auntie Rosa. You are free to call me that if you want to. Your shoulder is the issue, yes?"

"Yes, ma'am."

"Let me help you," she grumbles as she steps up to me. I look away as she works, mumbling under her breath as she using a stinky mixture that smells only slightly better than her as she wipes on my skin. After she's done, I sigh with a smile as she steps away. The relief is instant, the pain magically gone despite the added stench.

"She's really good at that," Jasper mutters as he rolls to his back as soon as he knows she is gone.

"What's wrong with her?"

"Auntie Rosa was a rotten witch. Do you know what that means?"

"Not really," I shake my head, "I just know they are monsters, not darklings."

"True, but do you know why?"

"No."

"See, as with all rotten witches, she was born a human but decided sometime in her life to use dark magic. Humans cannot handle the foreign magic so; their body starts to deteriorate and rot while their souls remained trapped within. All the while, a darkness eating away at their mind as they continue to prolong their lives. Auntie Rosa only looks so good because she used the same magic that is destroying her body to also maintain it. She isn't a darkling, as she isn't of dark energy. She was created, just as monsters were."

"So...but..."

"Why do we have a monster within our walls?" He asks.

"Yeah."

"Monsters aren't one hundred percent evil just like lightlings aren't one hundred percent good. The issue isn't as black and white as you might want it to be. Some monsters still hang onto their human side like Auntie Rosa, while others abandon it completely. Other monsters act more like animals like stone trolls, only fighting when provoked or when under control of someone else."

"How do you know which ones are good?"

"When they aren't trying to murder you."

"Solid reasoning," I mutter, picturing that giant gray thing that had almost crushed me, "was there a stone troll out there with us? Was it what tried to squash us?"

"Yes."

"That isn't bad?"

"Marcus controls it, otherwise it would just be munching on rocks somewhere."

"That sucks."

"It does," he shrugs, "that's why I tend to run and dodge them when I can versus straight up fight them."

"Another question," I say, "though you obviously don't have to answer it. Dante said you left? What does that mean?"

"Oh, I just don't live with them anymore. I left, like, a few months ago. I just pop in every so often to help out whenever they need me to. It stopped feeling like home whenever Ryder was gone. I stayed for as long as I could but, at some point you have to take care of yourself. Dante is a little butthurt about it."

"I probably would be to," I laugh, "considering what you can do."

"That's the problem," Jasper mutters, though he doesn't seem to be talking to me, "I want to be more than just my abilities."

"Is that the same issue Auntie Rosa? You kind of gave her the cold shoulder."

"Oh, no. She just blames me for Ryder's death, or disappearance would be the better word."

"That must suck."

"It used to," he shrugs, "but, I stopped caring a while ago."

"Liar," I mutter and he glares up at me. He doesn't correct me, though, as he lays back down and twists around. I follow his lead and lay down on the other pile, unable to sleep with the dark voice still lingering on my mind.

16

Strange Concoctions

Ryder occupies my dreams, images of him and Jasper fighting tormenting me as I struggle to move somewhere in the distance. Both look so intense and I hate the feeling that spreads through me, one that tells me that I am somehow at fault for their erratic behavior.

"Hey," I scramble awake and blink around wildly until my eyes land on a kneeling darkling. Jasper smiles before raising a bowl of muck in his hand, "I got you breakfast."

"What is it?" I ask as I grab it from him. It smells like grass and little bits of white float underneath the brownish thickness.

"It's a strange concoction of fish and plants," he shrugs, "it tastes horrendous but it makes sure we get all the nutrients we are missing in this kind of environment."

"Yay," I mutter as raise it to my lips, not bothering to ask for a spoon. I slurp it up, ignoring my usual manners once I realize how hungry I am.

He is right.

It is the worst yet most filling thing I've ever consumed.

"Jasper," a man walks in with a wide grin before pointing at the dark hallway, "another abnormality on Peach, yours?"

"Unfortunately, no," he replies, "I have to stick with Theo until we can get him home. Next time, though, definitely."

"What if it's Ryder?" Theo asks, causing the man to pause, "I mean, it isn't hard to imagine him coming after me. It was his job to protect me."

"Wait, *our* Ryder?" The man asks.

"Yes," Jasper nods, looking back and forth between us. He places his hands on his hips as he straightens up before letting out a sigh, "you're right. If they found a way in, perhaps they can show us a way out. I can't handle distractions, Thallius. I only want you with us."

"Done," he nods and darts away.

"He's a dark elf, isn't he?" I ask as he leaves. He has green skin like Stella, though quite a few shades darker.

"Yes," Jasper grins as he pulls on his trench coat, "ready?"

"Definitely," I reply, a grin of my own spreading across my face. It's impossible not to mirror his excitement as he leads the way out of the small room.

"We are going to be moving at a fast pace, okay?" Jasper explains, "you're going to have to keep up. I don't know how your shifter powers work but anything you can do to help will be appreciated."

"Okay," I choke out as we make it to a spiraling staircase. I can see it leading to a whole in the ceiling of the cave, on that looks very similar to the one we had come through the night before.

My shifter powers...what will he think when he finds out I can't use them? He already thinks I can't protect myself, though he has reason to, and I don't want him to think I am any more pathetic than I already am.

Thallius pops up beside us, bounding up the stairs with an actual sword strapped to his side. Jasper gestures me to follow after him as he, as I find he usually does, takes the rear.

"Okay," Thallius speaks up as we all three make it to the surface. It looks the same as the street I had appeared on with nearly identical broken buildings, cracked asphalt, and eerie silence waiting for us with the sun sitting high in the sky. The other two immediately start walking and I hurry to catch up after I pull my gaze away from the city around me. As terrifying as everything is, it is also strangely fascinating.

"You said Peach," Jasper says, as he glances over at Thallius. I'm a solid five feet behind and I'm not gaining as they continue with the same brisk pace, "near Auntie Rosa's old place?"

"Yes," he nods, "which would make sense if Ryder did find a way to come through."

"He won't linger for long after he finds out it's destroyed," Jasper replies, "when did we find out about it?"

"A little over an hour ago."

"Where else would he go?" I ask, causing the both of them to stop and look back at me, "wouldn't it be better to figure out where he would go instead of going where we know he isn't?"

"He might have stayed near there because of the siren. The shadow demons are staying out longer and longer after sunrise. He might still be in the area," Thallius comments.

"Or perhaps he headed toward the college," Jasper mutters before letting out a groan, "he wouldn't know about our removal."

"He'd be heading straight to Marcus."

"Okay," the teenager nods at the dark elf before nodding at me, "Theo and I will head to Auntie Rosa's old place and see if he's around there or if there are hints that it was in fact him who came through. Thallius, head toward the college and see if he's there. Don't make a move until I get there if you do find him. We'll make our way over with or without him after we check it out just don't get caught before we get there."

"Done deal," Thallius nods. He turns to walk away before pausing and glancing back at us, "Jasper?"

"What?"

"Don't die, okay?"

"I'll try not to," he mutters as Thallius disappears down an alleyway. Jasper turns back toward me before turning back around and starting down the road once again.

"Marcus is a pretty bad guy, isn't he?" I ask him as I finally fall in pace with him. He's not moving so fast after his friend's absence.

"He wasn't always, but people tend to change when faced with the trauma he was. In fact, he and Dante used to be friends."

"What changed that?"

"The D.M.M.A.? The civil war that trapped us here? They are two sides of a coin, Theo. Either one could have turned vengeful. We're just lucky it wasn't Dante."

"Should I ask why?"

"Probably not," Jasper chuckles as we turn a corner. At the end of the new street, a collapsed building awaits us. He doesn't speak as we come up to it, his purple eyes staring off at the shards of glass and wood.

"Ryder?" Jasper calls out, his voice echoing off the empty buildings around us. I follow suit, walking off in the other direction. My eyes land on something bright sitting outside of a nearby building and I dart forward before calling out to Jasper.

"They were here!"

"Who is they?" Jasper asks as he jogs over to me. I hold up the pink smart phone, the phone lighting up to showcase a picture of me, Ryder, and Stella. We had taken that a few days into school, standing outside of Mrs. Sagle's class. Luckily, she had caught Ryder by surprise so he's sporting a confused grin instead of an annoyed frown that always followed whenever she suggested a picture.

"Ryder?" he whispers as he pulls the phone close to his face, "who is the girl?"

"Stella."

"So, they were here and saw the collapse," Jasper mutters, "which means they probably did head toward the college. Come on, it actually isn't too far of a walk."

"Okay," I nod, my heart jumping in my chest as I follow after him. Ryder is here, he will know what to do and how to handle the mess I'm in.

He'll know how to get Jenny to come back to me.

The walk is silent with only a few bumps in the ground where Jasper pulls me into an alleyway to avoid one of those robotic monsters. When we reach a long roadway, I frown when I realize it is lined with what I assume used to be palm trees but now look like someone large stuck a bunch of sticks in the ground.

"Come on," Jasper says and pulls me behind one of the many buildings that line the road. Thallius is there waiting, a smile on his face as he greets us both.

"So, they weren't there," he says, the statement obvious.

"Nope," Jasper replies, "I'm going to assume he came here. Any signs of him? It would have been him and a girl."

"Yeah," Thallius sighs, "they're getting the grand tour with Marcus and that witch. They're a few blocks down."

"So, they haven't gone inside," he sighs before turning toward me, "you are going to stay here. I'm going to create a distraction and Thallius will be getting them out of there."

"Got it," the dark elf nods before darting away from the building. They've done something like this before, I realize as Jasper watches him leave. He moves to leave as well before I grab his arm. He pauses and turns back toward me, pulling his arm out of my grasp.

"I can't just sit here while Jenny is right there. I can...I can get her to come home. This isn't her, Jasper, someone must have done something to her."

"We can't risk it, Theo," Jasper groans, "that would be putting everyone at risk."

"Fine," I lie as he turns and darts out into the open and charging down the road. Letting out a heavy breath, I follow the way Thallius went and scurry down the sidewalk. I can hear their voices as I move past a few scattered buildings, my heart jumping when I hear Jenny's.

"Come on, darkling boy," she chirps and I peer around the corner of the nearest wall. Both Stella and Ryder are bound by...is that barbed wire? It's wrapped tightly around their chests, keeping their arms stuck at their sides. Dark, black bags sit on their heads. Jenny walks between them, her arms hooked through their elbows seeming without a care of how much it causes their skin tear at the wire. Marcus stands in front of him, raising his arms and gesturing toward the far building.

Before he can finish his sentence, his body flies back and slams through one of the dead trunks of a palm tree. The wood explodes with a snap as the vampyr rolls to a stop a few yards away. Jasper steps out around the corner and Jenny unhooks her arms as she steps away from her two prisoners.

"Marcus has told me so much about you," she giggles, her voice raspy as she steps toward him, "finally...I get to play with you!"

She doesn't look like Jenny anymore. Her face is covered in grime, something she should hate. She was always such a germaphobe. Her wild red hair is cut short against her head and her eyes are wild as she tilts her head. Her clothes are nothing like what she disappeared in, instead wearing a ripped-up robe that covers just enough for it to not be inappropriate.

"About all the times I beat him?" Jasper retorts as he ducks under a blast of fire. Fireballs jump to life in her palms and a grin spread across her face as he continues, "I'm surprised he would admit to such defeats."

"He said you were too arrogant for your abilities," she tells him, "you could be so much more with us."

It is then that I notice the dark veins taking over her exposed neck, looking just like Auntie Rosa's blemishes. Jasper had said that humans get those from using dark magic. Perhaps light witches are the same...

She's using dark magic.

She truly has changed, hasn't she?

That, however, doesn't stop my want to save her from whatever hell she brought upon herself.

"Stop!" I call out just as Marcus climbs to his feet. Jasper glares at me as I step between him and my ex, blocking her attack as I turn to face her, "Jenny? What...what are you doing?"

Does she even recognize me? She tilts her head as she sees me, her eyes narrowing as if she's struggling to comprehend who stands in front of her.

"Theodore Emerson," she whispers, her voice softening as the name leaves her lips. Her mouth twists into a small smile before her sunburned face contorts into a frown, "you shouldn't be here."

"Jenny," I repeat her name, ignoring Jasper's yell from behind me, "I don't know why you're doing this but, it isn't too late for you, okay? You can still walk away from this. I can help you…we can go home and it'll be just like it was."

"Theo," she shakes her head, "always so optimistic. I can't."

"You can," I counter as I step toward her.

"Correction," she chuckles bitterly, the fire in her hands dwindling slightly, "I don't *want* to. Go home, Theo, there's no place for you here."

"Not without you."

"I'm not going back," she shook her head, "you can't make me."

"Why not?" I ask, ignoring the tears that blur my vision, "you have a mother who loves you, Jenny. You have friends and family who want you back safe. You have so much to live for. Why do you want to throw all that away?"

"I am free here," she shrugs, "before I was suffocating in expectations I couldn't reach and they were stifling my abilities, Theo. Telling me I can't do this, can't do that…that would be bad…whatever. My own mother showed me all this power and then told me I couldn't use it. No, here I am free to use my power. Here I am free to use it as I please."

"To kill people?"

"To do whatever I want," she argues, her voice hardening as the fire strengthens in her hands, "whether that be to kill or to save or literally whatever. I've had enough of this. Unless you want to become a scorched corpse like your friend soon will be, I suggest you step aside."

"No," I shake my head, "I won't let you kill anyone else."

"So be it," she says as she raises her fists, "ready to burn?"

"Sorry," Jasper speaks up from beside me. He has a new cut on his forehead but looks otherwise okay, "but not today."

"We'll see," she screeches out as she throws her hand forward. Jasper ducks under the way as a fireball fly past him. He pushes Theo toward where Thallius is busy untying my friends. I stumble toward them, tearing my eyes away from the witch and hurry to help free them.

"Theo," Stella cries out as I pull off the bag. She wraps her arms around me and I hug her close, my heart hammering in my chest when I realize how dangerous this truly is. Blood coats her arms and she winces in pain as I pull away.

"Are you okay?" I ask her, looking her up and down to try and find other less obvious injuries.

"I'll survive," she says before stepping away to allow me to pull Ryder in for a hug of my own after Thallius gets him free. He awkwardly pats my back, a smile of his own on his face.

"You're alive," he grins as we pull away, "I…I thought you were dead when we found Marcus here."

"I know," I grin. His eyes focus on something behind me and they grow wide as he steps away from me.

"Jasper?" Ryder calls out, stepping into the street as his twin faces off against an angry witch and a vampyr.

A grave mistake.

Jasper's head snaps toward his brother just as Jenny sends a fireball toward him. I watch in horror as it slams into his chest, sending the twin flying back against the asphalt where he stays motionless. Ryder and I both charge forward but people grab us, pulling us back.

I turn back toward Thallius and Stella only to find them both gone. Ryder ignores Marcus's orders to stay put as he elbows the person holding him. He runs to his brother, dropping down to his knees to access the damage.

"Grab him," Marcus orders and one of his goons darts forward to yank him up. The vampyr giggles as he fights against it, turning toward me with a wide grin, "I should be thanking you, shifter. Usually when I get to see Jasper, he's in and out. You got him to stay in one place long enough for me to drain those annoying powers of his. He didn't even know what hit him. Come on, the dungeon awaits."

17

The Dungeon

The dungeon isn't a true dungeon. Instead, it's an old classroom with literal cages just big enough to fit one person in each. We each get pushed into one while an unconscious Jasper gets practically thrown against the metal links. I watch him flop down as the gate closes in front of me. My head snaps toward it as I stumble forward, my ears instantly popping as the man laughs on the other side only...only I don't hear it.

Why can't I hear anything?

I can't even hear my own breathing...

Soon, the goons leave us alone. Ryder is pulling on the fence, his face turned toward his brother. I can't even tell if Jasper is breathing from here...

"Theo," a voice speaks, allowing me to hear everything including the scream that leaves my lips. Jenny stands there with the open gate, her eyes a little less crazy as she leans against the frame.

"Jenny..."

"Why wouldn't you just walk away? Now Marcus isn't going to let you go if he even decides to let you live."

"Why do you care?" I grumble, "you were about to burn me to a crisp anyway."

"I only said that because Marcus was there," she sighs, "I was just surprised to see you. I didn't know you'd come after me."

"Well, I didn't try to come after you. I was kind of forced into it. But, I'm here, Jenny, and you were just so willing to kill me for it."

"And I'm sorry," she sighs as if it's enough to relieve her of any guilt. A grin widens on her face as she reaches for my hands, "but, don't you see? This is so great. You're here and now we can be together...forever. We just have to deal with Marcus. It shouldn't be too hard, right?"

"Jenny, no," I shake my head as I pull my hands away from hers, "you're not well. We need to go back...we need to go home where they can help you."

"No, we don't," she shakes her head, "w-we can live here. You can help us take Marcus down and we can live our happily ever after. Don't you see, Theo? We can solve your shifting issues. No one will blink an eye if you never change. They will all love you no matter what because you're with me."

"Because you love me?" I ask in a small voice.

"Because I love you," she answers back, lying easily.

"But you don't."

"I don't what?"

"Love me," Theo answers, "I may be slow at these kinds of things but, I'm not stupid. I eventually get it."

"Why would you say something like that?" she asks as she steps forward to cup my cheek. I nudge her away, pushing harder than I mean to and sending her stumbling back.

"Was anything about our relationship real to you?" I ask her, "we dated for six months before the attack. Was any of it real to you? Did you even like me at all?"

"Theo-"

"Answer the question," I reply. It hits me now, how everything had happened. How the warlock got through the safety net my father kept in place in our little community…the memory of Jenny just watching as the warlock tormented us…our whole relationship lacking any true meaning beyond how I pictured it…

"I-"

"How long were you planning on leading the warlock to me? How long did you know the danger you were putting me in so that you could abandon your family and come *here*? Was *anything* real?"

"Theo," she stutters out, looking like a fish out of water. A strange feeling of pride floods through me as she struggles to defend herself. That is the thing about Jenny, she always had something to say. Finally, she steps forward and grabs my arm, "I never wanted to hurt you, okay? But now we can put all of that in the past-"

"But you would hurt all these people? I heard the stories…I've heard what you've been doing…"

"They aren't *people*, silly," she rolls her eyes, "they're darklings…basically monsters. They don't deserve to be live. In fact, they should be honored to die by *my* hand!"

"You can't actually believe that," I mutter, my heart dropping as her words weigh on me. If this was the real Jenny, I risked all of our lives for nothing.

"Oh, come on," she waves her hand toward the doorway, "because one darkling helped you out, you forget all the centuries of war that happened between our people?"

"Just because we are of light energy," I spit back, "doesn't mean we are always in the right! You also have no right to talk. Witches spent decades doing horrific things to humans. There was a reason everyone wanted your kind dead."

"That's different!"

"Right," I nod, "it's even worse because you guys are considered the best of us lightlings because you were *chosen* by the Fae. What would your mother say?"

"Don't bring her into this."

"I'll bring whoever I want into this," I snarl, "I loved you. I risked my life, and theirs, for you. This is what I get in return? An evil witch that is terrorizing darklings that are just trying to survive?"

"You speak as if they are innocent."

"We were taught about the wars," I argue, "we were taught about both sides and the atrocities the lightlings did and vice versa. No one is innocent, Jenny, especially not in war."

"You are a naïve fool."

"And you're an arrogant bit-" I start but the sound of crunching glass interrupts me. Jenny sighs and steps away, kicking the gate closed as she does so. I suck in a breath as that same, deafening feeling falls over me and I finally realize that there's magic involved.

Marcus steps into the room with a wide grin on his pale face. His eyes linger over Jasper's cage, who remains still, before coming back to mine. Jenny steps to the side and he says something to her, something

187

that leaves a sour look on her face. She doesn't, however, stop him from stepping up to me and pulling the gate open.

"Theodore Emerson," Marcus grins, "Jenny has told me so much about you. You would be a great addition to our team."

"I'm not joining any team."

"You'd get to be with your girl," he gestures back toward Jenny, "and you can be free of the confines of reality. A father that doesn't love you...a society that only sees your flaws...you won't have to hide anymore..."

"I'd rather die," I say, mustering up as much strength as I can put behind it.

"That can be arranged," Marcus concedes as he turns back toward the witch, "I'm sure our lady can find someone who would have fun with it."

"Certainly," Jenny says, her mouth twisting into a wicked smile. She spins on her heel and disappears through the doorway. The vampyr grins as he kicks the door closed while turning toward the doorway himself. He doesn't notice my hand shoot out nor the wince of pain I let out as it slams on my fingers.

I stop it from bouncing back open as he leaves, holding my breath as I listen for any footsteps to return. With a sigh of relief, I dart toward Ryder's cage and pull the door open. He stumbles out, immediately moving to help his brother.

"Jasper," he mutters as he pulls his brother out of the cage. He's unconscious but breathing with a nasty burn on his chest. Ryder looks up at me and I nod as I look around. There's a small table in the corner and I hurry toward it. Luckily, it has wheels and

I pull it over before helping Ryder lift him onto the hard surface. It isn't a perfect fit, as his legs are dangling over the side, but he's well enough on there that we can wheel him away.

"We need to hurry. Do you know how to get out of here?" I ask him as I pull the top toward the doorway.

"Leaving so soon? A voice speaks up from the doorway. I sigh in relief as I spin toward it, Thallius's grinning face greeting me as go back to wheeling Jasper over.

"Thallius," I say, "is Stella with you? We need to get out of here."

"He's no friend," Ryder mutters, pulling the table away from him. Thallius tilts his head as he looks around me to peer at the conscious twin.

"Ryder," he smiles as he pushes me to the side. My back slams into one of the cages and I glare at his back as he steps toward him, "oh, how I have missed you."

"How...how did you worm yourself back into Dante's good graces?" Ryder asks.

"Save a few idiots and give him your word," he shrugs, "he's rather easy to forgive. It was your brother that took some time but, eventually, I was the only one he trusted. What a turn, isn't it? I do wish you hadn't found your way out of the cages but we all know that neither of you are worth anything without Jasper. You just made this all a little more entertaining."

"Oh, you wish," Ryder snaps as he pulls Jasper's table behind him. Thallius grins as he reaches down and pulls out his sword. Now, this isn't like Jasper's blades that are barely the length of his forearm with the hilt included. No, it is a full-on sword like from movies that explore Arthur and his magical buddy.

Dude...it would be awesome if it isn't so terrifying.

"Unfortunately, I can't kill you," Thallius says and points his blade at Ryder's chest, "but I have free reign on the useless shifter and the unconscious one there. Think you can distract me enough to get them both out of here before I kill them? That's also not considering the fact that everyone here wants to kill you so it's kind of impossible to escape."

"So, you think it's better that I sit here and let you murder them?" Ryder argues, though he doesn't exactly sound confident. Though I have never seen him truly fight, I know that this isn't fair. Even with his mental abilities, can he really defeat such a foe?

"Oh, did I forget to mention? The spell that blocked Jasper's abilities," Thallius giggles, sounding like a child, "also blocked yours and you never were much of a fighter."

"Theo," Ryder nods toward Jasper as he darts forward. Thallius chuckles aloud as he moves too, their bodies slamming together as I hurry toward the table.

Jasper is dead to the world but at least he's breathing. I turn the table as I move toward the door, Ryder keeping Thallius distracted as I push his twin to safety.

Jenny steps back into the room just as I make it to the door. She, like before, giggles as she kicks the table over. I catch Jasper before he can fly to the side and she steps closer, fire again sparking up from her hands.

"You don't get it, do you?" She shakes her head, her eyes no longer wild. Instead, she looks almost sad as she steps toward me. I back up, struggling under Jasper's weight, "your death will be meaningless. Join us..."

"No," I stammer out. I hear Ryder cry out behind me, pulling my gaze away from my old friend. Ryder is on the ground with blood falling past his nose and one of his shoes are twisted to the side...no, his entire ankle is backward.

"Ryder," he shakes his head, "that was too easy. I expected more of a challenge. Now, it's time to watch your people die."

A hot blast slams into my back, sending be flying to the side. Jasper falls out of my grasp as I slide across the ground. Jenny steps up, towering over Jasper's body though her eyes never leave mine. She leans down and grabs Jasper's collar, pulling him up as she raises her other hand. A fireball dances in her hand as Thallius leans down beside Ryder and pulls him up for a better view.

"Stop..." Ryder calls out, groaning as he struggles against the dark elf's hold. I force myself to my feet, holding on to the cage as my legs shake. Tears cloud my vision as she watches me, her face twisting into a sick smile as she brings her hand down.

My entire body locks up as the world around me freezes. Shaking, I collapse to my knees as my entire body vibrates painfully. I fall forward, my fingers snapping as I catch myself from falling face first.

"G-get a-way from him," I growl out as I look up, my back arching as my arms grow...stronger.

191

Thallius takes a step back from Ryder, letting the him fall back. Jenny's fire is gone, a thin line of smoke floating up from her palm. Jasper falls from her grasp as she stares at me, her face wide with shock.

Luckily, Jasper's eyes finally open. He scrambles back on all fours like a crab, his eyes widening at the sight of me.

Is this it?

Do I finally get to shift?

I don't feel much of the shifting itself. There's just an intense vibration to my body, one that only dies away when I'm standing on all fours. I feel taller and my body feels, oh, so much *stronger*. Sharp canines peak my curiosity as I run my tongue over them and I am instantly reminded of what my father can turn into.

With a cackle, I look down at the white speckled paws. Most of my coloring is a golden brown with white dotted throughout. I can't see all of me but judging by the looks on their faces, I must look as cool as I feel.

Their reactions are hilarious. Jasper just looks appreciative as he rolls out of the way, moving toward his brother as I face the other two. Thallius darts into the hallway and Jenny...Jenny simply straightens up as she raises her fists, apparently over the initial shock.

"You think I'm scared of you?" She asks, her voice shaking slightly as she steps back, "a first-time shifter?"

"You have to admit," Jasper speaks up, using one of the cages to stand up, "that is pretty terrifying."

Me?

Terrifying?

She rolls her eyes as she moves slightly so she can face both me and Jasper. I step forward, the movement sending a jolt of surprise through me. I move so freely, though it's also strange since I am technically walking on all fours.

The smells are the worst. I can smell Jasper's charred flesh and I can smell Ryder's blood. Jenny has this rotten stench about her and...what's that new smell?

Jenny's eyes go wide for a moment before she crumbles to the ground, revealing a familiar dark elf. Stella's magic seems to have worn off as her skin isn't her usual pale shade. She has a black eye and her sleeve is tied around her arm, a dark stain breaking the blue color.

Despite her injuries, a grin breaks out across her face as she steps up to me. I grin back, though I don't know how noticeable that is in this form, before turning toward the twins.

Jasper is kneeling next to Ryder, his hands on his twisted foot. Ryder is nodding, his eyes glaring at the ceiling. I wince as I watch Jasper snap the foot back into place, a yelp leaving his brother's lips. Stella steps toward them but Jasper is already whispering a spell, sparks dancing past his fingertips as they hover over Ryder's ankle.

"Okay," Jasper says as he helps Ryder to his feet, "it's still going to hurt a little but it's not broken anymore. You're Stella?"

"Yes," she says, nodding her head as she steps up to Ryder's other side, "let me help him. You know how to get us out of here, right?"

"Yes, ma'am," he nods as he heads toward the door.

"Wait," Ryder groans out, "we can't leave her."

"Why not?" Jasper asks, glancing down at the unconscious witch at his feet, "she's still breathing."

"No," he shakes his head, "she...she isn't possessed but, she's not herself."

"What do you mean?"

"There's something wrong with her mind, Jasper."

"Can you fix it?" Stella asks, her eyes finding mine. She seems to understand exactly what I'm feeling as she lets Ryder lean against the wall as she moves to grab the table, "I mean, we have to try either way, right?"

"Right," Ryder replies, turning to look at his brother. He glares right back, his eyes searching his twins before he lets out a sigh.

"Fine," Jasper shrugs, "but if I say leave her, we leave her."

"Fine," the other two answer in unison. Jasper turns to me with a sigh and Stella pulls Jenny onto the table with Ryder being more of a hinderance than a help. Finally, she's laying there and Jasper turns toward us with a grin.

"With our bud here," Jasper gestures toward me, "stealth isn't exactly an option. We also, though, don't want to fight. We're just going to have to book it. May not be the smartest plan, but it's what we got. Oh, and if anyone sees Thallius, he's *mine*."

We all nod, no one willing to challenge his word as he leads the way through the doorway. There is something about him and the confidence that he has that demands attention. It isn't, though, like that of my father. He is loud and intense while Jasper holds a more level confidence, one more reliant on actions than his commands.

The hallway we step into is narrow, so narrow that my new shoulders bounce against them as we run down it. The first few turns are empty until we burst into a large room that looks to be an old cafeteria. Marcus and Thallius stand surrounded by...shadows?

No, shadow demons.

"We still have some sun," Jasper says, nodding toward the windows across the room, "if we get out there, the shadow demons can't get to us."

"How are there so many?" Ryder coughs out, using the table for balance.

"Your guess is as good as ours," Jasper shrugs, "they've been here for over a year now. If we can get outside, we will be fine."

"How do we do that?" Stella asks. Jasper looks up at the roof and frowns.

"What if I bring the sunlight to us?"

"What do you mean? Your power is back?" Ryder asks.

"They can never subdue it for long," Jasper answers.

"Can you protect us?" Ryder asks, "the last time you did it..."

"I was an unexperienced child when you last saw me," he shrugs before grinning back at his brother. Ryder smiles back as he pushes the table so that it is right beside Jasper.

"Theo, get as close as you can," Ryder tells me as he pulls Stella closer to the sleeping witch. Jasper raises his hands, his eyes glowing as he looks upward. I gasp and stumble as the ground shakes violently below me. Thallius calls out from below, darting forward just as the walls start to crumble.

Too late I realize it was a challenge, one that Jasper doesn't take up as the roof caves in. I close my eyes and cover who I can, hoping against hope that Jasper knows exactly what he's doing.

18

The Kidnapping

Clouds of dust surround us, the piles of wood and stone slowly coming into view as it dissipates. The sun warms my back, chasing away any shadows that threaten to emerge. I push myself away from the others, coughing slightly at the dirt in the air. Stella is checking Ryder for injuries while Jasper steps out onto the debris, searching for something beyond what I can see. I look at Jenny and her still form but, luckily, she is still breathing.

Hopefully, Ryder can fix whatever is wrong with her head.

"Jasper!" Ryder calls out, "we need to go."

"Right," he mutters, a frown on his face as he turns toward us. He raises a hand and Jenny's table lurches up, floating in the air and away from the crumbled building. Stella and Ryder follow it, stumbling over the shards of wood and metal.

I bound after them, giggling to myself as I jump across the same distance. My laughter sounds more like cackles but I don't think too much of it as Jasper runs up behind me.

"We need to hurry," Jasper says, "the sun isn't going to last long."

"Look at you," a dark voice speaks up, echoing off the quiet streets and stopping any progress. Everyone freezes and attempts to find the speaker, though I know we aren't going to find one. I let out a gasp as fear shakes through me, my body shifting back to my human form. Jasper catches me before I can fall before wrapping his trench coat around me, his face turned the opposite way as I button it across my chest. The voice continues with a chuckle, the exact same as the one I heard when I first arrived, "just barely here and already causing a ripple. You have your witch. Do you think she'll be able to save you when you fail? I'd say her mind to too far gone but, you can put your faith in whoever you'd like."

"What is this?" Jasper asks, his voice barely above a whisper. Even he seems to feel how dark the presence is. Still, though, he shows no fear as he steps away from me with his blades at the ready.

"I'm your worst nightmare."

"I'm sure I've had worse," Jasper challenges.

"You haven't," Ryder speaks up, standing in front of him as if to protect him, "look, we're here. I'm here, just like you asked. I'll do whatever you need me to as long as you leave them be."

I stumble away as shadows gather behind Jasper. He moves to turn toward it but a dark hand wraps around his neck and keeps his face forward. Ryder spins around, stepping forward as the dark being whispers in Jasper's ear. His eyes go wide, his eyebrows furrowing as he tries to fight against his words. For a moment it seems as if he's winning until his body goes limp in the shadowy arms.

"Silly mortals," the Shadow Guy chuckles as Ryder darts forward. He raises his hand and Ryder skids to a stop. He groans in pain as he falls to his knees, held to the spot by an unseen force, "so keen on fighting even when they know they'll lose."

"Let him go," I growl out, my inner animal finally having a voice. Somehow, my fear for my friends overrides that crippling fear for my own safety.

"You think you have any control of me?" He laughs before turning toward Ryder, "you've already seen a part of the puzzle. He'll be returned to you once you do as promised."

"Wait!" Ryder screams out as the shadows, with Jasper intertwined, slide through the ground below as if it's water. He stumbles forward, dropping to the ground and running his hand over the solid stone.

"We...we need to leave," Stella speaks up, her eyes on the setting sun. She steps forward and places a hand on his shoulder but, he shrugs her off, "come on, Ryder...we can't do anything for him now. We have to get somewhere safe."

"But...Jasper..." Ryder coughs out. I step forward, carefully pulling him to his feet. He looks at me, tears in his violet eyes. I do the only thing I can think of and hug him, Stella following suit after a moment.

"We can't just leave," I speak up, "Jasper was right there. There has to be some sort of clue as to where he took him."

"We do have another issue," Ryder says, pulling away from us. He turns away, his eyes on the sky before he continues, "he knew where to go for safety. We don't. I doubt we can just hide in a random building when we have Marcus actively hunting us."

"I know," I nod, "they're underground. We can probably drop into any manhole and find a way to them."

"You sure?" Ryder asks, "the last time I was here, they were crawling with monsters."

"Which is worse?" Stella asks, "hanging up here where we know we'll die or trying down there where there's a chance?"

"Fine," Ryder sighs before gesturing for me to lead the way. I glance back at the where Jasper once stood and clench my teeth before forcing myself to look away. With a groan, I hurry forward as Stella and Ryder take charge of pushing Jenny along.

"He said I will know the rest," Ryder mutters aloud. I don't bother looking back as I try to remember the turns we took on our way here as well as trying to spot another manhole cover, "and that I've seen part of the puzzle. What have I seen?"

"Here!" I call out as I find one. I yank it off before the smell of sewage hits me. I stumble back, gagging slightly before turning toward them, "you go first."

Ryder rolls his eyes as Stella climbs down without complaint. He nods toward Jenny and I move to lift her up as he climbs down. Carefully, I lower her down feet first, my arms aching as I wait for Ryder to grab her from below. Finally, I follow and pull the cover up over the hole. Below me, Ryder is already creating one of his light spells.

"You're carrying her," Stella says, pointing toward Ryder struggling under Jenny's weight. I nod as I pull her over my shoulder, my newfound strength still flooding through me even out of my animal form.

As terrible as this situation is, this is pretty cool.

Unlike where I had been before, there is a layer of murky water below us. There is no other light at either end and have absolutely no idea which way will be best. Stella and Ryder are both looking at me but seem to realize that I am clueless pretty quick.

"Well then," Ryder sighs as he looks back and forth, "we'll go this way. I don't *feel* anything on either side."

Both me and Stella agree and follow him through, the water impossible to avoid. I shudder as it soaks through my shoes and my jeans, the smell attaching itself to us as we walk through. The area twists and turns, a never-ending walkway. It isn't too long until I hear the sound of rushing water behind us. I turn around too late as a wall of water slams into us, sending us flying back. Jenny falls out of my arms as I slam into a wall, spiraling out of control as the water pulls me forward.

The water pushes us through until the ground drops off, sending us falling through open air. I get one glimpse at a wall of flames before I spin around and slam into darkness.

The shock of the freezing water leaves me breathless as I lay suspended in the dark, unable to move as I struggle to get my body to agree to my commands. My limbs feel heavy and I struggle against the moving water, struggling to find which way is up.

Out of all the things that could have killed me here...

A pair of hands grab my shirt and yank me upward, forcing my body back to life as I kick toward the surface. Ryder and I both gasp for air as we break through the surface, my limbs still heavy as I struggle to keep my head above the dark waves.

"You good?" Ryder asks, his teeth chattering as he too struggles to stay afloat.

"No, I'm very much not good. I dropped Jenny...she has to be-"

"No," he shakes his head, "I can't feel them. They aren't down here with us."

"Where are they?" I ask, turning toward the cliffside. Above us, there is a hole with water dripping past it. There is a dark being, one illuminated by the fire on the other side. It is humanlike, with a faceless head and limbs that end in sharp points instead of fingers. It is partially out, its head looking down at us.

If they are up there with that...

"There's a dock," Ryder says, tearing my attention away from the monster. His head falls below the water for a moment before he pops back up, "come on."

Luckily, the flaming city gives us enough light though it makes everything red. I finally get to see the cursed side of the city that became its only identify. I find the dock Ryder found and swim toward it, averting my gaze from the flames as I struggle to fathom how much was lost when it first happened.

There's a narrow staircase meandering up the cliffside, steep and unsafe. I hate the thought of climbing up it, though I have no choice. It is the only way up and away from the water.

We both swim toward it and I make it there before Ryder, who is probably still bogged down by that ankle. I keep my thoughts away from Jenny and Stella, knowing full well if I focus on them for too long I'll break down.

Ryder seems to have the same thought.

I pull myself onto the old wood. I yelp and scramble up more as the planks crumble beneath me, sending me back into the water.

"Theo!" Ryder calls out. He has made it to where the stone stairway meets the dock. The wood is supported by the stone and I sigh in relief as I swim toward him. It takes me a moment to notice the panic on his face as he focuses on something behind me.

I can hear wild splashing behind me, my heart dropping when I realize we were never alone in the water.

I hate the ocean.

"Hurry!" He calls out as I reach the stone slam. He pulls me up just as something slams into the hard rock. I yelp out as we both stumble toward the stairs as the rock crumbles underneath us.

The water is still for a moment, the silence eating away at me as I stand frozen. Something was chasing me, that much I know. What lays hidden under the waves? Some forgotten sea creature that found a home in Maybelle?

"Oh god," I gasp out as a long limb stretches out of the water. I had been grateful for the light of the fire but now…now I get to see something that will forever haunt my dreams.

The long, dark limb tilts downward and Ryder pulls Theo out of the way as it slams into the remaining stone. We stumble up the stairs as it slowly lifts itself out of the water.

It reminds me of a spider leg, though it is as smooth as glass and pitch black. It finds its balance on the stone and the rest of its body rolls up into a standing position. Like what I saw above, it has no face…just a black oval that tilts back and forth. Shadows billow past its limbs as it starts forward, standing over seven feet tall.

We both book it up the stairs, Theo keeping his eyes forward as he races behind Ryder. The biggest thing I learned from the many horror movies I watched is that you never look back.

I don't until I hear a loud splash below. I glance back, sighing in relief as I watch it struggle in the water before the waves eat it up. The stairs had crumbled beneath its weight, leaving a large gap below.

I'm not, however, about to slow down.

"We're going to die!" I voice my fear as one of the dark limbs slam into the staircase a few yards above us. Ryder doesn't reply as he jumps over the gap without hesitation. I groan and follow suit, forcing my body to jump into the air. My ankle twists as I hit the staircase and I stumble forward, catching myself on the wall and scraping up my palms. I glance back as one of those dark things pull itself out from the stone, coming from within rather than below.

I clench my teeth and dart forward, ignoring the pain that radiates through my ankle. If Ryder can run with his injuries, I can too.

Luckily, we make it to the top without another attack. I keep my eyes on my feet, running my shoulder along the rough wall to keep myself from falling toward the edge. I can see the dark water below as well as the shadow monster trying, and failing, to climb up the slick wall. The other one is still struggling against the stone, its head turned toward me as it pushes and scrapes at the hard wall around it

They can't make it up there...

No.

Everything is fine.

Everything is fine.

Everything is fine.

"Theo," Ryder's voice interrupts his mantra. I glance up and sigh in relief when I see him standing at the top. Once I make it to him, I fall to my knees and place my hands in the cool dirt, digging my fingers into it as I try to calm my breathing.

I sit back on my heels, turning my focus away from the dirt below me. A yelp leaves my lips as I scramble away from a worn stone slam, my heart jumping to my throat as move away from the tombstone.

"Whoa," Ryder says, using his body to stop me from scrambling the fast way back down to the water. He helps me balance myself and holds onto my arm until he knows I won't fall back.

Tall, brown grass nearly covers all the other tombstones that lay dotted around the small hillside. Above the tiny cemetery, a small beaten down church awaits us.

"Ryder?"

"That…that's the part of the puzzle I saw," he stutters out as he too turns to face it, "I…I dreamed of it since I…since I first left Maybelle. I mean, I've always known of it. Me and Jasper used to dare each other to sneak inside. We never did."

"Do you feel anyone in there?" I ask. Ryder shakes his head, glaring at the small building. I shake my head as I turn away from it, not willing to even entertain the thought of stepping inside. Already, I can see a group of those dark beings just outside the cemetery.

"Ryder," I say, causing the other to turn toward me, "why aren't they coming after us?"

"Think about it, Theo," he says as he glances back at the church, "what would cause monsters like those to stay away?"

"I don't know," I mutter, frowning as I realize something almost scarier than those shadow beings, "fear. They're scared of whatever is in there."

"Or their master is keeping them at bay. Perhaps whoever is tormenting us also controls them. He wants us here."

"What do we do?" I ask.

"What else can we do?" Ryder shrugs as he starts toward the church.

"Ryder," I call after him as I glance back at the group. They move as I do, stalking forward as he moved closer to the church. I groan as I follow after, "we can't just march into danger! We don't know what's in there."

Ryder doesn't answer as he marches forward. He doesn't seem bothered by the shadow beings or the potential doom that inevitably awaits us in the church. Even now, Theo can feel the ground shake as if moving to some unknown beat.

"Theo," Ryder says as he pauses before broken steps. He glances back with a smile that he probably thinks is reassuring. Instead, I focus only on the fear in his eyes, "everything will be okay."

"I know," I nod, trying to convince Ryder of his own words but we both know that nothing will end well within those walls. My friend disappears into the darkness and I take a deep breath as I follow after him.

"Everything will be okay," I repeat under my breath as I step forward, the wood bending under my feet. A bright light stands just beyond clarity, only interrupted by Ryder's silhouette. I pause, my entire being begging to turn back.

We shouldn't be here.

Nothing *living* should be here.

"Ryder?" I whisper as I slowly walk up to his still form. I gingerly grab his shoulder but he doesn't move. His eyes are faced downward, staring at a spiraling bright mass sitting in the bottom of a giant hole in the floorboards.

I step in front of him, carefully pushing him away from the edge. Once I feel like he is safe, I frowned as I lean closer toward his face.

All I see is white.

All the color is gone from Ryder's eyes.

19

Ryder's White Eyes

The ground shakes violently beneath us and I fall back, slamming into the floor below. Laying there for a moment, I breathe in and out until it comes out easier before pushing myself up.

"Ryder!" I call out. I am in complete darkness, the only light coming from a ring of light directly above me.

A manhole.

"What?" I mutter aloud as I spin around. At my feet, without the water we were met with last time, is Jenny. She is sleeping, looking just like she had before she left only with the added-on grime. I bend down and pull her up into my arms before I start down the rocky hallway, calling out Ryder's name as I do.

"Theo!" Stella's voice echoes from somewhere in front of me and I rush forward, my legs aching under her weight. Finally, I find her standing above Ryder.

"Stella," I smile as I set Jenny down carefully and kneel beside Ryder, "I thought you were dead."

"Same, but about you," she mutters as she kneels at his other side, "where did you two disappear to?"

"I don't even know how to tell you," I mutter, my mind reeling. The scrapes on my hands are real...the whites in Ryder's eyes are still there...it wasn't a hallucination.

"Ryder," I mutter as I softly shake his shoulders. He's alive, that much I can tell. I just don't know what's happening with him.

"Theo?" A voice speaks up from the darkness. Stella stands up, putting herself between us and the stranger. As soon as he steps into the light illuminated through Stella's extended fists.

"Dante," I gesture toward the two unconscious bodies around me, "I..we..."

"You aren't too good with words, are you?" He mutters as he steps past Stella and kneels down beside Ryder. He turns his eyes toward Jenny and scowls, "you grab Ryder. I got her. Where...where is Jasper and Thallius?"

"That's a long story," I say as I pick up Ryder. He nods before growing quiet, his eyebrows furrowing before he lets out a sigh.

"We'll talk when everyone is taken care of."

A large part of me is relieved. An actual adult is here. He will know what to do. He can take care of Ryder and Jenny and figure out where Jasper is. Adults always have a plan. They always know what to do.

He has to know what to do, right?

We will be okay.

Without a word, Dante lifts Jenny into his arms. I follow suit with Ryder, Stella following silently as we pass through the sewer system. We walk through the door I remember from before, back when they slid a bag over me.

How did we get here?

Dante takes us into the large room where we are, again, meant with stares. He leads us to a long line of dirty hospital beds and drops Jenny onto one. Someone immediately darts forward and ties her limbs to it. I don't question them as I carefully place Ryder on one a few beds down as Dante suggests.

Auntie Rosa, as Jasper calls her, steps into view, bending over Ryder as before she and Dante whisper back and forth with each other. I try not to stare or focus on the smell that's coming off her. Though most of Maybelle is unfamiliar to me, the smell is slightly familiar. It is as if someone had sprayed citrus flavored disinfectant spray over rotting food, only adding to the horrid stench.

"What happened?" She asks, her demanding voice echoing off the walls as she glances back at me and Stella. I glance down at my friend and his eyes that remain the same pearly white.

"I don't know," I answer truthfully, "we, uh, we were at a church by the fire and-"

"You stepped inside?" Dante coughs out, "no one has ever stepped inside and came out the same except..."

"Except who?" I stutter out, my stomach dropping when I see the horror in his red eyes.

"Jasper," the sickly woman answers for him, "is he here? He and Thallius might be better at explaining the situation."

"No," Stella speaks up, "Thallius...he's a traitor, I guess. He tried to kill us and Jasper. He was working with Jenny."

"W-what?" Auntie Rosa speaks up, "you don't know what you're talking about."

"Do you want to go to the college and ask him yourself?" Stella challenges.

"What about Jasper?" Dante asks, glancing up at me, "where is he?"

"I don't know. He, uh, he was taken."

"By who?"

"We don't have a name for him," I say, sitting down on the end of Ryder's bed, "he's just...he's the reason we are all here."

"What do you know about him?" Dante asks, stepping away from the bed. Auntie Rosa just sighs and gets to work trying to fix Ryder. Stella follows as we step closer to where Jenny sleeps.

"Literally nothing," I tell him, "he just started showing up and telling us that we need to come here after I got marked by a warlock."

"Marked?" He tilts his head. I nod as I pull up my shirt, the weird mark sticking out across my chest. He leans toward it, his hand sneaking out and running over it, "Salem."

"Like, Massachusetts?" I ask, leaning down to look at it.

"Do you know the story?" He asks, his voice low.

"Everyone does," I shrug as I drop my shirt, "even humans."

"It was right after witches went into hiding," he explains, "most came to the United States to avoid such tragedies. When everyone saw that humans were now accusing their own kind, they knew any beings so unlike them will be given the same fate. That's why Maybelle was created. A darkling was needed to fully create the protection they needed here so he promised safety to all of them in return. What we need to figure out, though, is why Salem is involved in this. There was no true witch killed at that site."

"This doesn't make sense, does it?" I mutter, "why would he have me come here if-"

"You idiots," Jenny chuckles from her bed, finally awake, "Salem is not a place, nor can he be found in recent history."

"It's a being," Dante mutters.

"The dark guy," I reply as I fold my arms across my chest.

"The dark guy?" She giggles, "he is the starter of wars! A being created by Chaos itself, a being existing since before man was even a thought. He...he wants to watch us burn this world and it will be so easy...We have no choice, Theo. We must join them...we must join them so we can live past the suffocating blackness that is already taking over this realm."

"Them?" I choke out.

"They will bring this realm into darkness," she says, her eyes tearing up as her face twists in horror, "just as they did to the others. You can't face it, Theo…you can only try and save yourself."

"Do you know what's happening to Ryder?" I ask, not bothering to acknowledge her words. There is no answer she can give me that can satisfy the horror that comes with her words.

"Him?" Jenny turns her head to look at him, her eyebrows raising as she looks back at me with an almost innocent expression. The mood shift is almost disorienting as I watch her mouth twist up, "he stepped into the church, didn't he? Saw something he shouldn't have, didn't he? Forget about him, babe. He's a goner, just like his brother."

"What?" Dante asks.

"He belongs to Salem now."

20

Our Dark Friend and His Name

Surprisingly, no one tries to kill me in my sleep while I lay in their medical area. Perhaps it's because of Auntie Rosa's constant presence as she works tirelessly over Ryder, who hasn't improved in the two days he's been here.

Jenny has remained relatively quiet, her eyes focused solely on the roof above. Auntie Rosa had promised to look at her once she figures out what's wrong with Ryder, a task that grows more and more daunting as the days pass by.

"Hey," Stella speaks up as she comes up to my bed. She's hands me one of the two cans she holds before sitting down at the edge of my bed. I sit up and stir the spoon around the peaches.

That's all they have here.

Canned food, fish, and that weird fishy concoction.

"So," I say, looking across the few beds at Ryder, "any ideas on how to fix him?"

"No," she shakes her head, "it isn't something we can fix. There's nothing medically wrong with him. It's like he's trapped somewhere and we don't know how to get him out."

"Fun," I mutter as I shove a spoonful of peaches into my mouth. A loud gasp pulls my attention away from my breakfast and I jump up from my bed. The can falls from my hand as I dart across the room.

He's awake.

"Ryder?" I say as I make it to his bed just in time to stop him from scrambling off it. He looks at me, his breathing heavy as he struggles to find words.

"T-Theo…" he mutters out finally before Stella pops up on his other side. He turns toward her with a small smile before falling back against the bed, "what happened?"

"You tell us," Stella replies with a choked laugh.

"I…" he carries off as he looks to the side, his eyes narrowing. I follow his gaze to where Jenny lay with her head turned toward us. Ryder jumps up and, after stumbling for a moment, and hurries toward her.

"You're mostly intact," she mutters with a grin as she steps up to him, "how…interesting."

"You know what Salem wants me to do, don't you?" Ryder asks.

Salem?

He knows of him too?

Jenny glances around at all of us before nodding her head, her face dropping as she does so. She looks almost tired, as if the thought is tiring itself.

"Do you know how I'm supposed to do it?" Ryder asks.

"You're awake and alive, I'm surprised. Salem doesn't usually leave anyone unscathed. After all, look at me. To answer your question, your task is nearly impossible. I think he means for you to fail."

"You know I have to try."

"Do you even know what you're doing?" She asks, "such potential for disaster just to save that brother of yours."

"Not just to save him," Ryder shakes his head, "to save everyone here. He will kill us all."

"Stupid boy," she mutters, "hasn't anyone told you not to make a deal with the devil? Trust me, okay? I tried."

"Ryder?" Stella speaks up and grabs his arm, pulling him away from the tired witch. I follow, my own mind whirling with questions, "what is going on?"

"I know what we have to do," he says with a nod, "but, I don't know how we are going to pull it off."

"Just tell us what it is," I cut in before Stella can speak up.

"We need to figure out how to break a life curse."

"A life curse?" Auntie Rosa chuckles, coming up from behind us. She steps around Stella and grabs Ryder's chin, forcing him to look up at her, "if anyone knew how to break one, I doubt we'd still be stuck here. Your eyes seem to have returned to their normal state. How are you feeling?"

"Unless they knew the true reason for the curse," Jenny speaks up, her voice barely above a whisper, "and understood that it was better to stay trapped than to damn the world."

"So, you also know what the church hides," Ryder nods at her, pushing Auntie Rosa's hand away from his face, "you know the danger it poses."

"Have you ever truly considered why the witch would curse her city, forcing her own people to be stuck within? Why would she damn those she worked so hard for? Oh, wait, you never questioned who she was before she brought this all upon you."

"How do you know all of this?" I ask.

"Salem was here," she says, vaguely gesturing to herself with her bound hands, "with him, came history and knowledge I shouldn't possess. I don't think he meant to give it to me but, here I am. It comes and goes...sometimes I know all, other times I know nothing at all."

"And sometimes you're just flat out crazy," Stella mutters, "why would we need to know the true reason?"

"You can't break her curse without knowing her," she sings out, "you can't break her curse without understanding her sacrifice."

"What exactly did she sacrifice?" I ask, folding my arms across my chest. The other two seem to get it immediately, leaving me in the dark.

"Her life," Stella tells me.

"Who would know that?" Ryder asks, "you?"

"I never said that," she smiles, her eyes on the roof above.

"Ryder?" Stella asks as she glances over at him. I watch his eyes glow slightly before a sigh leaves his lips.

"As she said," he shrugs, "she knows very little about it."

"Okay, so we have to figure it out," Stella nods, "any ideas?"

"Theo?" Jenny speaks up again, her voice breaking, "do you remember that game we used to play?"

"What game?"

"We made our own boardgame with our own pieces and everything. Life was so simple then," she says with a genuine smile. She no longer looks like a crazed witch. Now, she looks like a scared teenager, one in way over her head, "we would use the actual street of your little town to plot out our main points. Remember, Theo? We had to get to the market to win?"

"Yeah," I smile, the memory resurfacing, the nostalgia overpowering the confusion that follows. We weren't even dating yet. It had been some part of an assignment for her school that we kept messing around with. We made pieces out of repainted army men and we made the board by painting a large piece of cardboard. I frown at her as she stares at me with wide eyes before muttering, "market..."

"What is it?" Ryder asks.

"Market," I say louder, the realization drawing on me. I grin at Jenny and she smiles back as I spin around and leave the small medical area. I hear Stella and Ryder follow me as I find Dante and push my way through the crowds toward him. In his corner, there are a group of people dressed like Jasper and bent over what I assume to be a map.

"How is the search for Jasper going?" I ask him as I peer over his shoulder. The map below him is large and separated by a wavy blue mass which I assume is the canal me and Ryder had fallen into. One side is scribbled out in red and orange crayon. The other side is filled with x's and branching off gray lines, one I assume to be the sewer system we're currently in.

"Not very well," Dante asks as he nods at the few surrounding him. They scatter and he turns toward me with a sigh, "what can I do for you?"

"I need this map," I tell him, "and a marker."

"Why?"

"Just do it, Dante," Ryder speaks up, "we'll explain in a second."

"Crayons will have to do," he mutters and hands it over. I lean over the map, grinning as I do so. Finally, this is something I can do. Jenny gave me a puzzle, something to focus on while everything else is falling apart.

"Want to tell us what's happening?" Ryder asks.

"When we first met each other," I tell him as I trace a finger over the canal, "we created this boardgame as part of a school project. We never actually played it and I don't even know what grade she got on it."

"Okay..."

"I think you're right, Ryder. Jenny isn't herself. She was giving me a message, one she couldn't just flat out say because she's still connected to Salem. The market wasn't the goal, the bank was."

"Maybe she just forgot?" Stella offers.

"No," I shake my head, "Jenny isn't one to forget something like this. We were bank robbers, competing to see who can rob it first. The market was on the other side of the board."

"She gave you a hint as to where we can find that information," Ryder mutters, "but, I couldn't see it when I went into her head."

"Salem could be blocking you," I tell him, "that's why she can't just say it because he is still in there. He'd have the power for that, right?"

"Right," Ryder nods with a grin, "all I saw was jumbled memories and Marcus's face. She...there's this darkness in her mind, that's what's mudding up her head. Perhaps she can see past it every so often. I didn't feel Salem, but I doubt that means anything. If he wanted to be felt, he would have been."

"I don't get it," Stella speaks up, "why wouldn't Salem want us to figure this out. Wouldn't it help us do what he wants?"

"Because it isn't what he wants," Ryder mutters before letting out a sigh, "I...in his vision, he showed me what we needed to do. The barrier was never meant to keep us in. It was created to keep the portal from opening. Now, it's...it's in some sort of limbo, not truly open but not closed because the barrier was created before it could finish opening."

"That's what's in the church," I mutter, the bright light popping up in my mind, "he wants you to finish the job...to open the portal."

"Yes."

"A portal to where?" Dante asks.

"To Hell," Ryder answers.

"So, we close it. Easy, right?" Stella questions.

"We can close it," Ryder repeats, rubbing his hands over his face, "and, if we close it, we won't have to face Salem's wrath. The portal will take the island with it."

220

"And the alternative?" Dante asks.

"If the barrier falls," Ryder closes his eyes as if it is painful to continue, "and gets what he wants, the portal opens and all of Hell gets released into this realm. He promised that he'd save a select few but..."

"Well, that's super grim," I mutter as I lean over the map. The world...us...it is all too much. No movie, no story, nothing can prepare me for what that image might be.

I glance up at Dante but he seems just as bothered as the rest of us. Why are we the ones making the decisions? Shouldn't someone step up? Someone older? Someone who *knows* more than us?

"What are we supposed to do?" Stella asks, her eyes also going toward Dante. He opens his mouth to speak but nothing comes out, standing as lost as we are. Ryder doesn't speak as he leans and traces his hands over the map, stopping where I imagine the church is.

Focus, Theo, I tell myself as my heart threatens to beat out of my chest. My knees lock up, straining against themselves as I struggle to control my breathing. This...this...

"Theo," Stella says, stepping up to him and sliding her hand into his, "breathe, okay? We'll figure everything out but, you need to breathe."

"I...I know," I nod, my hands shaking in hers. I close my eyes as Jasper's words come back to me. I freeze, I freeze...what did he say?

*Focus...focus on **one** thing...*

"One thing," I mutter aloud as I breathe through my nose. Everyone is looking at me, each waiting with varying levels of concern. I keep my eyes

221

on the map, finding one thing to focus on. I let out a shaky breath before saying, "to slightly change the focus, there are two places the market can be depending on if she considered the burning part of it or not."

"We can't just ignore the choice you three need to make," Dante speaks up.

"We get it," I snap without looking up at him, "okay? We know what happens when Salem gets what he wants. I...I will literally break down if I focus on the fact that everyone we know might die no matter what option we choose so...unless you have a better option, we better get to it, right? Salem won't save any of us...you have to know that he won't actually save anyone..."

"I'm just saying we should consider choices for more than a second..."

"I don't think we have a lot of time to choose," I tell him, "considering that he's doing whatever to Jasper and whoever else he conned into helping him every moment we sit here and wait."

"At least we have something we can do before we make that choice," Ryder mutters as I circle the two areas on the map. Ones at the very edge of the city while the other one is more inland, "I've never really been to these parts."

"This one is in the old shipyard," Dante points toward the outer one. He taps his finger on the inward one with a sigh, "and you know this one, Ryder. This was where you disappeared. It's in the old medical district. We don't really go anywhere near there because it was the D.M.M.A.s main point of entry after they fled the city. It's flooded with trackers. We've been trying to take care of them but Marcus doesn't make it easy."

"Trackers?" Stella asks.

"These large robots with ribbon arms," Ryder comments.

"They suck," I nod as I straighten up, "we have destinations. How exactly are we getting there?"

"Dante," Ryder sighs, "are any of your people willing to help us out with this?"

"Yes," he nods, "we'll handle the one by the outpost. It requires more of a stealthy approach. As long as you guys are out with the sun, you should be fine in the dockyard because we have an opening relatively close to it. I'll have someone show you the way."

"I have to step in, Dante," Auntie Rosa steps up behind us. We all turn toward her as she straightens up with her chin pointed upward, "sending a bunch of children out and about isn't going to solve anything. They're more likely to get themselves killed."

Finally, an adult who sees an issue.

"What would you suggest, Rosa?" Dante sighs, "you really think I can even keep them here if I wanted to?"

"You are the leader here," she shakes her head, "you have the power to do whatever you deem necessary!"

"We both know that's not my role here," he tells her.

"I'm not going to let you," she spits as she steps up close to the vampyr, "kill him again."

"Kill who?" I ask, turning toward Ryder. He looks just as annoyed as Dante does.

"You can keep looking for someone to blame," the vampyr nods, "but never yourself. He was your responsibility, not mine."

"You-"

"Enough," Ryder speaks up, "Dante is right. You can't stop us. Theo, grab the map. Dante, send whoever you can our way whenever this conversation is done."

"What was all that about?" I ask him as he leads the way through the large room as I roll up the large map.

"Auntie Rosa used to be my guardian," Ryder explains, "I guess she gives Dante some of the blame for me being taken."

"Should she?" Stella asks, coming up on his other side.

"No," he shakes his head, "there was nothing anyone could have done to stop me from going out that day...not even Jasper."

21

Shifters Don't Cry

Everyone is going to die and there is nothing I, nor anyone else, can do about it. There is no winning, no saving, no *triumph* if we beat Salem. All that awaits us is tears and turmoil, no matter who we can save.

The broken city matches the thoughts that crowd my head. It stands dark and ominous, just like the task before us. I can't help but wonder what would have happened if we had done what Ryder had suggested in the first place and went to my father. At least someone would know where we are.

His original threat seems so small now...

I can't bring myself to worry about my father, even with the thought of an upcoming apocalypse. To me, he is unstoppable...an unmovable, and unfeeling, mountain. Nothing can bring him down, not even Salem.

What about everyone else? I ask myself, I may not have anyone else but...

I shudder at the thought as I try to keep my focus on Ryder's back. He and Stella are walking a yard or so ahead, speaking quietly as we make our way through the broken streets. The buildings are thinning out and I assume that's because we are getting closer to where we need to go.

I frown as I wipe my face, brushing away water. Leaning back, I look up at the clear sky. Wiping my face again, I realize that I'm crying. The unwanted tears don't let up as I glare at the other two, hoping they won't look back at me.

Shifters don't cry...my father's voice rings in my head as I struggle to calm myself down. We aren't supposed to show weakness, we aren't supposed to let up but...why can't I stop?

I had been strong enough to keep my cool around Ryder and Stella but, as soon as they stepped ahead, I broke like glass. How is this not weighing them down? How can they just walk about like...?

"You okay?" Ryder calls out without looking back. I smile, knowing he already knows the truth but he isn't about to turn around and make me feel even more pathetic.

"Fine," I mumble as I use my shirt the wipe my face. I speed up my steps and walk beside them, keeping my breath steady as I clear my head of everything except for the task at hand.

Someone knows how to break the barrier and we just need to find them.

"Wait," Ryder whispers, both hands shooting out to stop me and Stella from moving. I frown as I listen, gulping when I hear footsteps. He pushes toward one of the nearby buildings, neither of us complaining as we do as he instructs.

Before we can enter it, though, a wolf-man steps out still draped in the shadows. Well, not a wolf man. He has the features of a wolf with the long snout, paws at his feet, and sharp yellow nails stretching out of his fingers. He even has the large pointy ears. That is where the likeness to a wolf ends. He stands on his hind legs, his arms far longer than his legs. There is no hair on his body, just horribly stretched skin...

I dart left, not noticing Stella and Ryder darting in the opposite direction until it's too late. Without looking back, I charge into the alleyway, ignoring the snarls behind me.

Before my mind can completely process what's happening, my body is shifting. I catch myself from slamming into the ground, my powerful legs launching me forward.

Without a thought of where I'm going, I dart in and out of alleyways and through the broken streets. I follow the salty and slightly fishy smell that leads me away, hoping that it meant the ocean.

By the time I stop running, the sun is hanging low in the sky. The large expanse of greenish blue lay before me, again bringing out an awed gasp just as it did when I first saw the ocean with Jasper. The familiar line of warehouses greets me as I walk forward, following the water as my body starts to ache.

I feel like a coward, immediately leaving my friends at the sign of danger.

"Ah, jeez," a familiar voice speaks up and I spin around with a growl. Thallius grins at me as he tilts his head, "see, the initial shock of you was terrifying but now...you still look like a scared little boy even in that huge body."

Anger flares up within me, the animal mind screaming for a fight. Behind him, two of his goons stand on either side of another. His dirty white button up is familiar enough but the bag over his head and the barbed wire that keeps his arms at his side only add to my newfound fury. Thallius sighs before continuing, "run along, little coyote."

"He ain't very little," one of his men mutters behind him.

"He's nothing," Thallius chuckles, "but a lightling child that has never seen a fight. Move along or I will move you along."

I don't, instead planting my feet and letting a growl rise up from deep in my throat. The two behind him stumble back, dropping their hands away from Jasper.

A grave mistake on their part.

As soon as their hands left his body, they fly back. Thallius spins around just in time to see them slam into the buildings on either side. He steps toward Jasper but I move quicker, slamming my head into his back. His body flies forward and Jasper steps to the side and lets him faceplant into the hard asphalt.

Jasper struggles against the binds for a moment before he seems able to mentally grab onto the wire. I watch in awe, as I always do when he shows his abilities, as the wire float around him as it slowly unwraps itself from around his body.

Using my mouth, I snatch the bag off his head. He looks me up and down with a grin before turning toward the dark elf that is only now pushing himself to his feet. Turning back toward us, Thallius groans as he pulls out his literal sword.

Jasper tilts his head to the side, sending the blade flying to the side. Thallius charges forward, swinging his fists toward the teen's head. It's as if something is weighing down on him, causing his moves to look sluggish. Jasper dodges past his attacker before lunging forward, wrapping his arms around his back. With a frown, Jasper lifts him up into the air and falls back. Thallius's head slams into the ground over his shoulder with a deafening *thump!*

Thallius doesn't move as Jasper walks over and undoes the sheath attached to the dark elf's belt. He attaches it to his own before willing the sword into his hand and sliding it in.

"Thanks for the rescue, bud," Jasper smiles as he steps up beside me. The teen grins as he glances over at me before back down at the unmoving body, "what am I to do with him?"

Jasper stares at me for a moment as if waiting for me to speak. After a moment of silence, he sighs and walks over to where Thallius sits struggling against his hold, "see? He can't talk in his animal form. What other shifter rumors aren't true?"

"You're supposed to be the smart one," Thallius groans out as Jasper lifts his hand, making the dark elf float as he starts down the road, "why are you refusing to see the better path?"

"You just tied me up with barbed wire," Jasper mutters as he rubs his side, little dots of red popping up around his torso, "there is literally nothing you can say that will convince me to even listen to your poison."

Thallius opens his mouth to say more but Jasper doesn't give him the time. Instead, he flicks his wrists and sends the dark elf flying after one of his goons. I hear him crash into the building but Jasper doesn't wait to see if he gets up. He starts walking the opposite way, not bothering to see if I follow.

"We need to get you some clothes," he says as he ducks into a building, one undistinguishable from the rest. I squeeze through the door as he jumps over a counter. He disappears on the other side before popping back up with a duffel bag in his hand. He grins as he gestures me forward, "I have these little goody bags all over the city. There should be enough clothes for the both of us. They might not be the best fit but, it'll be better than nothing."

I nod as he sets out a pile of clothing on the counter before stepping deeper into the building, leaving me alone.

With a sigh of relief, I let my body shift back. From my fathers earlier attempts to get me to shift, I know that it isn't exactly healthy to be shifting for long periods of time when first starting out. You are supposed to treat it like a baby walking, a few shifts at a time.

I fall against the counter, my body aching as I struggle to keep myself on my feet. My hands shake as I pull the clothes on, enjoying the coolness on my skin. By the time I'm dressed, Jasper steps out. He's wearing a red t-shirt and jeans that are too short for him as they show off his pale ankles. Of course, his trench coat hands off his shoulders but he also has Thallius's sword strapped to his side."

"So," Jasper asks as he pulls the duffel bags strap over his shoulder, "what are you doing out here alone? You should already know it's infested with monsters."

"I was originally with Ryder and Stella," I tell him, looking toward the door, "but we got separated."

"Hm," Jasper nods, his eyes narrowing slightly as he grins, "why are you *three* out here? Doubt you'd sneak out all this way just for me."

"No," I frown, "but we probably would have if we had known you were out here. We, ah, we are looking for someone. Maybe you know of them?"

"Someone living out here?" Jasper tilts his head, his gaze toward the light from outside. He sighs before speaking up, "last I heard, there was this old crone living in an old ship in the harbor. I don't know if she survived, though. Most of it crumbled underwater a couple months ago."

"Okay," I nod, "so, we have something, cool. We just need to find Stella and Ryder first."

"Actually," Jasper sighs as he peers up at the sky, "we need to wait."

"Shoot," I mutter just as the sirens go off. He pushes me inside and leads me toward a heavy metal door. It takes me a moment to realize that it used to be a freezer. He pushes me in and shuts it behind him, the small metal box feeling far warmer than it was created to.

"Hopefully," Jasper says as he creates the light in his hands, "our friends know to do the same."

"So, Ryder seems surprised at the amount of those shadow demons we saw?" I ask him just as screams break out beyond our safety. Others mix with them and I shiver as the roof above us shake.

"Yeah, they never used to be this bad. One day they were just here," Jasper shrugs, "and all we really know is that they are killing machines, far worse than any other monster in the city. Marcus claims to control them but I've seen them take down as much of his men as Dante's. They don't differentiate between us and the monsters either. They just kill...everything. We also never know when they're going to be out and about either. It used to be out at night and only sometimes. Now, they're slowly growing more and more prominent during sunset. They're easy enough to avoid, if you know what to look for, though. We just tend to stay in because once they see you, it's almost impossible to get away."

"That's terrifying," I shudder, picturing those large ones by the water.

"Can I ask you a question now?" He speaks up, "since we're going to be stuck here for a while?"

"Sure," I shrug with a smile, "I'm basically an open book."

"So, Jenny is your crazy ex," Jasper starts, "but, I thought shifters mate for life. Was she your someone?"

"I..." I tilt my head before shrugging, "I don't know."

"Did you love her?"

"Of course."

"Did you, though?" Jasper asks again as he leans against the metal that surrounds us, "I mean, you're so young. Do you even know what love is?"

"I..." my first instinct is to argue and claim that age has nothing to do with it. I have, after all, been arguing about that fact for quite some time. She was my girlfriend. Of course, I know she never truly loved me but...hadn't I loved her? We did all the couple-y things like dates and handholding. In that entire relationship, we had never even kissed once. She had never outwardly expressed her actual feelings but, neither did I.

Had we actually, truly even been together?

"I take that as a no?"

"Shut up," I grumble.

"That's good, right?" Jasper asks, "I mean, I've only read about shifters and their particular mating habits but, based on what I've read, it's devastating to lose their partner."

"I don't know. Most shifters don't mate anymore. They date and marry as they choose. There are a few of us 'pureblood' shifters left," I explain, using my fingers to air-quote pureblood, "but that number is getting lower and lower every year. People like my father want to keep pushing it. He has a plan for my marriage and everything."

"Really?" He asks, "I thought arranged marriages were looked down in today's society, well, American society."

"Not in shifter society, apparently."

"Does he already have a lady picked out?"

"Yes," I nod. I have pushed those memories so far back that I had nearly forgotten about it. My father would call me every other week to discuss meeting another shifter girl and her family. He immediately told me that it was for marriage and, even as a kid, I knew what marriage meant.

Marriage is forever and I never have liked the thought of forever.

It's strange how small my arguments seem now.

Jasper doesn't reply and silence falls over the room. He leans back and his eyes slide close but I don't question him because of what happened last time. I sigh as I too lean back, glaring at the gray, rusty roof above me.

I can't sleep. For the entire night, my animal side begs to be released at every sound from outside our small safety box. It is a strange feeling, one that throughs me for a loop as I struggle against it. It seems to change *fight, fight, fight* but, I have never been a fighter before.

It's as if something I can't see is taunting the animal within.

22

Aren't Cursed Souls Just Zombies?

When I wake up, Jasper in gone. The only light comes through the small creak in the door, a thin line shining directly in my eye. I lift my hand and block it, groaning as I roll to my side.

"Yo, you awake?" I hear Jasper call out from beyond the door. Before I can answer, he pulls the door open and pops his head in with a grin, "good. It's time to get moving if we want to make it back in time."

"Gotcha," I mutter as I let him help me to my feet.

It isn't long before even the warehouses start to fade. Jasper pulls me to a stop as we look down a sharp incline over looking the large harbor. There is only one boat, though half sunken, sitting alongside one of the docks.

It sits idle like everything else in this city, free of its creator's will.

"Is that it?" I ask him.

"Yes," Jasper nods.

"Shouldn't we try to find Stella and Ryder first?"

"It might be better if we take care of this first since we're here. This is, after all, the most dangerous part of the city."

"What?" I ask, my voice lowering to a whisper. My first instinct is not to question him as he knows this city best.

"Listen," Jasper frowns slightly. I do as he says, tilting my head as I wait to hear what he does.

"I hear nothing."

"Exactly," he nods as he steps down the incline, "nothing. Not even our monstrous friends from the college dare venture this far."

"Why not?" I ask.

"Let's hope we don't find out," Jasper mutters as he leads the way down the muddy incline and onto the docking yard. As we step closer to the dock itself, I realize that I drastically underestimated the size of the ship.

It'll take days to search this thing.

"Know how to swim?" Jasper asks as we step onto the dock. I glance over the side, glaring at the soft waves as they hit against the wood.

I've always hated swimming.

"Yes," I say, clearing my throat. The deck of the large ship is tilted with half of it under the dark blue. Luckily, the door downward stands on the half above the water.

"Is this even safe?" I mutter.

"This entire city is unsafe," Jasper shrugs, "we just have to do what we can. I don't think she could have survived, at least not here."

"Yay," I mutter as I step onto the deck. The tilted floor sends me stumbling a step to the side before I correct myself. I hear Jasper chuckle behind me, hating the blush that follows.

"Keep your eyes open," Jasper tells me as I make it to the door. I nod as I grab the nod and pull. The door stays as it is until I yank it, the metal screeching as I stumble back. Listening to the sound of the splashing water echoing from the depths of the boat, I frown at the smell hanging in the air.

A smell that I only became familiar with when I got to Maybelle.

The smell of rot and decay...the smell of something *dead*.

It is only after that realization that I notice something moving in the darkness; a strange humanoid creature that is slowly stumbling forward...

"Move!" Jasper calls out from behind me. It takes a moment for his word to register in my mind as a gargled moan erupts from the darkness. It sounds like someone is choking on water.

"Come on, you idiot!" Jasper is right behind me, yanking me out of the way as an arm reaches out toward me. We slip back, sliding down the deck and toward the water. Someone steps out into the sunlight, bringing memories of bad horror movies flashing in my head.

"A zombie?" I scream out as the body stumbles out of the doorway. The smell of rot hits me like a brick as the woman, or what used to be a woman, struggles against the slippery surface below her.

Just like those cheesy horror films, she is covered in grime and dried blood. Half of her head is just gone, leaving a slap with a half-smile and wide eye that is a sickly yellow. Her left foot is flopping about, as she actually walks on the bone of her leg. A low, inhuman gurgle leaves her lips as she steps toward us.

"What are we supposed to do?" I ask as we stumble onto the dock. Jasper tosses the sword at me and I catch it, luckily without it hitting anything, "what if she is who we needed to see?"

"She is," Jasper answers as he wipes out his arms and catch his blades, "but, we have to kill it, obviously."

"G-go for the head!" I stutter out as he steps forward. The zombie immediately takes a swipe at him but, Jasper steps to the side, easily dodging the attack. He swings his blade out, the sharp metal sliding through her neck.

"You know," Jasper says with a grin as the zombie crumbles down, "true zombies don't exist. This here is a cursed soul."

"Are you going to tell me what the difference is?" I ask as he kneels next to the body.

"Remember the dark veins on Rosa?" He asks, "or your ex?"

"Yes?"

"If Auntie Rosa stops using her magic to fight the darkness that is infecting her," Jasper explains as he pulls a leather-bound book from somewhere within her clothing, "she will become what we call a cursed soul. Jenny is on her way to becoming one as well. Mortal bodies, and souls, of lightlings and humans cannot take on dark magic. When they do, their souls are cursed to their newly decaying bodies. As it eats away at their brain, they slowly start to go crazy and get very, *very* hungry. They eat whatever is available whether it be garbage, animal, or human."

"How exactly are they different from zombies?"

"Zombies are a stupid movie trope that makes them far less scary than they actually are. These things can still talk and act relatively normal for weeks. They aren't immediately these crazed monsters until the very end. There have been several cases in the past with these guys going on killing sprees and only found out when they became like this girl here."

"You said their souls are trapped," I say as he hands me the book, "what happens to them when you kill them?"

"Moves on? Gets stuck in limbo? No one really knows what happens after even if you have a natural death."

"Think there's anything in here?" I ask as I undo the cord that keeps the book secure.

"Hopefully," he shrugs, "you never told me why you need it."

"Well," I start but Jasper's head snaps up. Following his gaze, I see both Stella and Ryder running up. I laugh as I hurry toward them with a wide grin on my face, "guys!"

"Where have you been?" Stella asks as she punches my arm, "we've been looking all over for you. We finally decided to follow the map to see if you somehow knew where to go."

"Yeah, I found Jasper," I say pointing behind me. When they return confused gazes, I glance back and realize that he is in fact not here. The zombie-er, cursed soul still lay dead and I still hold Thallius's sword. Before I can question it too much, though, a familiar voice pulls at my attention.

"*Theo…*" a voice sings out to me, echoing off the water around us. My heart skips a beat as I spin toward the noise, unable to accept the sound that invades my ears.

That voice...I haven't heard it in years but, it still brings tears to my eyes as her beautiful flashes behind my eyes.

That voice belongs to my mother.

"Theo?" I can hear Ryder call out from behind me but his words mean nothing to me. My mother...she can't be here. Warnings ping off in my head as I know she's impossible. I had watched her die when I was seven. I remember it as clear as day and yet...I can't stop myself from hoping to see her one last time...

"*Theo*..." her voice sings out again and I can finally pinpoint where it's coming from. Standing at the end of the dock, a figure stands hidden behind heavy fog. I hadn't noticed it before, as it stretches over the dark waves.

I can see her...I can see her reaching out toward me...

"Theo!" Ryder's voice tears me from my daze, his arms yanking me back and keeping me from stumbling toward her. In a second, the fog is gone, revealing what truly stands before me.

"What is that?" I cough out as she steps toward us. I find myself frozen again, unable to run from what faces me. They too seem frozen in fear, unable to move away from the terrible monster that grins at us.

Her skin seems to shine, reflecting off the water below the dock. Her thick, dark hair floats above her head as if she is forever suspended underwater. She is nothing but skin and bones, her pale skin nearly translucent as it stretches across her body. Her large hands aren't human. Instead, her fingers are stretched out and sharp, looking more like the talons of a predatory bird. Her arms, elongated toward her knees if she'd let fall to her sides, reach out toward us.

Her eyes glow white as she tilts her head toward us, no pupil or color sit. At first, I mentally compare them to Ryder's and Jasper's when they glow with their abilities. They, however, glow more like search lights. The siren's lips stretch out unnaturally as she smiles, revealing rows and rows of razor-sharp teeth much like that of a shark.

I take her in, still frozen as my legs are stuck in cement. I can't tell if it is a magical side effect of being near that *thing* or my own cowardice. Luckily, I'm not stuck for too long because Ryder gets over his fear quicker than I and pulls me back.

I don't turn away from her as I stumble back, watching in horror as her mouth stretches open. Her skin peels apart, drips of dark blood dripping past her lips as her smile stretches toward her ears.

That is all I see before I collapse, pain shooting through my entire body as it lets out a piercing scream. Though I know I fall, I don't register my body hitting the dock. I squirm as the monster's scream echoes through my body, opening my eyes long enough to see Stella and Ryder in the same state.

She is on a whole different level from the monsters I've faced before, though I mostly just ran. I have never felt pain like this, pain I can feel from the tips of my toes to my eyelids.

Come on, Theo, think of a way out of it.

That's the problem. I *can't*. I can't linger on any thought of escape of escape for long enough to implement it before the pain overcomes every thought I try to hang onto.

Come on, Theo, get up!

As suddenly as it came, the sound gets cut off, leaving me in an aching mess on the old wood. At first, I think it is Jasper. After all, he had disappeared right before the thing showed. Instead, I'm met with another surprise

Dante stands behind the creature, a blade through her neck as she slowly falls to the side and splashes into the sea.

"Is everyone okay?" He asks as he darts forward. Dante pulls me to my feet before moving toward the other two.

"Weren't you checking the other place?" Ryder asks as he stands up, holding his head.

"Yes, nothing was there," Dante sighs as he looks around, "we have a bigger issue."

"What's up?" Stella asks.

"You and Theo aren't meant to leave this place alive," he sighs, "Salem...Salem has Jasper."

"No," I shake my head, "he...he was just here."

"Yes," Dante groans, "he's under Salem's control. You three were meant to split up. You were meant to find Jasper."

"He led you here to kill you," Ryder mutters out.

"No," Jasper's voice spoke from the shore, "I wasn't supposed to kill him, the siren was. Just proof that plans don't always work out. Either way, this is where most of you end. Just not you, Ryder, Salem has a use for you."

"Jasper," Dante calls out, "I know you're still in there. Don't make me fight you."

"But, Dante," he grins wickedly, twisting his blades in his hands, "I really want to fight you!"

Both Dante and I start forward, gaining a giggle from Jasper as he nods his head to the side. Something invisible slams into my side, launching me off the dock and into the water. I crash through the waves, the coolness breaking the residue confusion the screaming monster.

I kick my way back to the surface, sucking in a gulp of air as I swim toward the old wood. Pulling myself up, I can see that Jasper has yet to take Dante down. Ryder stands back, watching the fight with narrow eyes and Stella stands behind him with a terrified look in her bright eyes.

"That was a jerk move," I mutter as I roll to my feet. As I watch them circle each other, I realize where Jasper learned how to fight. They mirror each other, blocking the others moves seemingly without a thought.

It is Dante that makes the first mistake. He lets Jasper dart past him, his movement followed by his blade swiping through the air at the vampyr's feet. He cries out, blood flowing from his ankle as he topples to the side and disappearing over the edge of the dock.

Jasper straightens up and Ryder steps forward, snatching the sword I had somehow kept a hold of. His twin doesn't let him do much as he sends him flying back and rolling like a skipping stone across the deck.

Stella darts forward after him, spells dancing past her fingers as she does so. Jasper slices them out of the air with his blades, getting closer and closer to her as he does so. I charge forward and push her out of the way just as he makes it to her. His blade nearly misses me as I stumble away, his smile faltering as he turns to face me straight on.

His eyes are stark white, just like Ryder's was.

"Jasper," I say, holding up my hands in surrender, "I don't know how far gone you are but...you are stronger than him. Break out of it."

"Silly boy," he mutters sounding so much like Salem as he lunges forward. I duck past two swipes, impressed with myself until his leg kicks out and knocks me off my feet. My back slams into the wood and before I can even register his movement, he is on top of me.

"You will die," he says as he raises a blade high, "you will break the prophecy..."

"Jasper," I mutter as his hand falters for a moment, "this isn't you...I know that. This isn't your fault."

I close my eyes as he brings the blade down, waiting for the pain that is sure to follow...

When no pain comes, I open my eyes. The blade still hangs in the air, Jasper's hand shaking as he stares hard at me. The whiteness of his eyes seems to be faltering, his violet coloring slowly peeking its way through.

He blinks, the color coming back as the white tries to invade again. With a yell, he brings the blade down. I scream out but the blade doesn't go straight down. Instead, it bypasses my face and plunges into Jasper's gut.

"Jasper," Dante appears again, soaked, and catches him as he slides off me.

"I...I couldn't let me kill him," Jasper groans out, his hands reaching toward his blade that is sticking out of his stomach. A dark blotch surrounds it, almost indistinguishable from the red of the shirt, "I...I couldn't think of anything else to do..."

"I know," Dante nods, his eyes furrowed as he pushes Jasper's hands away, "don't touch it. We'll get you back and take care of you, okay?"

"Rosa won't like that," Jasper chuckles, a noise that is instantly followed with a groan. Ryder appears beside them, his brows furrowing at the comment as Dante lifts him into the air.

"What happened?" He asks as he helps me to my feet.

"He stabbed himself to stop from stabbing me," I tell him.

"Theo," Stella cries as she throws herself at me, crying into my shoulder before continuing, "I'm so sorry! I tried to help but...I was so scared, I couldn't conjure up anything."

"Don't worry about it," I pat her back, "I know how that feels. Do you...do you think Jasper will be fine?"

"I don't feel the presence on his mind anymore," Ryder says, "but that wound...it's not going to be a fun recovery."

"Did you find anything?" Stella asks, coming up on my other side as we start walking. Dante is walking in front of us, his strong stride quickly leading him away.

"No," I shake my head, "she was a...Jasper called her a cursed soul before we got there. Um, he did pick up a book from her, though."

"Do you have it?" Stella asks. I nod as I pull it out of my pants. Luckily, I had slid it away before the siren. Ryder grabs it and untwists the leather cord that binds it closed. He flips it open and immediately sighs.

"It's an old daelic language," he mutters, "I can't read it."

"Yeah," Theo mutters, leaning over it, "they don't teach that at the academy."

"Yeah," Stella shakes her head, "it's an old darkling language created to keep our legends and secrets out of D.M.M.A. hands. Many of our own kind can't even read it."

"Jasper can," Dante speaks up as he stops above a manhole, "but let's get him taken care of first."

"Why does he know?" Stella asks, her voice hardening with suspicion. I immediately grow defensive, though I don't know the answer either, "I mean, even most darklings ourselves found those who used it traitorous and against their call for peace."

"I would be careful with what you're saying," Dante says, his voice getting low as I dart forward and lift up the metal plate, "I highly doubt you've spent enough time here to truly understand who your people are."

"I'm just saying," Stella mutters as Dante hands Jasper over to me. I shouldn't be as annoyed as I am. Sure, I've spent time with him and would be dead without him. She got to meet him while he was possessed. Definitely not the best first impression.

"And he's just saying," Ryder grins, "that you don't really have a say in what's right or wrong here. Jasper isn't about betraying his people, he's just about knowledge. The difference between surviving and dying is sometimes based juts off of what you know."

They continue talking but I turn my attention toward the problem at hand. Jasper's paler than ever, his face contorted in pain as I lower him into the darkness. I release him at Dante's word before slowly climbing down after them.

By the time we make it to the little medical area, Auntie Rosa is standing beside one of the beds. Her eyes go wide as Dante lowers Jasper down on one of the beds. He has long since lost consciousness, though he does wince as she grabs the hilt of the blade.

"Everyone out," Dante orders as he shoos us away, "I let you know when you can come see him."

Ryder sighs as they both follow me to that little room that me and Jasper had been assigned to. Stella plops down on Jasper's mat, a heavy frown on her face as she leans against the wall. I sit across from her, trying not to judge her too hard on her comments about Jasper's potential traitorous attitude.

"Look," Stella speaks up, "I'm sorry about what I said, okay? I...he just attacked us and I think I have a right to be a little cautious of him."

"He also saved us from Marcus in the first place," Ryder cuts in before I can, "and he's been keeping Theo alive since he got here. He wouldn't have done that if he was going to kill us anyway."

"I know," Stella sighs, "and I know I have no right but, you have to understand, though, right?"

"I think so," I answer before Ryder can, "but you also have to understand that everyone else has the right to defend him. He stabbed himself to stop from killing me."

"Yeah," Ryder nods, "pretty obvious possession."

"Okay, okay," she sighs, "I get it."

23

The Notebook and the Promise of Mayhem

Three days pass before Dante gives us any word on Jasper and even then, we still aren't allowed to go see him. He's alive and that's all that matters to me. Stella and Ryder, on the other hand, have grown restless.

"Can't we find someone else to read the notebook?" Stella asks, her voice barely above a whisper as we sit around a small table. Cans of various foods sit in front of us, none of them making a move to eat as I dig into mine.

"I know," Ryder replies as he stirs his peaches, "but, as you said, most darklings don't even know it. It died when the D.M.M.A. stopped being prominent here. I also don't think anyone else would speak to us even if they did."

"Why not?" Stella asks.

"We're lightlings," I reply, "they don't trust us. Someone tried to kill me the night I got here."

"Really?" Stella coughs out.

"Yeah," I shrug, "our buddy Jasper saved me, though. I don't think he likes it here either. He said he moved out."

"He moved away from everyone?" Ryder mutters, his eyebrows furrowing together.

"He said something about it being too much," I tell him, "you'd have to ask him."

"Oh, wait," Stella says with a chuckle, "we can't!"

"Actually," Dante says as he steps up to our table, "he's awake. You three are free to go see him."

"Really?" I grin as I jump up. Ryder follows my lead and we hurry over with Stella hanging back. I don't pay her any mind as I find Jasper sitting up, shirtless with white bandages covering his stomach.

There is the teen that saved my life seconds upon meeting. The one that has been able to sense almost every attack before it came. Here he is with his face already stuffed in the journal, jumping when I place a hand on his shoulder.

"Oh," he grins, "hey, Theo."

"Hey," I grin back as Ryder steps out from behind me.

"Ry," Jasper pushes himself up. Ryder smiles as he steps forward, pulling his brother into a hug. Before I stop myself, I lean forward and wrap my arms around the both of them and effectively ruin the brotherly moment.

"Off," Jasper laughs and we pull away. He lifts up the book and lets out a heavy sigh, "this is all the writings of an insane person. What exactly am I trying to find?"

"How to break a life curse," Ryder tells him as he sits by his feet. I hop on the bed next to him, glancing back at Stella as she stands leaning against the wall a few beds down.

"A life curse," Jasper mutters as he sits himself up straighter. He winces, his eyebrows furrowing for a moment. Ryder reaches forward and arranges the pillows for a more comfortable backing as he continues, "the one that has kept us trapped here? Who all knows about this?"

"We don't know," I say, glancing at Ryder, "us and Dante with some of his men."

"Many want it to stay as is because they fear what comes with it. You do know what's hidden in the church, right?"

"A portal," Ryder nods, "how did you know that?"

"I went in about a year ago or so," he shrugs, "the border is connected to it. Messing with it can open the doorway to wherever it leads, damning not only us but the rest of the world as well."

"Unfortunately," his brother says, "we don't have a choice. Something bigger is happening, Jaz, and we have to stop it. The first step is breaking that curse."

"You're going to face an army," he shakes his head, "if anyone finds out what your doing. Both Dante's people and Marcus's even if either leader tells them not to."

"That's great," I mutter.

"Yeah," Jasper shrugs, "anyway, I'll do what you want, I just need a reading buddy."

"Why?" Stella asks from her spot on the wall.

"This is in a dangerous language that has the potential to drive the reader insane. I need someone

251

here to make sure that I don't get dragged down that far."

"Okay," Stella grumbles as she pushes herself off the wall, "I'll help."

"No, thank you," Jasper shakes his head and elbows me, "I vote Theo."

"Why me?" I ask with a grin I can't help. I like Jasper, he's the first natural friend I've made since Jenny but, does she really count?

"Someone needs to go see who all found about this little plan of yours," he says, "and someone might want to go check up on Jenny. She's been muttering some strange things. Besides, I know Stella isn't fond of me and Ryder would probably be more useful trying to figure out who all knows about the life curse. You're my best bet at getting actual help without wasting Ryder's abilities."

"It's nothing personal," Stella mutters. Ryder chuckles as he grabs her arm and pulls her away from the hospital beds. I can see her trying to defend herself to him but he only laughs as they disappear into the crowds of darklings.

"You're also the only one that will help me move," Jasper says after they're out of earshot. He twists his body so that his legs are hanging off the bed. I hurry over to him as he pushes himself off the bed, catching him as he doubles over.

"I didn't agree to this," I tell him, "you shouldn't be trying to move around."

"And you shouldn't be in Maybelle," Jasper retorts as he points down toward the end of the beds.

I can see a dark doorway leading into darkness, "I just need something to help us get through it."

I nod as I help him limp over to it. As we make it there, he pulls away from him and instead opts to use the walls for support as he leads me down a meandering decline. The familiar light spell leaves his lips just as all the light from behind us disappears. It illuminates a small, cramped hole I doubt even a kid can get through.

"Jasper?" I ask just as he waves his hand with a new fae word leaving his lips. Suddenly, the hole disappears and opens up into a large, well lit space. Piles of books, scrolls, and other loose pages fill the space. A large table sits in the center with open books covering nearly every inch of it. A pile of blankets sits in one corner while there are piles of clothing scattered throughout.

"This was my room before I left," Jasper explains, answering my question before I can word it, "it would be too much of an effort to grab any of it so I just decided to hide it. I knew I'd be back often enough, either way."

Jasper carefully lifts a few piles of books of the table and gestures for Theo to join him on the bench as he sits down. I do as he says and he sets the journal down, open to page I can't decipher.

"So, what exactly do I need to do?" I ask him.

"Nothing much, actually," Jasper shrugs, "this is actually the language of the vampyr priests back in Dante's realm. It wasn't one that the common population knew, hence why both Dante and Marcus

253

are blind to it. It does, however, share the same basic structures as the fae language. They hold power and, if not careful, can cause quite a mess."

"Like, casting spells?"

"Not exactly," he says, "they were a very secretive bunch so they protected most of their books by imbedding spells into them. The reader ends up damning themselves without realizing it until it's too late."

"You want me to stop you from accidentally casting a vampyr spell?"

"There's a low chance that this journal is actually set up like that but, yes."

"How?"

"The spells are not necessarily the strongest," Jasper shrugs, "so, if I look like I'm about to kill myself, slap me. Hopefully, that's enough."

"Hopefully," I repeat as he leans over the book. I watch him like a hawk, noting down every twitch and mumble that might be pointing toward a negative reaction to the words on the page.

Jasper seems to be in his own world as he flips through the pages, reading faster the deeper into it he goes. I want to stop him and ask what's happening, curious to know what epic tale can leave such a hungry look on a teen's face as he frantically flipping through the pages for more.

"Okay," Jasper says as he makes it to the halfway mark. He looks over at me with a wide grin as he pushes the book closer to me, "I think I found what we need."

"Well, spit it out," I tell him.

"To break a life curse," he explains, "you have to do three things. First, you have to know exactly why the witch gave her life to cast the curse. She wanted to stop the portal from opening, it's written in the margins here. Number two, you have to go to where she cast it. You have to be right on it, otherwise it isn't going to work. Usually, though, there's going to be some sign around it."

"Sign?"

"Yes, like weird plants or a vampyric symbol," Jasper shrugs, "isn't really specific on that aspect. There is nothing in the margins here...maybe she never found it."

"What is the third thing?" I ask, sitting forward with my own curiosity getting the better of me.

"A sacrifice has to be made," he says, his voice growing low, "just like the sacrifice the witch made."

"What? Someone has to die?"

"That is what the book says, Theo," Jasper says, gesturing toward the worn pages, "I don't know what else to tell you."

"There has to be another way," I mutter as I reach forward and trace over the strange symbols covering the pages. Jasper doesn't say anything as I slowly flip through the pages. Slowly, the language shifts into English, though I can barely read any of it. As Jasper had said, it is the writing of a madwoman. Soon, it turns into a singular phrase...one that makes my heart heavier each time I re-read it.

"That doesn't sound nice," Jasper says as I flip through the rest of the pages. A stick figure sits in every corner, growing larger and more prominent with every

255

page. It is as if I'm watching the woman go more and more insane the deeper into the book I go.

The last page is what bothers me most. My stomach drops as I lean away from it, the book falling from my hands and slamming down on the table. I don't know what it is about that makes me want to run…that makes the stuffy air around me feel almost suffocating.

Something tells me that the old cursed soul had every right to be terrified. It isn't just some crazy person's s ramblings.

No, it is a warning.

MAYHEM IS COMING

WERE ALL GOING TO DIE

24

How to Break A Life Curse

Sitting alone beside Jenny's bed, I watch as Dante's people clear out the remaining beds. Jasper remains but he is nowhere to be seen, probably hidden away in his old room. I want to talk to him, the message hanging heavy in my mind. Everyone else seems to have taken it as just some insane person's hallucinations but, there is something about it that weighs heavily on my mind.

The large area had been nearly completely cleaned out, leaving only a few beds and supplies for us. Dante didn't tell them all the details; however, he expressed the importance of getting to safety. They're moving as far away from the portal as possible, camping up along the shore. Last I heard, a select few are preparing boats for when everything does go down.

Jenny hasn't opened her eyes in a few days as the infection has spread too far or so they tell me. Her mind is deteriorating faster than expected. Dark veins dance under the skin of her face, stretching across her cheeks and reaching toward her eyes.

She doesn't have long before she fully turns into a cursed soul.

Both Ryder and Jasper suggested a quick death, something that I immediately shut down. I know it's selfish, I've seen enough scenes about someone turning and the mess it creates but...I can't bring myself to kill her or let someone else do it.

Ryder said there wasn't anything else to get out of her, not even after digging into her head. Everything was drowned out by a single phrase, repeating over and over, the same one that preoccupies mine.

"Mayhem is coming," she whispers, her green eyes opening wide with fear. She turns her head toward me, the dark veins in her eyes nearly overtaking her irises. She keeps muttering the words over and over again until she freezes, her mouth snapping shut and falling back against the pillows. Her eyes still hold mine as if she was trying to tell me something.

It's almost as if she's saying a name, not a concept...

"She's nearly there," Ryder says as he comes up from behind me, "it'll be best if we take care of it now, Theo. Let me take her away, okay? You don't have to be a part of it."

"Take care of it?" I cough out bitterly, "you mean take care of *her*. You mean *kill* her. Can't...Can't we fix her?"

"She is going to turn into a cursed soul," he tells me, "see the veins? She's too far gone. No magic can do anything for her. If we don't take care of her now, we'll be her next victims."

"No," I sob out, "you aren't killing her. We can fix her. You know she didn't mean to do all those bad things. She's not a bad person...she doesn't deserve this."

"I don't think she was," he nods, "she was just in a bad place, okay? But, Theo, it won't do anyone any good to keep her alive. She's in pain. The most humane thing we can do is take that pain away."

"I…"

"Theo," Jasper says as he limps over to us, "no healer can fix the infection, it has spread too far. It's the soul that's cursed, not the body. The body just follows after."

"So," Stella walks up cans in her arms, interrupting any other conversation, "everyone is out. Dante is out there making sure no one else sneaks in. So, you two know about what we have to do so out with it."

"To break a life curse," Jasper speaks up, "you need to do three things and I think you both are going to hate it as much as Theo does."

"What do we have to do?"

"You have to know why the witch did it, where exactly she did it, and you have to make the same sacrifice," I tell him. Jasper nods his head slowly as he turns to face the other two.

A sacrifice must be made…

"Someone has to die?" Stella chokes out as Jasper grabs the cans from her. That is the thing about Jasper. He always has to have something in his hands.

"Well, it obviously can't be you or Theo," Stella chokes out as she starts to pace around the small space. Jasper's head snaps up as he opens them.

"How is that obvious?" He asks as he hands out the cans. I should be excited. After all, I get beans instead of the normal fruit mixture that I have been getting since I got here. However, the circumstances make any positive emotion virtually impossible.

"There's a prophecy-" I start but Jasper interrupts me with a slurp of his peaches. He chews for a moment before sighing.

"The prophecy of the six," he says after he swallows, "the one that calls for six kids to save the world from some almighty darkness. You...you think Theo and Ry are part of that prophecy?"

"Obviously, that's why they're here," she shrugs, obviously still salty about the whole "attack".

"So, Theo and Ryder are part of the prophecy. What about you? You're just along for the ride?"

"I guess," she shrugs and turns back toward Ryder. Her voice shakes as she continues, "anyway, it has to be me, right? I have to be the one to die. I'm the only one who can do it."

"Lies," Jasper mutters as he takes in another mouthful of peaches. Everyone turns to look at him and he rolls his eyes before gesturing toward himself, "do you not see me standing here? I feel like I'm the better choice."

"What?"

"You're not the only one who is on this ride," he shrugs as he put his empty can down, "I'm going to do it. I have to make sure it's done right, after all."

"What?" she snaps, immediately offended before realizing what he is doing. She still looks like she wants to argue, but she doesn't speak.

"Jasper," Ryder chokes out but, he can't seem to form the words. We all know that it has to be done and he is probably the best option. That, however, doesn't stop tears threaten to fall out of either of our eyes.

Jasper's face doesn't betray him as he faces us without a look of fear or sadness on his pale face. All he does is reach back and pull something out of his jacket pocket.

"I thought you might need this," he says as he hands a scroll over to Ryder, "it's the spell that closes the portal so having Stella with you wouldn't be the worst idea. We both know you were never the best at casting them. I wouldn't do anything Salem tells you to, especially if it's casting a spell."

"Thanks," Ryder says as he takes it from him. Jasper eyes my untouched can of beans and I hold it out to him, knowing my stomach can't handle even that. He takes it without question and slurps it up before limping out of the small area.

"I'm going to go make sure that Dante has everything taken care of," Stella mutters, ducking into the darkness after Ryder's brother. Ryder watches her leave, his face almost pained before he turns back toward me.

"Why haven't you told her yet?" I ask him. He turns toward me with furrowed eyebrows.

"What are you talking about?"

"You know what I'm talking about."

"I...don't know," he shrugs, finally giving in, "definitely wasn't something I was thinking about, Theo, considering everything else."

"I know," I tell him, "but, I've wanting to tease you two about it since before we even got here. It's so obvious that you two like each other. I'd totally support it by the way but...even if you did, you're never going to be able to do anything about it, are you? We're all going to die, aren't we? If we close it, Salem will kill us and our families. If we don't, everyone is going to die anyway. There's nothing waiting for us when we succeed. Even if we don't die now, the crap we go through for the prophecy has to be even worse, right? We aren't going to move on to grow older and have relationships and…my father, Stella's people…"

By the end of it, I realize I am rambling as the realization hits me again. Sure, he can tell Stella he likes her and she might like him but…what can they do about it?

If we die, aren't we also damning the world?

"It's a hard thing to accept," Ryder smiles bitterly as he glares down at his open can, "right? Never being able to see where your goals and aspirations took you."

"You don't seem torn up about it at all," I mutter, "I'm the only one that actually seems worried about everything."

"I'm not," he shrugs, "well, not about myself. I'm more torn up about you and Stella because, well, here we've always been prepared to die before we were ready."

"What?"

"When you grow up in Maybelle," he whispers, glancing around as if to keep this conversation private, "people are dying around you left and right. Hell, I even saw my brother die. Or, I thought he died. I still don't know how he survived. But, we learned at a very young age that living was a privilege that we had to fight for. I never fought under Dante but he has a moto that I always respected. You survive because of others and others survive because of you. Basically, saying that surviving Maybelle is a team effort that everyone has to participate in. We all protected each other and we were all prepared to die for another, had this in my mind even as a child."

"What does this have to do with us?" I ask.

"I will not feel bad for myself for dying so that others can survive," Ryder says with a small smile, "you shouldn't either. You need to get out of your head, Theo. This is bigger than us, our families, or our futures. Don't think about it as you...think about the entire realm as a whole. Think of all those families, all those people that will die alongside our families. There's no winning for us, Theo, but we can make life better for everyone else."

"I think...I think I can accept that," I nod. Ryder pats my shoulder before walking out of the small area.

Everything is going to be okay.

"Alright," Jasper pops back in, dressed in his usual attire with his black trench coat. He still limps around, though it's far less prominent, "we're going to move closer to the church. I have a safe house set up a few blocks from there. We'll make our way to the church in the morning to avoid the shadow demons that surround it."

"Sounds like a plan," I nod before turning toward Jenny, "what are we doing with her?"

"Dante already said he'd come back for her," Jasper tells me. I nod, glancing back at her as I follow him into his room, "I just want to grab a few things before we head out."

"So, Jasper," I say as he gathers a few random items and stuffs them into a bag. He pauses, glancing back at me before straightening up.

"What's up?"

"I'm sorry."

"About what?"

"Everything," I shrug, "you're going to die tomorrow."

"Sure," he shrugs as he goes back to collecting small items, "but, that's not your fault."

"Still. It still sucks. I know I haven't known you all that long but...I'm going to miss you, bud," I say, using the same thing he's been calling me. He grins as he slides the bag over his shoulder.

"Don't worry," Jasper grins, "I'll come back to haunt you."

"Good," I chuckle but I can't stop my voice from breaking. He holds out his fist and I bump it, grinning for a moment before letting out a sigh. Pulling him into a hug, I say, "thank you for everything."

"Sure thing," he chuckles as he pats me once on the back and pushes me away, "I'm just glad I was there to save you. Now, we should get moving if we want to get there before dark."

I nod, watching him leave before gazing over the now quiet space.

I close my eyes, trying not to linger on the fact that I am going to lose one of the few actual friends I have. Not only that, but Ryder is also going to lose his brother...someone he just got back.

How is any of this fair?

265

"Nope," I mutter aloud as I blink away the tears and turn around. Standing in the narrow doorway is Jenny.

"I told you," she cries out, "I told you!"

"Jenny," I step toward her. Her eyes are wide and crazy, looking just like that zombified woman at the docks, "you need to go back to the bed, okay? We can help you."

"Ha!" She chuckles, "by killing me?"

I wince as a giggle shakes through her. She gestures to herself before tilting her head toward me. With a whisper, fire leaps up from her hands as she steps toward me.

"Killing me?" She whispers this time as she lifts her hands as her voice turns into a broken scream, "killing me?"

I duck under the table as she sends a fireball past my head, knocking it over as I do. The fireball crashes into one of the book piles, sparking a fire that dances across the room.

"You will die," Jenny calls out, "a pointless death!"

By the time I make it out with the smoke digging into my lungs, she is gone. As I stumble out, it is Jasper that catches me before I can crumble to the ground.

"Jenny?" He asks as he leads me away.

"Yes, did you see her?" I ask, nearly coughing my lungs out.

"No, I saw the empty bed and came to check on you. Let's get you out of here," he says, leading me to the ladder. He follows behind me, smoke slowly filling out the now empty corridor.

"Jenny escaped," I tell Ryder as he helps me to my feet. Stella glances down at the hole as Jasper climbs out. She moves to close it but he stops her, kicking it to the side.

"I'm not leaving someone to suffocate," he says, "besides, it will just drive her more insane. We just need to watch out for her. It won't be long before she's a mindless body."

"Okay," Ryder nods, "let's get moving."

25

The Sacrifice

Sitting alone, I lean back against the dirty wall of what used to be an apartment. There are some plushies scattered about, each standing as a reminder of what the portal cost this city. The sun rose a while ago, the warm light stretching across the room and showcasing the grime and ash that covers everything in this part of the city.

Downstairs, I can hear them moving and the slight mutterings of a conversation. I can't bring myself to go downstairs and engage with them as my mind is preoccupied with Jenny and the task that awaits us. Everyone else has a job, something they are supposed to do except for me. Everyone is an important aspect except for me.

Me? I'm just a burden...someone they're going to have to keep alive.

"You look glum," Jasper says as he kicks open the door. I glance over at him before pushing myself off the bed.

"Is there any other way to look?" I ask him, "I mean, don't you plan to die in a few hours?"

"Sure," he shrugs, "but I already knew it had to be me when I read the line."

"How?"

"You think I'd let any of you sacrifice yourselves?" Jasper tsks, "I've been training my whole life to protect everyone. This...this is what I was raised to do."

"That isn't very fair to you," I mutter as I lead the way downstairs.

"What's fair doesn't matter here," he mutters as we step into the main room. Ryder and Stella stand over a table, both matching the same glum expression I do. Jasper is the only one that doesn't seem bothered as he walks around the table and points down at the small map they had etched into it.

"It's time," Jasper says a grin spreading across his face, "we have hours before sundown so we should be free of those shadow demons. Marcus may or may not show up so we need to get this done quick. We don't exactly have an army to back us up."

"Okay," Ryder nods as he points to the x, "me and Stella will head to the church. Jasper and Theo will try to figure out exactly where the life curse was cast."

"Good deal," Jasper nods. I try to match his energy, forcing a smile onto my face as I watch them go over the best routes to take in case Marcus is already waiting for us.

"We have everything we need?" Ryder asks, his eyes solely focused on his brother. His brother grins as he places his hands on his shoulders.

"Everything will be fine, okay?" Jasper promises.

"I hate it when people lie," Ryder mutters with a sigh. Like me, he forces a smile on his face before stepping forward and wrapping his arms around Jasper. I follow suit, squeezing them both like this is our last chance because…well, it is. When Stella finally joins, Jasper has had enough and shoos us away.

"Enough," he chuckles, "let's get moving before anyone gets cold feet. We got this."

"Obviously," I say, sounding far more confident than I feel. Part of me wishes that I was going to the church instead of watching Jasper die, however, Salem awaits them. I shudder at the thought of the dark being, dreading what waits for them inside those old walls.

As we step outside, a large group of darklings await us. At first, terror runs through me because my first thought is Marcus. Dante steps out of the crowd, distilling the fear with his wide, confident grin.

"Good morning, fellas," he says, "you didn't think you guys were going to have all the fun, did you?"

"What is this?" Jasper asks as he steps forward.

"There is already an army waiting for you," Dante tells us as he slaps a hand down on his shoulder, "we all decided that we wanted to stand by you. We trust that you guys are making the right choice for more than just this city."

"They all know what's coming?" I ask. Dante nods, his grin wavering slightly. Again, I am reminded of Jasper's and his similarities. Putting on a strong face to make sure those around them comfortable.

The large group moves as a silent wave, the only sound coming from our feet hitting the asphalt. It is a nice, steady rhythm, something that oddly calms my nerves.

"Hey," Stella says, falling in line beside me, "in case this doesn't go as well as we hope, I want you to know how much I appreciate you."

"What?"

"You are the only lightling I've ever told about my darkling side," she says, "you never judged me or looked at me any differently. I was so scared for so long to tell anyone and...perhaps...perhaps that is only my parent's fear living through me. Either way, I'm glad that you were the first lightling I ever told."

"Me too," I grin, "I'm glad we met you. You're really cool, cooler than any witch I've ever met. Definitely cooler than Ryder."

"Definitely," she agrees, glancing back at the twins walking beside each other a few yards behind us. I follow her gaze and frown as it grows sour, "look, I know you like him and it's fine but...I can't drop it. Jasper was with Salem and there is nothing lingering in his mind? He gets no repercussions for what he did?"

"Stella-"

"Do you know what people call him around here?" She asks, answering her own question before I have a chance to, "they call him a monster, Theo. Even his own people don't trust him so why...why are we so eager to?"

"He has done nothing but help us," I argue, though her seeds of doubt slowly sprouting. What if he is like Jenny? Slowly growing bad as the infection spreads...I shake the thought out of my mind before continuing, "no. He won't turn against us. He wouldn't do something to hurt his brother. I trust him."

"Why? You've only known him for a few days."

"And I've known you for so much longer," I remind her.

"That's not the point," she sighs, "just, be careful, okay? Me and Ryder won't be there to have your back."

"Sure," I mutter as she steps away from me, leaving me alone to walk along darklings I've never met. Jasper replaces her without a word as Ryder disappears somewhere to my right.

"So, what exactly is the plan?" I ask him, "has it changed with our new additions?"

"Not really," he shrugs, "while Dante and the rest of them are entertaining our friends, we are going to sneak away. Stealth is key here as we don't want people following after us. While I perform the spell, you need to make sure no one is gets to me before I can finish it."

"And you are still totally cool with this?"

"As cool as I can be, why?"

"I don't know," Theo sighs, "you are marching to your death."

"We've had this talk before...like, three times. Everything will be fine, bud," he shrugs, "I will break the curse and you will go on to save the world, promise?"

"Promise," I nod as Jasper holds out his pinkie. I smile as I link mine as he lets out a chuckle before dropping his hand. I let out a chuckle of my own before saying, "I haven't made a pinkie swear since I was seven."

"Ryder and I used to always use pinkie swears. Guess it never wore off."

"Guess not," I reply as he grabs arm and pulls me away from the crowd in into an alleyway. A flash of fear spreads through me, instantly reminding me of

Stella's words. The fear, however, is quickly replaced with relief.

On the other side of the alleyway is the church, the cemetery already crawling with people.

"We're almost there," Jasper tells me, "we'll move once the fight starts. It should be the distraction we need."

"Okay," I mutter just as battle cries ring out. Already, the bodies shift and move out of view. I follow Jasper's lead as he jogs forward, his body low. Once we make it to the cemetery, I look over at the battle that is happening around us. Darklings fighting darklings, monsters are scattered throughout. I see Stella and Ryder making their way through the crowd.

"Theo!" Jasper calls out. I turn back toward him just as a werewolf circles me. Before I can react, a shining, spinning blade slams into its head. I dart forward and yank it out, tossing it over to Jasper as I jog to him.

"Thanks," I mutter. We are almost at the church now. I bypass him as I gaze over the grounds, looking for any kind of sign that would point toward a curse. The sound of metal scraping fabric erupts behind me and I spun around to see Jasper pulling his blade out of the back of a rotting head.

"Another cursed soul," he mutters, his eyebrows furrowed, "Salem has been busy."

"Don't usually see much of them?" I ask.

"Never," he shakes his head, "the one I killed was only the second one I've ever had to deal with."

"Wait," I point toward a patch of grass, the only green patch in this city. Jasper nods and hurries over toward it, kneeling down and running his hands

273

over it. I jog over to him, clenching my teeth as I glanced around for anything else, "that has to be it, right?"

"Yes," Jasper nods as he takes out a small scroll from his bag. He unrolls it before tossing the bag to me, "that's for you."

"What is it?" I ask.

"Supplies, information," Jasper shrugs as he takes off his trench coat and places it over my shoulder, "I don't need any of it anymore."

Tears slide past my eyes as he steps forward, pausing in front of the grass. Jasper takes a deep breath before stepping on it. He turns to face the flaming city and spreads his arms out wide.

I watch in quiet horror as he opens his mouth to cast the spell that will kill him.

He never gets the chance.

A fireball knocks him off his feet, sending him crashing through a tombstone a few yards away and disappearing into the tall, dead grass. I spin around, ready to face whatever attacked him.

I had one job.

Jenny stands right behind me, a small smile stretched across her face. She doesn't look like a zombie. In fact, she looks more like herself than she ever has since we got her. She looks beautiful and...free, her bright eyes shining against the dirt on her skin. She grins at me, a look of defiance, before grabbing my collar. I make no move to stop her, completely dazed.

Her lips crash into mine, sending a frenzy of chills running through my body.

"Save the world, Theo," Jenny pushes me away before darting toward the blade of grass. She pauses, looking back at me with a wild smile, "I'm free now…don't-don't worry…"

I cry out as she casts the spell, her whole body going rigid. As if her body is made of sand, she slowly gets blown away, scattering into the wind. Only her clothes remain, standing a few yards from where she gave her life.

"Is that it?" I sob out, "is it done?"

A loud bang shakes the ground around me, forcing me to take my eyes away from the spot of perfect grass. The fire still burns, however, the buildings teeter and fall, crashing into one another in a horrible domino effect. Gravity pulls them downward, sending some tumbling off the cliff and into the water below. I stumble back as a large crack stretches out of the stone below me, someone pulling me away from the edge and toward the fighting crowd,

"You help them," Jasper orders, pointing toward our losing side as he takes his coat from my arms, "I'll get Stella and Ryder. Hopefully, they did what they had to."

I nod and turn toward the battlefield. Already, my animal is begging to be released and I almost give into it before the crack stretches past me. I stumble to a stop as the buildings beyond us start to shake. The battle freezes with me, both sides turning to watch their city begin to crumble.

Oh, right, we knew this was going to happen.

This is the End

The City will Crumble
Two Kingdoms will Fall
But Life…Life will Survive…

26

Ryder Skye and His Inability to Accept the Truth

Ryder doesn't hesitate to step into the church, Stella lingering behind as he steps into the familiar hallway. As soon as she passes through, his body is yanked forward. His body slams into the floor, the wood cracking as his back hits it.

Ryder rolls to his feet and narrows his eyes as he spins in a slow circle. He knows this space, he's been here before if only in a dream.

He follows the hallway down toward the main room of the church, ignoring the dread creeping up into his throat.

The old pews lay scattered about and shards of painted glass crunch under his boots. The end of the room is missing the wall, giving Ryder a perfect view of the burning city beyond. A giant hole sits in the middle of the room, something bright glowing from down below.

It calls to him...begging him to come to it.

Instead, Ryder focuses on Stella, or tries to. He waits to hear her footsteps but they never come. Spinning back toward the walkway, he steps forward

277

only to be launched back again. He slams into the wood, rolling dangerously close to the edge.

"Ryder Skye," a familiar voice taunts from the shadows, "finally. I've been waiting too long for you to piece everything together."

"Where is she?" Ryder asks as he scrambles to his feet, "this is between you and me."

"You brought her into this," he says as shadows form in the corner, creating a dark figure, "have you made your choice? Are you here to do as your told or do you think you can trick me with that small mind of yours. The curse is not yet lifted...do you wish to come fight me instead?"

"We're working on it," Ryder snaps, looking around to see where he can be hiding Stella.

"Working on it," Salem repeats before letting out a sigh, "you should have come prepared."

Ryder opens his mouth to reply but is interrupted by the ground shaking violently below him. He stumbles back as he struggles to stay on his feet. Ryder glances back, his mouth dropping upon seeing the buildings crumbling against each other.

They did it.

They broke the spell.

Jasper...

Salem throws his head back and laughs as the shadows wound tighter and tighter around the form until *poof!* They are gone.

They are replaced by something much more terrifying.

"Finally," Salem says, towering over Ruder in his newly physical form, "I'm free."

"What?" Ryder coughs out as Salem steps closer. He has to be over seven feet tall, his wild black hair sliding against the short roof of the church. His bare chest is the width of a truck and his arms are the size of barrels. He wears a vaguely Viking-style clothing with a large wooden hammer hanging off his back.

"Can't speak?" Salem laughs as he swings his arm out, catching Ryder in the chest and sending him flying. He rolls to his feet just as another fist swings his way. Ryder ducks under it and rolls away from the large being. He has the spell memorized but he needs time to actually cast it.

"Come on," Salem chuckles as he walks after the darkling. Before they had stepped within these walls, Stella had agreed to be the distraction. She is, however, nowhere to be seen. Ryder ducks and darts out of the way, desperately trying to come up with a new plan before Salem killed him.

Ryder isn't a fighter.

How is he supposed to win this fight?

"This is a useless game," Salem sighs, catching Ryder by the neck and lifting him off the ground, "open the portal and live."

"No," Ryder chokes out as he struggles against his grip.

"You mortals lack vision," he spits, "Mayhem will reign supreme no matter what you fools try to do. At least this way, I can find some use for you beyond his coming."

"I won't be the one to release him," Ryder says.

"Look into my eyes and tell me which is worse," Salem whispers, pulling the darkling toward his face. Ryder gasps as he is caught into the spiraling violet mess that is the being's eyes.

Eyes that strangely look like his own...

Ryder can't comprehend the flashing visions that run past his eyes. They are all a blur, leaving him dizzy in his wake. He can *feel* them, sending searing pain and blinding fear through his body.

Ryder can't take it. He desperately wants to beg to be released from whatever hell this is but, he can't even feel his body outside of the torture that engulfs him. He is floating in a sea of pain and fear and...he is slowly forgetting what anything else feels like.

"Feel it?" Salem's hungry voice asks, bringing Ryder out of it. He blinks, right back in his limp body and still hanging from the monster's grip, "that is all that awaits you if you disobey me."

"I won't damn the world to save myself," Ryder whispers.

"Fine," Salem waves me away, sending me to the ground, "if your pain doesn't inspire you, maybe your green girlfriend's will."

"No," Ryder coughs out, struggling to sit up. His body aches as Salem steps away from him, turning toward the dark hallway.

"Achne sporus," Ryder starts, the words coming easily to him. The beings back straightens as he turns to watch him. Ryder whispers the last few words just as the being lunges forward as if to stop him.

Salem doesn't. He pauses, his fingers a mere inch away from Ryder's body as he finishes casting the spell. The teenager can feel the power...he can feel something changing below as the ground shakes. Salem seems to not notice, his violet eyes on his before a wide smile stretches across his face.

"You mortals are always the same," he giggles as the ground shakes around them, "thinking you know more or can trick a being that has been alive since the very creation of this realm. So...unbelievably arrogant."

"What?"

"You did exactly as I expected you to," he shrugs, "exactly what I *needed* you to."

"No..."

"Silly, little boy," Salem says as he brings out his hammer and twirls it around in his large hand, "haven't you heard? You don't make deals with the devil."

The large being doesn't seem to notice Stella crouching down behind him, a knife in her hand. Ryder doesn't acknowledge her, instead glaring up at the large being. Salem stands with his back to the ledge and Stella stands directly behind him, standing so close to the edge...

"You think you know what's coming?" Salem taunts as he leans down and grabs the darkling's hair, pulling him to his feet. Ryder gasps out in pain but, he can't find the strength to struggle against his grip, "I'm the bringer of war...a literal *god* of lies. You never stood a chance. The funny thing is, Ryder, that this is your destiny...a prophecy to fulfill. Every since you were born, we always knew you were the key to draping this world in darkness..."

"No..." Ryder mutters, "no..."

"Let me guess," Salem pats his cheek, "they told you that you were part of this great prophecy...someone meant to save the world? One of the six?"

"Y...yes."

"See, they were close," he shakes his head, "there are two parallel prophecies, each taking place with the other. Depending on which one is fulfilled, the world will either become like all the others we've taken over or it'll remain in its original pathetic state. One calls for six, the other calls for only one...only one to unleash the monsters into the realm, one that is connected to the six, though can never be a part of it."

"Jasper," Ryder coughs out.

"Yes," Salem chuckles, "you're getting it! The one your people have terrified of for so long is actually the one born to save them. Well, was. I mean, you had him kill himself so that the world can't be saved. Brilliant, isn't it? How easy you are to manipulate...here I thought the world has changed...apparently no-Ah!"

Salem's grip loosens on Ryder's neck, sending him falling back to the ground. Dark blood runs down the back of his knee and Stella stumbles back closer to the edge as he spins around toward her.

"You little brat!" He spits, "you have no part in this!"

She sends Ryder a wink as she steps out of his reach, her heel hanging over the edge now...

"Oh, come on," she taunts, "you don't look so scary."

"I am the bringer of war, puny mortal!" Salem yells as he steps forward. The wood cracks under his feet as he raises his hammer. She grins as he raises it high above him, "you will die by my hand!"

"I'm counting on it," she says, her eyes on Ryder's as she falls back before the hammer hits. The wood shatters beneath the dark being, crumbling underneath him and sending him falling in after.

"No," Ryder sobs out as he crawls over to the new edge. The spiraling colors make no change, no indication that anything has fallen into the portal.

"Stella!" He calls out. He...he can't feel her, or the dark being for that matter. Ryder can't move from the spot, his body locking up as the ground shakes around him.

Ryder can't just leave her down there with that thing. She...he can't just let her suffer down there alone...

He looks back at the hallway and the doorway that can potentially lead to his survival. He has nothing here now...no family...no purpose...he just started the apocalypse and there is no way to save it.

"I'm sorry," he sobs out, closing his eyes and letting the tears fall. Ryder doesn't move as the ground shifts below him, falling out from underneath him.

"No!" A voice rings out and Ryder's fall is cut short as someone grabs his hand. Ryder looks up, his body being pulled in two different directions as he falls closer to the portal. Jasper lay above him, holding onto his hand as he struggles against the power below.

"Let me go!" Ryder calls out, "I can't just leave her!"

"I'm not losing you again!"

"Please," Ryder cries out, "please...I have to do this!"

"What about the six?" he asks, his body straining against the floor. Ryder can see the wood cracking underneath him...it isn't going to hold for much longer.

"I was never a part of the six," Ryder says, "it was supposed to be you. It was always meant to be you."

"I just got you back!"

"Go save the world, Jaz," Ryder smiles up at him, "and then come save us, okay? Hell can't be as bad as they say, right?"

"I can't just let you go," he cries out.

"I know," Ryder nods. Using his brother's arm, he pulls himself up just enough to reach up and touch his brother's forehead. Jasper's face goes blank for a second...just long enough for Ryder to slip through his fingers.

"No!" His brother's voice is drowned out by the loud humming of the portal below. Ryder twists his body to face the brilliant light as he hits it, muttering a soft prayer before his world goes black.

27

Theodore Emerson and The Rescue

The city is falling and there is nothing anyone can do to stop it. The fight had long since ended, the darkling scattering away. There are no more rivalries as they all flee together. Dante and Marcus stand on either side of the clearing, leading their people away from destruction.

Theo turns back toward the church after lifting up a fallen darkling and pushing them toward the rest. Bits of stone fall from the cliff, leaving the building sitting haphazardly on the edge as it leans toward the darkness below.

Jasper has been in there for a long time.

"No," Theo mutters as he hurries toward it, "no one else has to die today."

He jumps over cracks as they start stretching across the ground. Theo dodges past a few lingering darklings before bounding up the steps of the church. Before he can step inside, a body slams into his chest and sends them both falling back to the ground. Just as his back slams into the hard ground, the church crumbles backward and disappears over the side of the cliff.

"No!" Theo cries out as he shoves Jasper off of him. He scrambles to his feet and hurries toward the edge. Jasper grabs him, yanking him back as more of the ground crumbles toward the waves.

"What happened?" Theo demands, shoving the darkling off of him, "where are they?"

"They're gone," Jasper says, "they…they fell."

"Fell?"

"Into the portal…Ryder wouldn't let me save him."

"Wouldn't let you?" Theo asks, a horrible thought sparking up in his mind. Stella had warned him about Jasper right before the fight. He shakes the thought out of his head as he steps closer to him, "you are incredibly powerful. I've seen you bring down an entire building with just your mind. How can you not be able to save him?"

"Excuse me? You think I'd just let him fall?"

"I…Stella said there was something off about you…maybe I just didn't see it because you saved my life! You're all for the greater good, right? Why would you let him fall? He's part of the prophecy?"

"We can discuss this later," Jasper grumbles, "but, right now, we have to go."

"No!" Theo says, "you listen to me. Stella knew! Do you want to hear my theory?"

"Go for it," Jasper dares him.

"I think you let him fall," Theo says, "because you aren't for the greater good. You let him fall because you thought you should be the one of the prophecy that gets all the glory for saving the world. That's how you knew of it before we mentioned it. That's why you were fine dying because you knew you actually weren't going to."

"That is the stupidest thing I've ever heard," Jasper nods with a frown, "I don't have to explain anything to you."

"Because I'm right."

"Because the city is crumbling around us," Jasper groans as he, again, pushes Ryder away from the crumbling edge.

"Stop touching me, you monster!" Theo groans as he shoves hard against Jasper's chest. The other teen falls, his back hitting the ground. Theo watches in horror as the ground crumbles under Jasper's weight, sending him falling toward whatever lay below.

"No!" Theo calls out as he stumbles forward. A pair of arms stops him, wrapping around his chest. He twists his head around to meet his father's stern gaze. A cord is attached to him, pulling him up and toward the helicopter that hovers above.

Without a word, Theo and his father are pulled into the air. Theo watches in horror as the city falls below him. He can see dark shapes dancing across the sky as his father pulls him into the helicopter. He doesn't know what they are, but he has a nagging feeling that they just released something they shouldn't have.

. . .

Theo watches the cold water chase away all the blood and dirt that had clung to him in the past week. He has no interest in eating the warm meal that awaits him nor in meeting his father's stern gaze.

287

His father tells him that he is lucky. He made it out alive with very little consequence to himself. Every injury is an easy healing spell away from nonexistence and even the academy still holds his place. They blame it, after all, on the darkling he had with him. All he has to do is promise to visit a therapist regularly.

Funny...it's as if his father was arranging all this since before he even made it back.

Theo is lucky. He's alive and relatively well but...why doesn't he want to be? Everything that happened was so easily erased by his father. Stella, Ryder, Ja...Jasper...

"Hey!" A sharp knock causes him to jump and fall against the hard shower wall. He groans as he pushes himself back up and turns the water off. Theo dressed hurriedly before yanking the door open.

"Sorry," Austen smiles awkwardly, sitting below in a wheelchair, "you were in there so long I thought you fell or something."

"It's fine," Theo mutters as he tosses his towel into the hamper. He sits down on his bed and waits for Austen to leave. When he doesn't, he looks over at him with a raised eyebrow, "did you need something?"

"Oh, sorry," Austen says as he pulls a small phone out of his pocket. Theo stands as he recognizes the bright pink cover. He snatches it out of his uncle's hands before looking back up at him as he continues, "they found it in your clothes. Thought you might like it back. When did you get a pink cover?"

"I didn't," Theo says as he unlocks it. He traces his finger over the home screen, smiling at the selfie she had taken before they had left on that insane quest.

The quest that took away his friends.

The quest that made him out to be a monster.

The quest that was for nothing, as whatever prophecy there was can no longer come to pass.

Theo sighs as he plops back down, falling back against the mattress. Stella looks so happy...Ryder's even grinning as he's held against his will...

"Feeling okay?" Austen asks, his voice growing tight when Theo doesn't answer. He sighs and rolls away from the older man, closing his eyes as he tries to ignore the nagging feeling of guilt that always comes when he sees that awful chair.

"I feel fine," Theo mutters, sounding harsher than he means to. How is he supposed to tell him that the world is now doomed? How is he supposed to tell him that everyone is now going to die because some kids fell into a portal?

How is he supposed to tell him about a darkling prophecy that everyone refuses to acknowledge?

Acknowledgements

I just wanted to take a quick moment to acknowledge those who have helped me write this book. Without them, it would have been a lot less fun.

A huge thank you goes out to my family from my parents to my uncles as everyone has been majorly supportive.

Thanks to Oliviaprodesign from FIVERR who created the beautiful cover.

I also owe my very first reader a thank you. So, Mrs. Nelson, thank you for taking time out of your day to help me indulge in my dream of being an author.

You all rock!

Monsters Unleashed: City of Flames

Jocelin R. Deneweth is an English High School teacher who calls South Texas home. She has spent most of her life writing and has always dreamed of sharing her books with the world. If she isn't hiding away with a book tucked under her arm with a horror movie playing in the background, she is cuddling with one (or all three) of her dogs.

Monsters Unleashed: City of Flames is her first book.

Want more?

Subscribe to my website for updates, deleted scenes, and a free short story about our very own Jenny Church.

https://deneway911.wixsite.com/jocelinrdeneweth-1